THE FOURTH TIME CHARM

MAYA HUGHES

Cover Design: Najla Qamber, Qamber Designs

Cover Image: Rafa Catala

Editors: Dawn Alexander, Sarah Kremen-Hicks, Sarah Kellogg

To Dawn! Now that I've found you, I'm never letting go! :-P

CHAPTER 1

LJ

When I found the buzzing thing buried in my blankets, I'd launch it out my window.

Marisa always told me to put my phone into night mode after ten o'clock, but I hadn't listened. And I'd make sure to never let her know she'd been right.

Usually, my phone sat on the shelf by my bed, but I'd fallen asleep studying for finals while icing the growing bruise on my thigh. At least there were only three spring football practices left before summer break—I'd finally be off Coach Saunders's shit list for a while.

Why wouldn't the buzzing stop? My arms and legs were lead logs weighing my blankets down. Off-season weight training and practices sucked so much more than any hell week during the season.

Following my charging cable, I found my phone and saw notifications of five missed calls on the screen.

My heart rate spiked. The calls were from an unknown number. Was it the hospital? Had something happened to my dad?

Before I could tap the number, the phone jumped in my hand. I answered before the first ring.

"Hello?"

Sirens blared and truck engines rumbled and roared nearly drowning out the voice. I slammed my hand over my ear like it would help to block out all the background noise on the other end of the line.

A cleat spike slammed into my heart.

"LJ?"

"Marisa?" I shot out of bed and struggled to shove my jeans on. "What happened? Where are you?"

"Fire...my apartment...ambulance."

I strained to hear her over the power washer on steroids—no, it must be the fire hoses.

"I'm on my way. I'm coming!" I shouted into the receiver, not even sure if she could hear me. I buttoned my jeans, grabbed a t-shirt from my hamper and snagged some sneakers off the floor.

Rushing out of my room, I tucked my sneakers under my arm and wrestled with my t-shirt.

"Dude, where's the fire?" Reece rubbed his eyes, stepping out of his bedroom.

"At Marisa's."

"Are you serious?"

"I told her that apartment was a piece of crap. I should've found her somewhere better to live." My sneakers dropped. I tugged my shirt all the way on.

"Your shoes don't match." He said it like that was the most shocking thing we were dealing with right now. "Is she okay?"

"I don't know. I'm going there now." I pulled on one sneaker, grabbing onto the railing so I didn't fall and break my damn neck. Fear for Marisa clogged my throat and made it hard to focus.

I needed to get to her. I needed to see her. I needed her to be okay.

Sitting on the bottom step, I shoved my foot into the mismatched shoe and grabbed my key from my pocket.

Sweat beaded on my skin. I jumped from the top of the porch steps and scrambled onto the sidewalk, taking off for my car half a block away. If anything happened to her, I'd lose it.

I flicked on the headlights, rocketing down the empty street.

I got stuck at a deserted red light and banged my hands against the wheel, willing the damn thing to change. What the hell? It was three in the morning.

After two hour-long minutes, I vibrated in my seat, checked each way at least twice, and said screw it. I peeled out through the empty intersection, tires screeching.

In the distance, the smoke wafted into the air and flames glowed against the dark sky. The top floor of her five-story apartment complex peeked from behind the trees. A grenade of fear detonated in my chest and panic rose, blocking out everything but one thought: get to Marisa.

I gunned it the rest of the way. I reached the end of a long line of firetrucks and ambulances and nearly forgot to put the car into park. People stood on the sidewalks watching the apartment complex smolder and burn.

Out of breath like I'd been running wind sprints for an entire practice, I rushed up to someone talking into a radio.

"Marisa Saunders." I gasped, gulped for air. "Marisa Saunders. She called me and asked me to come get her."

The guy looked me up and down, talked into the radio on his shoulder and interpreted whatever came through as a squawk. "Ambulance #304. It'll be on the side and back doors of the ambulance."

"Is she okay?"

Sprays of water from the hoses blasted the air with mist and steam. The oranges and yellows danced in the air, embers and ash falling to the ground closer to the building. Had everyone made it out of there? The flames were mesmerizing, the heat warming the air and beating back the early spring chill.

"I don't know. They're checking all the residents for smoke inhalation. There have only been a few who've had to go to the hospital so far."

Panic gripped my chest, making it even harder to breathe than the smoke burning my eyes and lungs had managed.

I ducked under the yellow tape and rushed into the melee and confusion. Dodging people and shuffling and stumbling over cables and gear, I spotted the ambulance.

The back doors were open and there was someone on the gurney. Bare feet poked out from under a blanket. EMTs were on either side of the figure, but I couldn't tell what they were doing. Did she need oxygen? A burn bandaged?

Was it even Marisa?

The EMTs leaned back and she sat up.

She was wild haired and sooty faced, and she'd never been more beautiful. My heart triple jumped and I had to lock my knees so I didn't collapse.

Her gaze swept over the crowd and stopped on me. With a watery smile, she flung off the blanket and jumped out of the ambulance, ignoring the EMTs yelling after her.

I opened my arms.

She slammed into my chest, nearly knocking me over. I steadied us both and wrapped my arms around her.

"Are you okay? Are you okay?"

She squeezed me tight, resting her chin on my shoulder. A shiver rolled through her body and she held me even tighter. "Scared shitless for a while there. There's no way we could've jumped from the fifth floor."

I shuddered not even wanting to think about the danger getting any closer than it already had. "You're coming home with me, Risa. Are you okay?"

She nodded, her chin knocking into my shoulder.

I rubbed her back and squeezed my eyes shut. She smelled like the homecoming bonfire without the s'mores to soften the harsh edges of the scent. She'd been close to the fire—so close she was covered in soot.

I held her snug against my chest until she loosened her hold and pulled back. "What took you so long?" Her punch to my shoulder made me laugh. "I'm freezing."

"Only about six firetrucks, some police, and a stoplight that refused to change."

"The one on Hawthorne?" Her teeth chattered and she stared at the building.

"Yeah. I hate that fucking light."

The orange glow from the fire painted one side of her face. The other remained harshly shadowed by the light from the ambulance, which already had someone else in it. "It added another five minutes, didn't it?"

"It would've, if I hadn't run it."

"You did freaking not." She shoved at my shoulder.

"I did."

At least the fire hadn't kept her from jumping back into her normal role as a pain in the ass.

"What, was there a fire or something?" The corners of her mouth twitched and her gaze flew to the building where the flames reached even higher. "Oh yeah, I guess it's okay then, I'll allow it." She laughed, but the laugh turned into a cough and her eyes sharpened with panic.

Fear washed over me and I held onto her shoulders.

"Is she okay?" I looked over her shoulder to the EMTs who were already focusing on someone else.

She looked at me out of the corner of narrowed eyes. "Must have been some ash. I'm good. Chill the hell out."

Even thinking that was possible after I'd found her in the back of an ambulance was insanity.

The fine mist from the hoses made any body part not facing the charred building a hell of a lot colder. I didn't have anything for her. I should've stopped for a second and brought her a coat or sweatshirt. Or a blanket, or spare shoes —anything.

Shifting to face the ambulance, I asked again. "Will she be okay?"

"She's good. No singeing of the hair in her nose."

Marisa mumbled under her breath, "yippee."

"But she'll need a shower and her clothes need to go."

She shivered again and wrapped her arms around herself. Her lips were pale and she kept watching the flames.

My one objective had been to see that she was safe and now that I had, the list of other things she needed was getting long.

Marisa pulled her phone out of her pajama pants and sent a text. "I need to find Liv."

"You have your phone! Why the hell did you call me from an unknown number?"

She wore a mildly pained look. "I forgot I had it."

I held onto her shoulders and shook her. "You forgot you had your phone?"

"No need to get grumpy. I could've died in that fire, remember?" She pointed at the building still engulfed in flames.

"Do you think anyone died?" she whispered, looking over at me.

Her phone screen lit up and she answered. "Liv, where are you? Are you okay?"

She paused, pushing her phone tighter against her ear. The buzz of Liv's voice was barely audible on the other end of the line.

"Outside now. LJ is here, and he's about to get his ass kicked. He's hovering like I'm going to drop dead at any second."

I wasn't hovering.

Marisa put her hand over her phone. "She said they just finished checking her out and she sounds good."

We walked along the line of ambulances parked in the mini-triage set up on the street. A few ambulances cranked on their sirens and took off for the closest hospital.

"You shouldn't have been in that apartment."

"Not this again." She rolled her eyes, still shivering and chattering. "It was all I could afford, and it was a fine place to live. Well, until…" Her gaze darted to the fire, which reflected in her eyes.

"Liv offered to pay more than half the rent. You two could've gotten a better place together."

"I'm not a mooch. Just because she has money doesn't meant I'm going to take advantage."

"I could've helped."

"Again, not a mooch. Plus, you wouldn't be stealing lunch meat from the dining hall if you were rolling in enough extra dough to pay my rent."

This time her stubbornness had literally almost gotten her killed.

We walked past the rows of ambulances, checking for Liv. Marisa unmuted her phone pressed against her ear. "I can hear what she's hearing." She sped up, rushing forward.

The back doors of an ambulance opened and a vaguely familiar big guy stepped out, holding out his hand and holding onto it was Liv, Marisa's roommate. Then it clicked into place. Ford. Liv's maybe-boyfriend had made it here too.

Marisa dashed toward Liv and nearly tackled her like she had me. "I was so worried when you disappeared."

"I could say the same about you."

"Stop crying—you'll make me cry, and then he'll lose it again. He's trying to get me to go back to The Brothel, but I'm not leaving you here."

I did not lose it. "Liv can come too."

"It's okay. I know the football house is cramped as it is.

I'm going to go with Ford." Liv looked over her shoulder at the man.

He straightened. It wouldn't be the first time Ford had swooped in to save Liv—at least she wasn't drunk off her ass like she'd been at the last party she attended at The Brothel. There was no way he'd made it through the night without a puke christening from her.

Marisa shot Liv a look.

Ford stared down at her. "She's coming with me. You can too, if you need to."

My hackles rose. Did he think I wouldn't take care of her? I might not've had a pro athlete salary to flash around and fix everything—yet—but I could still make sure she was okay. Getting Marisa to my place was my number one goal. Get her warm, showered, and into bed. To sleep. Purely for sleeping.

"I'm good. I'll go with LJ." Marisa eyed Liv, ducking her head. "Are you sure?"

Liv held on tighter to Ford's arm. "I'm sure."

"Then I'll see you on campus? We need to figure out a more permanent living situation and what the hell we're going to do about our stuff..." Marisa stared up at the death trap that was once her building.

"Let's just get through the night and figure everything else out tomorrow. I need to take a shower. I reek of smoke." Liv tugged at her t-shirt.

They said their goodbyes and I walked her back toward my car. I wanted to scoop her up in my arms away from the wet, dirty ground, but it would've been like trying to carry a feral cat.

Her steps were slow and heavy. The adrenaline crash was hitting her hard.

I wanted to take her hand, but instead I wrapped my arm around her shoulder and guided her through the swarm of people who'd descended to stop the blaze and take care of everyone who'd been displaced. She didn't need any of them now—she had me.

I opened the door for her, and the fact that she let me showed me how tired she truly was. Normally, she'd rush around to the other side of the car before I got the chance to open it.

I slid into my seat, the adrenaline wearing off. "You can sleep in my bed tonight. I can take the couch."

She yawned and rested the back of her head against the window, while looking over at me. "I can take the couch of death. After I crash, it's going to take a marching band shooting fireworks to wake me up."

"You need a good night's sleep. You're sleeping in my bed." Saying the words out loud, a rev of desire streaked through me. The adrenaline rush of getting to her and knowing she was safe had faded, now there was a different feeling humming through my veins.

She rolled her eyes. "So bossy. I need a shower and then I can fight you on this. You need your bed. You've got practice tomorrow."

"I don't care. We've shared a bed before."

Instead of fighting me, she closed her eyes.

Good it was settled. Shit, it was settled. I was sleeping next to Marisa tonight.

We got back to the townhouse, one of a row of houses just off campus in various states of repair or neglect. Ours had been one of the more popular frat houses, until the frat had been booted for too many rule violations.

The house had been kept up nicely with all those frat dues, but the name they'd given it had stuck: The Brothel. Their other enduring legacy was the way that the house sprung parties like a leaky barrel when we least expected it.

The street was quiet; it was too late for even the weeknight party warriors. I pulled into the spot I'd vacated less than an hour ago.

I turned off the ignition and leaned back in my seat, rolling my head to the side to watch her.

Her lips were parted, and a gentle snore rumbled in her throat.

The streetlights haloed the nest of her hair. She was here and she was safe. I'd only been more scared once in my life, and I never wanted to feel that way again.

I could've lost her. Shoving those feelings aside, I focused on what she needed right now. A shower and real sleep.

Wrapping my fingers just above her knee, I squeezed the spot twice.

She jolted awake, her head whipping around.

"We're here." She must have been exhausted, because I made it to her door before she could open it.

"I had it," she grumbled and hopped out. "My toes are freezing." She wiggled them against the hard, dark concrete.

I glanced down at her bare feet. If I offered to carry her inside, she'd probably punch me in the balls, so I bit the inside of my cheek, watching for glass or splintered wood on the porch steps.

Inside, I got her straight to my room and handed her a t-shirt and some boxers before I sent her to shower.

Her quietness told me just how much she needed to get under the covers—for once she didn't have a quip or a biting comment.

The stench of smoke hung heavy in my room, more noticeable now that we were away from the fire. I sniffed my shirt and jerked away from the burning smell. The last thing I wanted was for her to walk in here and be hit with the stink of char.

I took off my smoke-soaked clothes and grabbed my towel off the back of the door, wrapping it around my waist. I dumped the clothes outside my door and grabbed fresh ones.

The water in the bathroom shut off and the door opened, the hot, humid air billowing into the hallway.

She stumbled back in and spotted me, freezing mid-hair-drying.

Dammit, maybe I should've waited to take my clothes off until I'd gotten to the bathroom, but it wasn't like she hadn't seen me in just swim trunks before. At least I'd gotten the towel on and she hadn't walked in on me totally naked like she had last summer after our water balloon battle.

"My clothes smelled like smoke too. I'm hopping in the shower."

Seeing her in my clothes did something to me—something that couldn't be contained by a towel. I clutched my sweats and t-shirt in front of my now-straining erection. My blood pounded in my veins and I didn't know how I was supposed to spend the night lying beside her. Maybe I should take the couch. I rushed out the doorway, poking my head back in.

"Get into the bed. I'll be back in a few." I flicked off the light, blanketing the room in darkness aside from the glow from the hallway.

The shower was quick and efficient and I kept myself from relieving the pressure that had built up when I saw her in my clothes. I cranked it to cold until my cock deflated and I could end my freezing torture.

Climbing out, I picked up her clothes from the floor and dropped them outside my bedroom door. I'd wash them in the morning and see if a gallon of detergent got the smell out.

If it didn't, I wasn't opposed to her wearing more of my clothes until we got her some new ones or she got to go back to her place to see what could be salvaged.

There was no sound in my room. For a second, I thought she might've gone downstairs to get something to eat, but then I heard her soft, gentle breaths coming from my bed.

I hung my towel up and crossed the room.

Marisa was spread out like a starfish, taking up most of the bed.

Chuckling, I took her arm and put my hand on her waist,

rolling her toward the wall. She grumbled, but let me move her, shifting her pillow and clutching it to her chest.

If I weren't a glutton for punishment, I'd have taken a pillow and blanket and gone downstairs to the couch of torture, or I'd have nudged her even further toward the wall and put my back against hers. But I couldn't help myself.

Sliding into the bed, I curled my body around hers, wrapping my arm around her. Just for tonight. Just because of how close I'd come to losing her. Just because I couldn't help myself.

Her hair smelled like me. As much as I loved that, I'd have to pick up some of her shampoo and soap when I got a chance.

"Night, Marisa." Closing my eyes, I breathed deeply, matching my breaths to hers.

Tonight, I'd hold her in my arms.

Tomorrow, I'd figure out how to deal with being in love with the coach's daughter.

CHAPTER 2
MARISA

I rolled over, running my hands over the blankets. The sheets were soft and comfy, like flannel. This wasn't my bed.

Shooting up, I looked around the room and it all came flooding back. Staying up late studying. Being woken by Liv. The choking smoke. The panic and fear. The blind crawl down the stairs and sucking in lungfuls of still-smoky air once we'd made it outside. And LJ.

Seeing him had calmed me in a way I hadn't anticipated. He'd been the only person to call after the fire. No way was I calling my mom or Ron, and his number was one of the few I'd committed to memory.

Seeing him standing next to the ambulance, though, I'd almost burst into tears. I'd only managed to hold them back because I knew how much it would freak him out to see me cry. Once his arms were around me, the fear had ebbed away, and when I was in his bed, sleep had come quickly. I barely remembered the shower, only his body wash that smelled like evergreen and orange zest even through the smoky burn still lingering in my nose.

The blinds were drawn on the two windows in the room. I

couldn't even tell what time it was from the light peeking through the slats. Sometime between 7am and 4pm, since it was light out. I wouldn't have been surprised if I'd slept through an entire day.

I had no idea where my phone was. I'd need to call work and let them know I wouldn't be in. All those student tour groups at the Philadelphia Museum of Art would have to carry on without me for a little while. I was sure no one would miss my museum curator jokes.

LJ's phone sat on the nightstand beside his bed, which was wedged into the corner of his room. His towel was hanging on the back of the partially-open door. The desk was neat and clear, and multicolored tabs stuck out of the neat stack of notebooks. Pens and highlighters were lined up beside them for easy access. His closet door was fully closed and there wasn't a thing on the floor other than his shoes. His room had always been neater than mine.

It made all those sleeping-bag sleepovers in middle school less like going on a fungal expedition and more like seeing how a normal house functioned.

Now my excuse for my messy room was that my days were filled with cataloguing and organizing, so once I got home all bets were off. Technically, I didn't need an excuse now. I didn't have a room—at least not one I'd be returning to anytime soon. I'd rather sleep on the train than go back home and commute in for classes and my internship.

My mom had probably turned my room into a speakeasy since I'd been there last summer. That had been the visit where I vowed I'd never stay at home again—not that it had been much of a home after my dad left.

Thoughts of last night kept intruding. Was this what shock felt like? Last night, I'd been so confused on seeing LJ and finding Liv. Now, the realities trickled in until they became a flood.

Fire trucks had lined the street in front of my former

apartment building. I could've died. A shiver shot through my body. I pulled my knees up to my chest and rested my back against the headboard. My throat closed up and I forced the air from my lungs.

The bedroom door opened and LJ walked in balancing a bowl on top of a cup in each hand. "You're up." He smiled and the tightness in my throat eased.

"I am."

"I brought you breakfast."

My heart triple stepped and I scooted to the edge of the bed. "You didn't have to."

"It's just cereal. I microwaved your milk." He shuddered, his lips curling in disgust.

"It's freaking delicious." I took the bowl balanced on top of my cup Jenga tower and set the bowl in my lap. And one sip from my glass of milk to settle my stomach.

He gagged and held out a spoon, while not directly looking at me.

"Do I even want to know where you were hiding that?" I eyed it warily, given his double-handed cereal delivery.

I slid it out of his grasp.

"You don't trust me?" he said syrupy-sweet before grabbing his desk chair and wheeling it closer to the bed, resting his feet near my crossed legs. Taking his bowl, he made a puppy dog pouting face, bringing his spoon up to his mouth and adding in a trembling hand for the full effect.

I burst out laughing. "Are you sure you want to play football? You should swing by the drama department." My perfectly soggy Apple Jacks melted in my mouth and flavored the milk for a bonus treat after all the green and orange loops were gone.

"Ye of little faith. These sweats do have pockets."

"Oh those were spoons in your pocket. I thought you were just happy to see me."

He snorted in the same cute way he had since the sixth grade. "Hardly. You snore like you're a tugboat in a harbor."

"If I snore, which I don't, it would be like Tinkerbell whispering sweet nothings to an angel."

There were so many things to do, so many real-world necessities I had to deal with, and I didn't want to do any of them.

"We should go to Kart-astrophe." I set my bowl aside.

"Why?"

"Why not? It's the weekend and it's not like I have anywhere to be. Or any laundry to do—except yours because I know it's piling up. Or any notes to study from." I shrugged. Go-karting was the perfect way to get my mind off the mortal danger I'd run up against.

"How about we take care of a few things first, like emailing your dean and professors to let them know what happened? My old laptop is in my closet, I can boot it up and wipe it and you can use it."

"I can use the computer labs."

"This is not a negotiation. You'll need a laptop, unless you want to be stuck in those computer labs during finals in a couple weeks. Did you call your mom already?"

"Why would I do that?"

"So she doesn't worry."

"She doesn't know about the fire, and she won't know."

"What about your dad?"

I ducked his gaze, checking out the trees outside his window. "What about him?"

"He works here. You think he won't find out about one of the biggest off-campus housing complexes burning to the ground?"

"Let's set a timer and see." I set my imaginary watch.

"Marisa…"

My eyes narrowed at the warning tone in his voice. "Fine, I'll call him."

He tossed my phone to me.

Grabbing it with one hand, I stared at the fully charged battery icon and my anger bubbled up. Ron didn't deserve to get a call to reassure him I was okay. How many years of radio silence had I sat through after he'd left my mom—left me behind? How many missed birthdays? Christmases? And every other holiday in between?

"Later." I dropped the phone beside me.

LJ shifted his gaze to the ceiling with his arms folded over his chest. The muscles bunched under his t-shirt and the gray sweatpants were unfair. Every other girl on campus got to ogle LJ, but not me. I was the best friend, the partner in crime, but never more than that.

After all this time, I should be used to it. Getting shot down senior year had been rough, but I'd learned to live within the boundaries of our relationship. It didn't mean I didn't sometimes want to break free from them.

In less than a year the draft would happen, and then he wouldn't be my best friend and a member of the Fulton U football team who were treated like campus gods. He'd be a professional athlete, with all the perks that came with it.

Ron hadn't even been a player or a pro—he'd stuck to college football and then dropped me and my mom for his chance at gridiron glory. I was his own flesh and blood. What were the chances I wouldn't get left behind once LJ signed the dotted line and got the big fat check?

The only reason LJ went out of his way to drag me back to our friendship whenever I tried to put space between us was because I'd saved his dad's life. But that magic would wear off eventually. The debt and the gratitude would get old, and he'd leave.

"What are you thinking so hard about?" LJ hopped onto the bed beside me, striking my same crossed-arm look and mirroring my expression.

The corner of my mouth quirked up as I tried to hold back

a smile. None of that meant I shouldn't enjoy my best friend while I still had him. Dropping my head to his shoulder, I sighed and stared at our legs next to one another. Mine were clad in his boxers with thick Christmas socks his mom had bought their whole family two years ago, and his in sweats, with his sock-covered feet resting near mine. If I wanted to screw with him, I could start playing footsie and see how he reacted. "Thinking about all the stuff I need to deal with today." I rubbed my hands over my face. "This is going to suck. Thank god you talked me into buying renter's insurance."

His chest puffed out and I rolled my eyes, jabbing him in the ribs.

"Gloat much?"

He rubbed his side. "I didn't say a word."

My head popped up and I glared. "Body language. It was gloating. A skywriter would have been less obvious."

"Can we jump off the LJ-is-a-pain-in-the-ass train for a minute? Let's write down everything you need to get done. We'll divvy up the list and knock it out."

"How about I go back to bed and pretend I didn't almost die in a fire last night?" I grabbed for the blankets to pull them back over my head. It was an overwhelming list and I hadn't even catalogued in my head everything I'd lost. There were so many little things I wouldn't realize were gone until I searched for them in a couple months or a year. The few things I'd picked up for my trip to Venice in six weeks. My freaking passport! Nope, I wasn't going to get up today.

He yanked the blankets back. "Nope. Let's go." He grabbed me around the waist and plopped me down in the chair like it was nothing, like he'd done back in middle school before wrestling had gotten a lot more awkward.

Spinning the chair around, he pushed me into the desk in front of a notebook and a piece of paper.

He held out a pen. "Write."

We spent the rest of the morning sending off emails to my deans and professors, creating a list of everything I could remember from my room, filling out the renter's insurance paperwork, setting up LJ's laptop for me to use, and going through his clothes to find at least a few things for me to wear. My emergency passport application appointment was in two days. I'd have to go back to Moorestown to get a copy of my birth certificate. Strangling myself with one of those velvet ropes they set out in front of art at the museum held more appeal.

By early afternoon, my brain was Swiss cheese.

"And your wallet. We'll need to replace all your cards. The campus ID card will be easy, but your driver's license and credit card will take some time." He'd bribed me with the promise of lemonade, which was the only thing that could have gotten me out of the bedroom.

I dropped my head to the kitchen table, banging it against the wood a few times. "Enough. Enough for today. I can't take anymore." Tilting my head to the side I peered up at him.

His face softened and he slid the papers he'd been flipping through back into the folder he'd scrounged up to keep everything in one place. "How about we get some ice cream?"

My head perked up. "Ice cream?"

"My treat."

"It would have to be, since the fourteen bucks I had are now burnt to a crisp."

We walked to T-Sweets, one of the busiest spots off campus with killer sundaes, hand-dipped ice cream, and, for people with no taste, soft serve. I got more than a few curious looks.

Usually girls didn't look like this in the mid-afternoon. This was more of an early-morning-walk-of-shame look, if the guy was nice enough to let you borrow some clothes.

LJ's black sweats were rolled at the ankles, even though he never felt that much taller than me. We were almost the same height, but somehow the laws of men's sweatpants didn't apply to women, and there was rolling involved.

His Batman t-shirt wasn't as baggy as I'd have liked. Being a double D did wonders for filling out a guy's XL t-shirt, not that anyone would be able to see it, since I didn't exactly have a bra. I kept his hoodie zipped up high and walked with my arms propping up the girls—I looked like I was smuggling two puppies under the sweatshirt.

At least it was cool out, still not in full-on spring mode, so that part of how I was dressed didn't get me too many glances. The real issue was the oversized guys' clothes and flip flops that kept shooting two steps ahead of me every couple of blocks.

"Why are your feet so big?" I grumbled, chasing after wayward foam and plastic.

"Pot, meet kettle. You've got some boats there too."

We made it to T-Sweets and found the usual line sticking out the front door. The five tables inside were taken. The crowd's eyes lit up when they spotted LJ.

I smiled as he ducked his head.

The attention always made the tips of his ears go red. Every step closer, more questions spilled out from people around us.

"LJ, where do you think you'll play after next year?"

"Ready for another championship?"

He put on his press-conference smile that hid his internal screams for escape, and replied like he had the answers written on the backs of his eyelids.

"Are you guys worried about this season with so many seniors leaving?"

I shoved my hand into his back pocket and yanked out his wallet. "I'll order for us."

"How do you know what I want?"

Waving the wallet, I joined the line, abandoning him to his

adoring fans. It was always a chocolate and vanilla swirl with rainbow and chocolate jimmies. Always.

He'd stand and stare at the menu, waiting for the line to move, and then he'd get to the counter and order the same thing every time.

The line moved quickly and I glanced out the window. In jeans slung low on his hips and a t-shirt that highlighted every sinewy muscle, he held court amongst the picnic tables in front of the shop.

He hated the attention. It made him want to go full turtle and crawl inside his shell.

I loved it. I loved watching him get the attention he deserved after the amount of work he put in on the field. I loved how he got so nervous in front of everyone, even though when we walked back with our ice cream, he'd remember every question they'd asked and how great it felt to sign an autograph or two.

He felt like he didn't belong in the limelight, but he did. He was the best person I knew. Too bad he didn't feel even half of what I felt for him.

CHAPTER 3
MARISA

Senior Year - High School

"I thought you were coming home tonight?" I shuffled down the stairs with my phone cradled against my shoulder and a death grip on the banister. The wood creaked under my sock-covered feet.

"This is an opportunity I couldn't pass up."

"Since when is Atlantic City a once-in-a-lifetime trip?" I winced. My hips ached. The bruises were intense. It was a small price to pay, but I needed some painkillers.

"Since I'm not paying and Frank is a high roller, so we're staying in a Presidential Suite."

"What am I supposed to do tonight?"

"Why don't you go to LJ's house? It's where you're always running off to anyway. Or call your father. Sorry, I forgot. He ran off to god knows where and didn't look back."

I gritted my teeth, steering her back to the only shitty parent currently speaking to me—her, and away from the only people I could count on.

"I'm not there that much." I made sure to never be there more than a few times a week during the school year, and I only slept over once every two weeks. During the summer, I let myself bump it up to weekly sleepovers and four days hanging out.

Overstaying my welcome wasn't something I ever wanted to do with LJ's family. I felt like I'd already overstayed my welcome with my own mother.

"It's not my fault your father decided he'd rather run off with all his extra special sport's groupies and leave us to make due. All those promises to send birthday money or Christmas presents and we've never heard a peep."

Another reminder and comparison, which wasn't helping my stomach trying to eat itself.

"The doctor said I should take it easy for a few days." Plus, LJ's whole family was still at the hospital after the bone marrow donation the day before yesterday. They'd been in Charlie's room taking shifts since the chemo had started.

"You looked fine to me two days ago. And shouldn't his family be taking care of you? They owe you after what you did. God knows, we're not getting child support from your father. They could throw us a bone."

I squeezed the bridge of my nose and attempted to pace around my room before giving up. Everything out of her mouth was always about how shitty everyone else was—trust me there was more than enough to go around between her and my dad, but I needed someone here. Now. I pulled my shorts away from my hips. The bruises made me look like I'd owed some bookies money, but they were yellowing. Still sore, though. "I did it because it was the right thing to do. We've known their family since I was in the third grade. They don't owe me anything." If anything, I owed them.

"You should've gotten something. Asked for some money or something. No one gives anything away for free. You'd be wise to remember that."

"So what are you giving up for your trip to Atlantic City?" I bit the inside of my cheek.

"Sounds like you're perfectly fine and back to normal after your little hobbling act at the hospital."

Yes, the limited movement walking out of the hospital after going under general anesthesia and having someone drill into my hips to harvest bone marrow had totally been an act.

This call needed to end. But my stomach and I weren't on the same page about letting her off the hook so quickly. "I guess I'm just too tough for my own good. Did you leave any cash?" If she was going to be gone for an indeterminate amount of time, I'd need to buy more food.

She let out a sigh like my request for money for food was the same as whining for a shiny new BMW for my birthday. "You're eighteen. You're strong and independent. I'm sure you can figure it out, sweetheart."

"When are you coming home?" Not that I minded her being gone. At least I wouldn't have to hear the hundredth nitpick about me or the millionth rant about Ron and how she'd given up on her dreams and goals to be with him and was left saddled with a kid. But she'd at least order some food or give me cash to buy some, if she were here.

She talked to someone who wasn't me. "The next hand of blackjack is starting and I'm Frank's good luck charm. I've got to go." The call ended.

I stared at the blank screen. After all these years, it shouldn't surprise me. I shouldn't have any expectations about my own parents. I flung my phone down like it had something to do with the person on the other end of the line always finding new ways to dig that knife in a little deeper. I blinked back tears and massaged my hip.

I'd made so many promises to myself that I wouldn't get my hopes up about her possibly remembering she had a daughter, but, without fail, I did. No matter how much I pretended I didn't care and it didn't matter, it broke something a little more inside me every time she didn't swoop in at the last minute to reassure me that everything would be okay.

Shuffling my feet and bracing my hand against my hip, I walked down the stairs. It wasn't as bad as it had been before, but I didn't want the pain or my mobility to get worse. It wasn't like there was anyone to help me.

Downstairs, I evaluated my food situation.

Half-empty ketchup and mustard bottles rattled in the fridge. The packages of turkey, ham and cheese I'd stashed inside earlier were gone. So was my deli pickle and the loaf of brioche bread I'd been drooling for. I'd used the last of my money to buy bread and lunch meat for sandwiches. Counting on my mom to cook anything for me would've led to starvation.

I slammed the fridge closed, sending the meager contents inside toppling over, muffled by the sealed door. She'd stolen my freaking food. I let out a scream of frustration.

Taking painkillers on an empty stomach wasn't ideal. Puking wasn't at the top of my list of activities for today, not that I'd have anything to puke up if I didn't eat, but the roller-coaster of nausea wasn't a line I wanted to stand in either.

I checked the normal spots my mom stashed cash and found only empty bottles. Back to the kitchen I went, confronted with what we had left. Cans of light tuna in water and dry cornflakes were my options.

Maybe a cereal and tuna fish sandwich? I grabbed the bread still sitting in the breadbox.

If the green fuzzy spots dotting the loaf were anything to go on, this had been here since the last time my mom had gone grocery shopping two months ago.

I grabbed the cereal box and opened the can of tuna, standing in front of them like a dare gone wrong. The corn-flakes could be like mini scoops. Like tortilla chips. Same thing, right?

A knock on the door broke me out of my debate on whether contemplating this as a meal made me insane.

I rushed to the door as quickly as my hip would allow, which probably looked more like a hobble. The pain of attempting to run was still better than dealing with the mush mixture sitting on the counter.

Nudging the curtain in front of the window in the door, I spotted a face I was always happy to see. His neutral look tied my stomach into knots.

My heart clenched and I opened the door, bracing myself for the news. "LJ, what happened?"

"I've been calling your phone for the last half hour. Where have you been?"

The phone I'd thrown down in disgust after talking to my mom was somewhere in my bed or on my floor. Apparently I'd been on my foraging adventure for at least that long. Maybe that was why my stomach rumblings were getting louder.

"Right where you found me. How's your dad?"

His face brightened. "He's good. They did the transplant today. It only took a few hours."

"Really? Already? I figured once they harvested it from me, it would take more time."

"Nope, they move quickly. Mom's bringing him home tomorrow. The doctors said he's doing well, which means…" He grinned, rubbing his hands together like his diabolical plan was all coming together. "I got this for you."

He shoved the bakery bag under my nose while turning his away. "I got you an everything bagel with strawberry cream cheese."

I snatched the bag out of his hand. "Seriously?" Peering inside, my saliva glands went full waterfall. "How can you not like an everything bagel and strawberry cream cheese?"

"Because my stomach has a sense of self preservation. Poor food choices aside, I've got a surprise for you."

I shoved a chunk of the salty, sweet, crunchy food into my mouth. "Surprise?" I mumbled around the dough. A seed or two might have escaped my mouth.

He tugged one of the napkins that were wrapped around the outside of the bag and handed it to me. "We're going on the senior trip." Wiping his hand off on my shirt, he gestured to his.

He was wearing our senior trip t-shirt. The same one I had been supposed to go on, but couldn't pay the full price for and had lost the deposit I'd saved for the whole summer to put down. That was what I got for believing my mom when she said she'd help me out with the rest of the cash.

I shook my head, stuffing my mouth even more. "Our whole class left three days ago."

"That doesn't mean we can't have one of our own." He rubbed his hands together with a state-championship-wide grin. The kind he hadn't worn in a long time, not since Charlie had gotten the results back from the doctor. Lymphoma.

"How are we going to take a senior trip?" I opened the door fully.

"You'll see. Get your shoes." He vibrated with an infectious excitement.

I turned, wincing and holding onto my hip. Now I could take my pain meds.

"Shit, what am I thinking? I'll get your phone and your sneakers." He barged into my house and looked around before rushing upstairs to my room. He hadn't been in there as much as I'd been in his, but he knew the way.

I shuffled into the kitchen and dumped my monstrosity into the trashcan before he could see. It would be an unholy smell when I got back, but I'd deal with it later.

The pain meds were on the counter. I downed them dry and shoved the bottle back into my pocket.

He jogged back down the stairs with my phone and shoes

in his hand. "Where's your mom? I thought she was going to be taking care of you after the surgery."

"A friend broke her hip, so she had to go visit her in the hospital." I folded my arms over my chest. My long sleeves covering all but the tips of my fingers. "She'll be back in a little bit."

LJ had a bad case of white knight syndrome. He was always the first to try to swoop in and save someone. Sometimes, it led to things like his dad's bone marrow drive, other times it led to him badgering me to get in touch with Ron or have a heart to heart with my mom about my feelings, and the flames of those two attempts still licked at the edges of my heart. So no, he didn't need to know my mom was out getting bombed somewhere with some guy she probably barely knew.

LJ would probably show up with a full list of rehabs and family therapists, but people could only be helped if they thought there was a problem. In my mom's eyes, her only problem was leaving for New York in less than a couple months.

"Cool, let her know where you are." He handed over my phone. "Did you want pants or are you good in those?"

I lifted an eyebrow. "How long have you known me?"

He handed over my sneakers and held up his hands. "I'll never get how your arms and hands are like ice blocks, but your legs are a furnace. Are you sure you weren't pieced together in Frankenstein's lab?" He shot his arms out in front of him imitating a reanimated corpse.

"Maybe I was." I did the Frankenstein's monster walk right alongside him, but mine was more convincing since the pain meds hadn't kicked in yet.

"We're already off to a good start. Come on, let's go."

He hurried me out the door and I didn't protest nearly as much as I normally would've because right now, choosing between going anywhere with LJ and staying stuck in my house alone with my barren cabinets was a no-brainer.

Opening his car door like he always did, he kept tight-lipped through all my questions.

"What do you have planned?"

He turned on the car and headed toward his house. "I've had a lot of thinking time being cooped up in the hospital. Contrary to what you might think, it's not a non-stop party in there." He winked, still smiling. It hadn't faltered since he walked inside.

The relief of the transplant being over had lifted a weight he'd been carrying for a long time. The whole family had. When we'd done the bone marrow testing drive at school, we'd hoped to get more people into the registry. A match was a pipe dream. Helping LJ coordinate it had been easy—anything for Charlie. When the news that I was the person they'd been looking for came, all eyes were glued on me.

For the past month, while Charlie had undergone chemo and we'd sorted through all the insurance red tape, everyone kept watching me. They'd whisper when LJ and I walked past in the hallways, or they'd ask tons of questions about the procedure and complications and what would happen to Charlie after.

At least now it was over. The school year would be finished in a couple weeks and we'd have the summer before college started. Before LJ and I would be going our separate ways. He'd be going to Fulton U and I'd chosen a school in New York.

The art history program there was one of the best in the world, right along with the price tag, but the scholarships and financial aid forms, which I'd had to fill out myself by digging through my mom's tax forms, would get me there. And the museums. I could spend the rest of my life and still not see every piece of art housed in all the collections in the city.

Art had always been an escape for me. I could check out books from the library and pretend I was a Renaissance woman who was a muse for a famous painter. Or imagine what it would be like to sit beside the lake covered in water lilies. Once I could take the train, I'd spent a lot of time in museums in the city. I was under twelve way into my teens for the free admission. Sitting and watching the paintings, and how people reacted to them and the other artwork. I'd try to imagine their lives, making up stories about where they were coming from or going.

Hiding out at the museum had helped when I didn't want to overstay my welcome with LJ's family. It was quiet, not too crowded, the perfect temperature and no one bothered me if I was there for hours. My escape to art became a love I couldn't deny.

We pulled up to LJ's house, where Mickey Mouse-shaped balloons arched around their doorway and floated from the railings leading up to their porch, swaying in the gentle breeze.

"How did you do all this?"

His eyes crinkled and he jumped out of the car before sliding over the hood and opening mine.

I stared at him, wanting to rub my eyes to make sure it was all real.

He held out his hand and I took it, gritting my teeth as I shoved out of the low bucket seat.

We walked up the driveway, which was lined with cut outs of the mouse silhouette on popsicle sticks shoved into the ground.

"Seriously? How did you pull this off?"

"You ain't seen nothing yet." He took my hand.

Electric sparks traveled from my fingers and wrapped around my heart.

We walked to the porch, hand in hand, all my aches and

pains washed away with a single touch. My body tingled and blood pounded in my ears.

His fingers tightened around mine as we walked up the solid steps. He opened the door and I gasped, covering my mouth with one hand, still keeping my fingers intertwined with his.

"Oh my god."

CHAPTER 4
LJ

PRESENT

———

A sharp pain jabbed me in my ribs, and I fought against my smile, keeping my face lax as the weight shifted beside me. It had been three weeks since Marisa moved into my house—into my bed.

Liv had shown up at The Brothel a few days after the fire, cursing Ford's name and swearing to Marisa that she would exact a vivid and slightly disturbing torture on him for whatever he'd done.

After a couple weeks of the two of them living on ice cream and mixed drinks, Liv had packed up her things, bought us a few cases of beer as a thank you, and practically floated out the door under the watchful gaze of her no-longer-broken-up-with boyfriend, so there was another sleeping option for Marisa—or me. But we kept sharing my bed. Lying next to her each night, I fought to keep my hands to acceptable points of contact like a brush against her back or arm.

Sleep also gave me a level of plausible deniability about the morning wood tenting my sweatpants. That had been much harder to control.

On my side, under the blankets with my back resting against the wall, I kept my hands in front of my face.

Her hair brushed over the back of my fingers, tickling them.

I shifted a finger, letting the strands slide against my skin. This close, her French toast smell invaded my lungs. Not the baked dessert, but the cereal. No one should ever let her anywhere near their stove or oven.

More hair brushed over my hands. Next the tickle moved to my neck and chin.

I wanted to slide my arm under her head and hold her against my chest. I wanted to trace my thumb down the curve of her neck. I wanted to taste her lips.

Having her this close for the past few weeks and having to keep myself under control had been one of the hardest things I'd ever done. After nearly losing her, I wasn't going to do anything to freak her out.

I kept my eyes closed, stilling my lips from the creeping smile trying to invade my muscles.

The hair traveled up my cheek, and I curled my toes against the twitching tickling feeling.

Then it shoved straight up my nose.

My eyes shot open.

Bathed in the late morning sun, Marisa stared back at me propped up on her elbow grinning with a lock of her hair pinched between her two fingers.

She burst into a fit of laughter.

"What the hell, Marisa?" I knocked her hair away, rubbing at my nose the same way I did on the field when a bug decided that, out of the entire world, my nostril was their new favorite spot.

She doubled over with laughter, curling into the fetal position while flailing and wiping the ends of her hair off on my shirt. "That's what you get for pretending to be asleep."

"How is trying to touch my brain with your hair a suitable punishment for fake sleeping after being woken up by your bed-shaking snores?"

Her eyes narrowed and she shoved at my shoulder. "I don't snore."

"You're totally right. The fog horn must have been all in my head."

"Fog horn!" She charged forward, her fingers diving to my vulnerable sides, digging in and revisiting the tickling from before back on me tenfold.

My legs kicked out and my body recoiled, trying to evade her fingers of punishment.

Her hands sunk lower, going for my stomach. She sat up and got onto her knees for maximum leverage and control. Her hair fell around her face above me like a curtain.

I jerked away, but there was no escape with the wall at my back. Having her this close, even with the tickle treatment, hadn't totally killed my erection. And I knew the exact moment she found it.

The back of her hand grazed the head of my dick and stilled.

She didn't yank her hand away. Instead, she kept it there with my dick spelling out precisely how revved up I was in Morse code on the back of her hand.

.. ..-. / -.-- --- ..- / -.- . . .--. / - --- ..- -.-. .... .. -. --. / -- . / .-.. ..
-.- . / - .... .- - ..-- / .. .----. -- / -. --- - / --. --- .. -. --. / - --- / -.... .
/ .- -... .-... / - --- / .... - --- .--. / -- -.-- ... . .-.. ..-. / ..-. .-. --- -- / -.-
.. .. -. --. / -.-- --- ..- .-.-.-

Her eyes widened. But her hand remained. She didn't jerk away like she'd been burned, although it felt like my skin was lit aflame.

I groaned, torn between leaping out of the bed and turning her hand, so she could touch me fully.

"LJ." The breathless half-question did nothing to kill the erection.

As if she'd heard my thoughts, her hand brushed along the head of my cock and she palmed it through my sweats.

We both sucked in a sharp breath.

I reached out and wrapped my fingers around her arm.

Her half stroke drew a groan from my lips.

Through the soft fabric of my pants, the heat and weight of her hand made it hard to breathe. I'd spent so many nights wanting exactly this.

I was tempted to pinch myself to test the reality. It would take a cleat to the chest to wake me if this was a dream.

Her gaze jumped from the blanket still draped over me from the waist down to my eyes.

She had taken the lead, her tentative movements more than a brush, but less than a stroke with the barrier between us. A gap of intention big enough to deny. 'Oh, I thought that was your hand' or 'I was joking and shoved a flashlight in my pocket to screw with you.'

I fought to keep my eyes from rolling back in my head. My mouth and lips were dry and my fingers itched to touch her.

I pulled her closer. "Marisa—"

Her hand slipped into the waistband of my sweats.

I grabbed her wrist and pulled it back out.

A hurried hand job wasn't what I wanted our first time to be.

I rested my forehead against hers. My lips inches from hers. My blood on fire in my veins and my dick growing by the second to full mast, heavy and ready for her touch.

"Marisa…" My voice came out strangled and tortured like my body was kicking its own ass.

She tilted her head, her eyes hooded with desire. This wasn't a drunken night of craziness. It wasn't something we could walk back from and chalk it up to the booze or late night loss of inhibitions. And I wanted it. I wanted her.

A sharp knock broke through the tug-of-war in my chest. "Marisa, you have a…visitor."

Her head snapped back and she looked at me. Her eyes scanned my body before returning to my eyes like she'd also thought she had been dreaming.

She dropped off the bed, looking more like she'd fallen out instead of jumping out. "It's probably Liv. I'll see what she needs." Her stunned breathless expression morphed into a smirk—a full, plump, kissable one which sent a thundering throb straight to my straining erection.

When she got back into bed, I wasn't sure I'd be able to tell her no. I wanted her just as much, had wanted her for too long.

All the reasons I'd held back before had been eroded with three weeks of nearly constant contact and nights with her beside me. Our friendship. My plans. Her dad.

Grabbing a hair tie off the knob at the top of my bed where there were at least twenty, she put her hair up before disappearing out the door.

I slammed my head back against the pillow, muttering every curse in the book at her former roommate's terrible timing.

What if Liv had found another place for them to live? What if she'd broken up with her pro hockey player boyfriend again and planned on occupying all of Marisa's time with ice cream and nail-painting whisper sessions?

I jumped out of bed and headed after her.

Yeah, I was an asshole.

This wasn't how I'd planned for this to go. There were so many plans swirling around my head for how to bridge the chasm from best friend to girlfriend. All of them had been flattened like a kicker put on the defensive line.

By the time I was halfway down the stairs, Marisa was standing in the partially opened door.

It wasn't Liv. The two of them would have been on the couch laughing or cursing someone's name by now.

Marisa had her arms crossed over her chest and was using her elbow to keep the door from opening any more.

The deep set of her frown was highlighted by the bright sunlight casting harsh shadows on half her face, not reaching the rest of the house with her wedged in the opening.

Who the hell was here?

Every protective cell in my body ignited to get between her and whatever made her fold her arms over her chest like that.

I jumped to the bottom of the steps and tugged open the door, ready to take down whoever stood on the porch giving her shit, but all those feelings withered and retreated as I stared back at the man in his mid-fifties in a Fulton U cap and polo shirt.

"Coach Saunders…" I licked my lips. The ones I'd been seconds from pressing against Marisa's.

"See, I'm perfectly fine." Marisa stepped back and stood beside me to fully block the doorway like she expected him to barge in without me there as backup.

Coach Saunders looked from her to me. "Why didn't you tell me?"

"Why would I? I'm safe. You were at the combines anyway, so it's not like you were even here."

"You could've called me." He wasn't looking at her. His eyes bored into mine.

My skin felt like it was blistering. Shit.

Marisa would've killed me if I told him about the fire. I'd badgered her about calling and she swore she would.

"The paramedics didn't even take me to the hospital. LJ picked me up and brought me here. I'm good. I've got people around me I can count on." That was a grenade launched straight in his face.

His gaze swung back to her, softening. Worry creased the deep lines of his face. "What about your things? Do you need new clothes? A computer? Or anything else before your trip?"

"I took care of it all. Renter's insurance is paying for most of it. I'll save a nice chunk of change on the checked bag fee, since I only have enough possessions to fill one."

He shook his head, pain and regret etched deep in every line. "I wish you'd called me."

She let loose a humorless laugh. "I'll see you at Monday dinner."

"I know you think I'm the bad guy, Marisa." He lifted the brim a few times like he needed to air out the furnace churning in his head before settling it back on his head. "All I want is for you to be safe and happy."

Marisa peeked over at me with a hide-and-seek smile. "I am." She stepped closer to me and wrapped her arm around my waist. Her fingers toying with the waistband of my sweats. Shit. This was monumentally bad. After three years of dinners, she'd never taken pissing her dad off this far.

My muscles went lockjaw tight.

His laser focus was back on me. His gaze swept over me from top to bottom, zeroing in on my crotch like he was about to rip my dick off with his bare hands.

I followed his gaze and with horror-movie realization saw the spot on the front of my pants. The slightly damp, definitely not pee spot as I stood with his daughter's arm wrapped around me.

I jolted, jumping back and pulling Marisa's arm from around me and dropping my hands in front of me.

She looked over at me, her eyebrows dipping before she folded her arms across her chest again.

My stomach plummeted.

"And I'm safe and happy." But she didn't sound it in the

slightest. There was an edge to her voice. "I'll see you on Monday." She closed the door without waiting for his reply.

With a long hard look at me that felt even more searing than the one from her dad, she dropped her arms and climbed up the stairs to my bedroom.

"Brutal."

I jerked at the invasion, turning to glare at Reece holding a mug and standing in the kitchen doorway.

"I don't need the commentary."

He stepped in closer, chancing a glance at the empty staircase. "All I'm saying is you need to make a choice, because you might not just be fucking yourself over with this thing with you and Marisa. Coach could take this whole house out. I know you two have been friends for forever. But he has your career by the balls. If he decides you're out, that's it. No draft. No pro career. No pro money."

"She's my best friend."

"Would she want you giving up your dream for her? For your family?"

My back stiffened. It had been a hard road since my dad had first been diagnosed. My parents had tried to shield me and my brothers, but there's only so much that can be hidden.

My parents had been struggling even after my dad beat cancer three years ago. It was the scariest time in my life, a time I never wanted to go back to, where we'd had to sit down and decide if we wanted a roof over our heads or to push forward with lifesaving treatment for my dad. If anything like that happened to someone I cared about again, I wanted it to be as easy as writing a check.

I'd waited so long for the time to be right. It had never been.

Not after our first kiss in my backyard treehouse in third grade, where she punched me in the nuts for springing on her.

Not after our second one at the seventh-grade dance,

where our braces got stuck together beside the pull-out bleachers in the gym, and we'd had to be separated by the school nurse. We'd spent the next couple years trying to live that down.

Not after I recreated the senior trip for her after she'd saved my dad's life and she had made it categorically known that she wasn't into me that way.

But keeping this inside was like wrestling with a part of my soul trying to break free to tell her.

"I love her."

He squeezed the back of his neck, shaking his head. "Will you still love her in a year? In two years?"

"I've loved her since we were fifteen. It's never going away."

With the all-knowing look he'd barely earned after having his cake and eating it too with a first-round draft pick and the woman he loved, he dropped his hand to my shoulder. "What's better for everyone? Waiting or thinking with your dick?"

"I'm not thinking with my dick."

"That's not what the stain on the front of your sweats says." He took a sip from his mug.

I tugged my t-shirt down lower. Did I have a neon fucking sign pointing to my crotch?

Waiting. Waiting even longer for her. I shoved my hands into my hair, resting my forehead in my palms. What choice did I have?

"If I tell her we can't do this because of her dad, she'll never forgive him. She barely speaks to him as it is." I looked to Reece.

"Isn't it better that she hate him, than hate you?" He disappeared back into the kitchen to leave me with those lingering words.

I was left alone in the empty living room. People laughed

and shouted outside on the sidewalks. The blinds were still drawn inside; the house only now waking up.

As much as I wanted the answer to be him, she deserved a shot at some kind of relationship with her dad. Her mom hadn't always been there for Marisa. A last-minute trip to visit a sick friend, a car breakdown or a work meeting that ran late. Anytime my parents took her aside to talk to her, she'd always reassured us her mom was just busy and was the go-to responsible friend, so everyone always turned to her.

During middle school, Marisa had hung out after school during my practices to get a ride home with me, and she'd usually stayed for dinner.

But her dad was trying. For over a year he'd been trying. Maybe what he was doing to me was fucked up, but I was also the one who showed up to every dinner he tried to have with Marisa to get her to open up. There was only one more dinner left before she left on her trip to Venice—a trip she should've been able to take years ago, if it hadn't been for me. If she hadn't sacrificed it for me.

Taking the stairs one at a time, I walked up to my bedroom and took a few breaths before pushing the door open.

Marisa was crouched by her backpack, dumping highlighters, pens and paper all over the floor. Her whole life was crammed into that bag and one of my dresser drawers. Other than the few clothes I'd given her, there wasn't much I could do to help.

My scholarship took care of rent, food, and a night out a few times a semester. I'd check in with the financial aid office and see if I could get a small student loan. Paying it off would be easy as soon as I signed my contract.

I wanted to be able to take her out and replace everything she'd lost. Get her brand new clothes, a top-of-the-line computer, and anything else she wanted. But I wasn't there —not yet.

After next year. After the draft. After I signed my first pro contract, I'd be able to take care of her and everyone else I cared about without a second thought. I'd seen the plans the drafted seniors were making.

Reece had been planning out an automated sneaker closet. Guys bought their parents brand-new homes. They paid for their siblings' college tuition. If they were smart with their money, people they loved never had to worry about anything, and they got the best medical care in the world.

I just had to get there.

Marisa shoved papers back into the now empty duffel. "I can't find my tutoring notebook."

I slid a few folders to the side and pulled the worn purple notebook from the stack.

"I know I had it," she grumbled and shoved more back into the black and gray bag.

I held out the notebook beside her, dangling it in my hold.

Her head snapped to the side and she looked at it and up at me.

I scrubbed my chin. "We need to talk."

CHAPTER 5
MARISA

N o, we most definitely didn't. Not even a little bit. We didn't need to talk because I didn't want to hear what he was going to say. He'd telegraphed it all loud and clear downstairs in front of Ron.

My stomach had knotted tight and painful when he'd dropped my arm, letting it flop to my side like a sunbaked fish covered in flies.

A couple minutes before, I'd sworn he was going to kiss me. I could almost feel his lips pressed against mine from the intensity of his gaze.

The ache between my thighs had plowed into me and I was ready to take our friendship to the next level. Obviously, I'd been a freaking moron for forgetting what our relationship was.

Once again, reading the room hadn't been my strong suit. How many times were we going to do this? Too many, it seemed. Only this time, I hadn't kissed him—I'd gone straight for his dick. Stepping up my game. Maybe next time around, I'd grab a strap on and some lube.

I'd gotten a big head thinking his morning wood was due to me. Maybe he had forgotten who I was for a second, just thinking of me as another woman who'd woken up in his bed, not Marisa, his best friend.

With any of the other women he'd slept with, it probably would have been, but not me. And then I'd gone for it and he'd stopped me. Who stopped a girl mid-hand job? Although it was more like a hand-internship or hand-volunteer-work than an actual job.

He'd been looking at me so tenderly in a way that made my heart thump against my ribs and made me feel lighter than air. I had been thinking he was holding onto my arm because he had to touch me. Instead, it was more likely because he'd been trying to keep me from going any further.

And the second I attempted to go for it, he was ready to head for the hills.

How stupid was I? And then he'd stepped away in front of Ron. Double rejection right in my face.

It wasn't like Ron hadn't cancelled three weeks of dinners for some scouting and recruiting trips he needed to go on. After all the posturing he'd done about how much he wanted to connect, he'd cancelled more dinners during the season than we'd actually eaten. Instead of making me happy, it pissed me off even more. He'd shown me exactly what was the most important thing to him.

I'd thought about calling Ron after the fire, but I hadn't, even after promising LJ. I kept meaning to, but other things kept coming up. Maybe it was a test. One where I waited it out to see how long it would actually take for him to realize his daughter might have died in a fire. Maybe.

And I'd gotten my answer: three weeks. It had been three weeks since Liv had woken me from my study hangover with an index card stuck to my face and smoke choking the air from my lungs. Panic had shot through me and all knowledge of exits and fire escapes were wiped from my memory as smoke burned my eyes and seared my throat. We'd crawled out of the apartment, tumbled down the stairs, and were met with firefighters and paramedics on our doorstep.

Three weeks.

It was a hell of a lot better than fourteen years, I guess. That was how long the radio silence had lasted before. I hated that I'd counted the days. Hated that I cared. Hated how much it hurt.

It wasn't like I expected him to come swooping in to rescue me. Liv and I had done most of the saving, and LJ picked up the rest of the slack, but three weeks?

I had a tutoring session in an hour and I couldn't find my damn notebook.

LJ dangled it beside me.

Making sure to keep my fingers far from his, I took it from his grip after he'd uttered those fateful words: 'we need to talk'.

Turned out they worked just as well on girls as they did on guys.

"I've got tutoring this afternoon." Flipping through my schedule taped to the front page, I bit back my groan. Of course today, I was tutoring Chris. The perfect addition to an already supremely shitty day.

"I know."

Why'd he have to say it like that? Like he'd committed my schedule to memory and knew everything about me. Well he mostly did, but like a best friend did, not like a guy who wanted to jump my bones.

"I need to get changed and get to the library."

"About this morning—"

"Nope, we don't have to talk about it." I stood and opened the drawer where my other clothes were, seconds from slamming my hands over my ears and screaming 'la la la, I can't hear you'.

"We should."

I lifted my head to meet his gaze, feeling like I was a rusty robot. "Why? I crossed a line. It won't happen again." Why had he looked at me like he was going to kiss me? Why had I given in to all the feelings I'd bottled up for so long? Why did I want it so bad?

"You didn't cross a line. I was there too." And he didn't look happy about it.

"With nowhere to go." I'd cornered him and felt him up. The cringe was real and intense. My mom's voice rang in my ears. They all leave.

"We were early morning groggy. You know, just…I'm not upset or freaked out. it's not a big deal."

Well, I wouldn't say that. "Right, my hand has just been one of many to paw your junk."

His neutral face dipped into a full-on frown. "I never said that."

"So if I slipped my hand into your sweats right now for a little handy action?"

His eyes widened and his whole body locked. Not in a hell-yes-more-of-that kind of way. More like please-don't-let-my-pain-in-the-ass-friend-paw-me-again kind of way. "Let's keep our hands outside our pants."

"So you're up for an over-the-pants handy? Might be a friction burn in store for you." I shrugged and stepped closer, shoving my shirt sleeves up to my elbows. "But if that's what you're comfortable with."

I'd push this past the realm of serious talk straight into slapstick. Better that than the alternative of getting called out for being willing to go through with it and hoping against hope he'd been about to kiss me earlier.

"Could you be serious for five minutes?"

I extended my hand. "Hi, I'm Serious. Nice to meet you." Dad jokes for the win at defusing insanely embarrassing situations.

He scrubbed his hands down his face and gave me the

exasperated look that told me we were okay. He pinched the bridge of his nose and looked up at the ceiling.

My smile wasn't paper thin anymore. It was a full on grin. Distraction mode activated!

"The next eight months make or break my future."

"And you've got it locked down. You were the best player in our high school." I'd take the diversion to LJ's worries about football and cling onto it like a crazy-glue-covered spider monkey.

"But it means going after it with a singular focus." An intensity burned in his eyes and I wished he was going after me with a singular focus.

Brush it off, Marisa. Focus. Isn't that what we were talking about? Like how his t-shirt was tight across his chest and his gray sweatpants made me want to climb him like a Redwood.

Focus! His lips were still moving. Lock up those feelings and throw away the key.

"Of course. I get it. I was at the sidelines for all those games. I badgered you through summer workouts in the gym. If there's anyone out there who wants you to make it, it's me."

His face softened. "I know, Marisa." He opened his mouth before snapping it shut like he was trying to capture words before they could escape.

"And as much as I'd love to give you another pep talk, I've got to tutor, so I can make rent and not get kicked out of this beautiful college townhouse." Taking my escape, I darted from the room and disappeared into the bathroom, closing and locking the door behind me. I held my clothes—not even mine, my borrowed clothes—to my chest and squeezed my eyes shut.

I had less than a year left until he was drafted, and I needed to figure out what to do next. This time I wasn't going to be left behind. This time I'd do the leaving.

———

THE WALK TO THE ATHLETICS BUILDING DIDN'T TAKE LONG. I shoved my long sleeves up and hitched my backpack higher. The championship trophies and mini banners lined the hallway along with the jerseys of all the drafted FU players over the years. LJ's name would be up there soon with LEWIS scrawled across the back, hanging beside Reece's, which they hadn't put up yet.

Inside the auditorium they used for team meetings as well as tutoring, I sent up a silent prayer that Chris wouldn't arrive. Signing in with the tutoring monitor, I reminded myself of how much I needed the cash.

"Good luck." The mentor added, spotting the name of who I'd be working with.

I found a spot and pulled out my supplies, wishing I had some holy water and a crucifix for this session.

Five minutes past our scheduled time, I closed my notebook. The study halls were mandatory for any player on the edge of eligibility due to their GPA, but tutors only had to stay until fifteen minutes past the scheduled start time, if the athletes didn't show.

Nine minutes after that, I slipped everything back into my bag. This would be the quickest cash I'd made all week.

The door swung open and he sauntered in like he'd stepped into a saloon.

My silent prayer became a not so silent curse, and a couple people glanced in my direction.

I sank lower in my seat and prepared for the pain.

Chris Farrell strolled down the steps, his grin widening when he spotted me.

This was going to be a long hour.

"We're calculating limits here." I checked over Chris's answers to his calc homework.

"Can't you just do this for me?"

The football player study hall paid better than tutoring at the student center, but it came with drawbacks. Mainly, asshole football players who thought they could be assholes because they could punt, kick, throw or pass a ball. Thankfully, I had no illusions that this only extended to football players, but the volume I interacted with showed me they went one of two ways.

They could be total marshmallows, or absolute d-bags who didn't understand why ladies weren't lined up around the block to blow them. The funny thing was, it was often inversely proportional to how good they were on the field.

"If I did it for you, you'd never pass your final exam, which is in…" I checked my imaginary watch. "One week."

"This is bullshit. What does calculus even matter?" He shoved his papers forward almost knocking them off the desk.

"You signed up for the class, not me. And you missed the add/drop window after warnings from everyone to let you know how close you were to failing the class."

He grumbled like a three-year-old. "I won't need any of this shit once I'm drafted."

From what LJ said, it wasn't happening. If anything, he needed to knuckle down and study his ass off, so he at least got his degree when his pro goals went up in a puff of smoke.

"I'll pay you a hundred bucks to take the test for me."

I glanced up at the team monitor in the auditorium dotted with other players working with their tutors. "Are you trying to get us both in trouble?" I seethed, gripping the edge of my desk. Getting fired or worse, drawing the attention of the coaching staff—like my father—to my low-key tutoring job wasn't on my list of to-dos before I left for the summer.

"You know all this shit. Have you taken your calc exam already?"

"I'm not taking calc."

His head jerked back and he stared. "What do you mean you're not taking calc?"

"I mean I'm not taking calc. I haven't taken it since high school."

"Then how the hell are you tutoring me?"

"Why do I need to be enrolled in a class to tutor you? I took it as a senior in high school." Calc wasn't easy, but I'd taken it to get a leg up on college admissions. It wasn't my fault that Chris barely paid attention, never took notes, and didn't do any of his homework.

"What are you majoring in now?"

"Art history." I wasn't going to lay out my course load in analytical chemistry and the chemistry of art, so I could take on preservation as well as curation work.

"Now that we're finished with the getting to know you portion of our session, can you get back to your problems?"

"You're not even a math major. No wonder I can't figure any of this out."

I squeezed the bridge of my nose. Think of the money. Think of the money and think of Venice. "You can't figure this out because you're not paying attention. Let's go over it again and I'll do a sample problem for you, so you can see the steps to solve it again."

"This is bullshit and I'm out of here." He flipped the notebook sending it crashing to the floor and stormed out. Whelp, at least I'd still get paid for the whole hour.

The tutor monitor called his name, but the door was already slamming shut behind him.

I cleaned up the papers and walked up to the front to sign out for my session.

"Only one week left, right?"

"One week too many." I scribbled my initials next to my sign-in and left. Instead of heading back to The Brothel, I took a detour to the Franklin Building. My department was tucked in with the history department, but the couches were comfy and worn in and no one was ever there.

Reprints of works by Klimt, Van Gogh, and Monet hung on the walls in ornate frames with their own lighting. The framing probably cost as much as a year's tuition.

Being here always relaxed me. It was quiet and out of the way, and I could stare at the paintings and imagine what it was like to be the first person to see the finished artwork. Or think about having a chance to preserve them so future generations could appreciate them.

They were eternal with their influence rippled out for decades and centuries after the artist was gone. I'd learned that was the kind of permanence you got with things, never people.

Taking my worn-in spot on the green leather sofa, I flipped open my laptop and scrolled through my emails. Italian names were sprinkled throughout my inbox.

Checklists, introductions and arrangements to be made. My first step to my new adventure. Italy. After so many years, internship application essays and interviews, it was so close.

Part of me was afraid to get my hopes up, that the trip couldn't live up to the hype, but the other part of me was screaming 'Italy, fuck yes!' from a convertible screaming down the Italian coast.

An office door opened, muted by the old carpet and hallways lined with bookshelves filled with dissertations and portfolios. "Marisa?"

I glanced up from my laptop. "Hi, Professor Morgan."

"Excited for your trip?" She was part of the reason I'd decided to focus on museum studies in my art history major. Her outfits reminded me much more of Indiana Jones than a stuffy museum tour guide, and her love of art radiated off her, from her tattoos to the ornate earrings paying homage to classic works of art.

She was my favorite professor and had gotten me my internship at the Museum of Art.

"Very—and a little scared. Thanks so much for the opportunity."

"You earned it. After your exciting spring break, I'm glad you'll get a chance to have some fun this summer."

"Me too." It also meant I didn't have to go home for the summer. Was it even my home at this point? Maybe I'd adopt the bohemian nomad persona instead of going back to my mom's house.

Not that going to Italy would ever come in second place to staying on campus or bumming around on people's couches for two months.

"When do you leave?"

"Two weeks after my last final, so I only have three weeks left." Nervous flutters took flight in my stomach.

She checked her watch. "Another faculty meeting for me. Email me any time you need anything, and if I don't see you before you go, then have a wonderful trip."

The walk back to the townhouse was longer than it needed to be. Every errand I hadn't gotten to over the past three weeks racked up in my head into what would've normally been a scary long list. But right now, it was perfect.

In addition to studying and taking my finals, I could pick up more tutoring sessions, which meant I could buy a new bathing suit and underwear for my trip.

The back-breaking couch of death was calling my name and whispering sweet nothings to me. Sleeping downstairs would mean I could wait for silence overhead before sneaking up to the bathroom.

At least there were only three weeks until I left for Venice. It would give us both some distance after the Wake Up Call of Regret. After the summer, things could go back to normal. Pretending things were fine wasn't new territory to me.

CHAPTER 6
LJ

My fingers dug into the dirt and grass. Panting, I was on my knees with sweat pouring down my face, blinding me. My heart jammed against my ribs with each beat as I gasped for air.

The sun beat down on me, baking my pads and roasting my body. We didn't usually fully suit up for spring practices, but today had been an exception. Sweat squished inside my cleats.

The shrill whistle blew above me.

Coach Saunders' feet came into view before he crouched down in front of me. "Is there a problem, Lewis?"

I gritted my teeth and pushed up off the ground. "No, sir." Standing, I let my arms fall to my sides, although all I wanted to do was brace my hands on my knees and try not to puke.

"Good." He blew the whistle and called for another set of wind sprints.

The whole team groaned and went to the end zone line.

Berk wiped his face with his shirt, but it was already soaked and didn't do much to stop the steady stream pouring down his face. "If these guys find out we're doing this because you're sleeping with Marisa, they're going to crucify you."

"All we're doing is sleeping."

"Hasn't stopped him from trying to burn a hole through your skull with his eyes." Another reason to keep things between Marisa and me platonic for now. It hurt almost as much as my calves.

The team of a hundred and twenty guys stood on the end zone line in two rows and Coach Saunders stood with the clipboard at his side flanked by the support coaching staff.

He sounded the whistle and we took off for another round of torture.

Fifteen heart-bursting, leg-wrecking, lung-burning minutes later I collapsed. Other guys puked and some wandered aimlessly like they were hallucinating or had decided screw this and were walking home.

After crawling off the field, I drained the ice water from my water bottle. Finally able to breathe in more than short pants, I set it down and began the long march.

On this sunny, bright day each step felt like one closer to my execution. Coach had his back to me, headset around his neck and clipboard at his side.

"Coach Saunders." I cleared my throat. Even after all that water, my mouth was sawdust dry.

He stopped, his back straightening, and turned to face me, face neutral, but gaze biting.

"Can I speak with you, sir?"

His gaze scanned me from head to toe before he issued a curt nod and took off toward the locker rooms.

I jogged after him, my muscles screaming with each step. "About yesterday."

"What about yesterday?"

"About Marisa staying over at my place…" The words took off like birds migrating, leaving my brain an empty pond.

He made a gruff noise.

"We've been friends for a long time and I wanted to make sure she was okay."

"From the rumble you made coming down the stairs and the state of you, it didn't look like you were only making sure she was okay." His words were clipped and blistering.

"Ask Marisa and she'll tell you we're only friends. Best friends, but it hasn't gone beyond that."

"But you'd like it to, huh? Has she shut you down?" His scathing chuckle grated with his enjoyment of my imaginary and not-so-imaginary blue balls when it came to Marisa. "Good for her. I can't imagine she'd want to follow in the footsteps of me and her mom." His mouth twisted in a grim line.

Marisa had never been too open about what happened with her parents other than her dad leaving when she was eight to take over the assistant coaching position at Ohio State.

He never came around much—ever, that I knew of. I hadn't ever met him before, and I hadn't made the connection between the two until Marisa told me she was transferring to Fulton U because her dad was the head coach here.

"There are two spring practices left. You need to think long and hard about how much your future in football matters to you." His pointed glare sent a pit plummeting to the depths of my stomach. "Dismissed."

Clenching my hands at my sides, I turned and left, walking back to the locker room. The threat was clear. Cross the line with Marisa and I was done. After three national championships he'd probably sacrifice our chances this season to bench me as much as he could. He could go out and recruit some of the best offensive linebackers out there to take my spot and the team would never miss a beat.

As much as I wanted to grab my phone and tell Marisa how right she'd been about her dad being an asshole, how he treated me and how he treated her were two different things.

I'd suck it up and deal with the fallout of making it clear we were only friends, and I'd try to toe the line through the end of next season, but then all bets were off.

Then he couldn't lord my future over me, and I could finally tell her how I felt—if it wasn't already too late.

———

FOR THREE WEEKS, SHE'D BEEN AVOIDING ME. SOMEHOW, INSTEAD of making it better, it made it a hell of a lot worse. We were about to spend the whole summer apart.

I pulled up to the airport departure lane, my car one of many offloading their passengers.

Marisa picked her bag up off the floor, double checked for her passport and wallet in the front pocket, and gave me a smile like she was psyching herself up for the first day of summer camp. The first smile in the three weeks since That Morning™.

She'd taken to sleeping on the back-breaking couch, until Keyton moved in a few of his things early, including a couch which hadn't been designed during the Spanish Inquisition. After that, I hadn't even had that as an excuse to get her back into my bed.

"Call me when you land."

Wrapping her arms around her bag, she looked over at me. "I will."

Nervous excitement radiated off her. It was her first trip out of the country. We'd picked the bag up the day after her emergency appointment after the fire.

"I can't believe you're going away for the whole summer." A grip tightened around my heart. Her freshman year she'd been in New York had sucked. I'd missed her—a lot. But I'd had classes and a whole season to gear up for. All summer without her would suck. The gym and my summer classes would take up some time, but there would be no water balloon fights, road trips to the shore, riding carnival rides until we were about to puke, or hanging out in the backyard soaking up the sun.

"Now you won't have to worry about me bugging you during workouts or forcing you to go out for late-night ice cream runs."

I didn't mind any of that one bit.

"The house will be quiet without you."

"Berk and Keyton will be there." She fiddled with the zipper on her bag. "Are you sure everyone's cool with me living there? I don't want to cramp everyone's style with my lady parts." She vaguely gestured to parts of her anatomy I'd been trying to keep my thoughts off for years now.

"They're hoping you'll help us ward off unwanted female attention."

She snorted. "Half the women on campus would plow through me in a heartbeat for a chance at any of you guys."

"Good thing you've got strong shoulders." I squeezed hers.

Her laugh was full this time.

"Plus, Berk's hung up on his pen pal and has been keeping a low profile since they've started trading dirty letters. Keyton is…" I shrugged. "Keyton. Who the hell knows? You're not cramping anyone's style."

It also meant she could stay in our up-to-code house where she didn't have to take on a random as a new room-mate now that Liv was squarely in the shacked-up category with Ford.

I had to subsidize her rent a little to make it work. I'd pay off the private loan once I got my signing bonus in the spring. The interest rate was ridiculous since my parents' credit was shot and I barely had any, but it was for less than a year. The stretch would be worth it to have her close, no matter how much that killed me.

She fiddled with her bag even more. "What if I hate it?"

"You won't. You've been looking forward to this since forever. All those paintings you've been forcing me to look at for years—you'll finally get to see them in person. Gondola rides for days. Maybe learn to cook some Italian food." I ducked my head trying to catch her eye.

"I make a great spaghetti already." She shot me a look.

I fought against the shudder. Every bite of her food was taking your life into your own hands. "You're right. But it's always good to learn new techniques. Maybe you'll up your game."

"Maybe." Silence descended on the car.

"Marisa—"

"LJ—"

We spoke at the same time. An uncomfortable chuckle followed by our gazes connecting.

I opened my mouth.

A knock on the window broke through the tension building in the car. I turned and glanced out at the cop.

"Drop off only. You've been here too long already." He walked on to the next car and did the same thing.

"We should get you inside." I popped the trunk and opened my door, climbing out and heading to the back of the car. "I'm glad you've finally gotten this trip. You should've gone ages ago."

"It's not a big deal. I figured I'd get there eventually."

"I know, but...I wish it had been when you were supposed to go."

She dropped her hand onto my arm. "LJ, enough with guilt tripping yourself. Sometimes I swear you're only friends with me out of obligation." Her laugh was reedy and a little stilted.

"Nah, it's also because of your wonderful cooking skills."

Her glare was precise, but her lips twitched. "More like the fact that I'm the only one who'll touch your dirty underwear."

"I never asked you to do my laundry." And I hadn't. But Marisa made it a Thursday night movie tradition to handle the folding, which I hated. Putting my clothes in the washer—sure. Them making it to the dryer before they got mildewy was debatable. Folding was an absolute no. She was probably the only reason I still had friends after freshman year when she'd come to campus and balked when she saw how long it had been since I'd last washed it all.

"It was that or watch you try to Febreeze your way through another year. No one needed that."

"Come on, it wasn't that bad." I wrestled her bag out of my trunk, hefting it up and out and setting it onto the yellow no parking lines across the front of the drop off area.

"Your clothes were a week from walking out the front door all on their own."

Marisa followed me and grabbed onto the handle of her bag. Her hand landed half on top of mine. The commotion of the airport was a background track.

Eight weeks. We hadn't been apart for that long since freshman year before she transferred. All those same crazy scenarios I'd run when she went to New York came roaring back. Would she be safe? What if she had the time of her life and never came back? What if she met some guy?

Her gaze was filled with uncertainty, excitement, and fear.

I wished I could go with her. I wanted to be her partner in crime, exploring Venice with side trips to Rome and train rides to Switzerland, Germany, and France.

"Let's go." A call broke through the hustle and bustle of the crowds around us. "Kiss your girl and leave. You're already over the time limit." The cop blew his whistle and went back to hounding people.

Marisa stared at the center of my chest before pulling the

bag from my grasp. Her arms wrapped around me for a way-too-short hug. "See you, L. Have a great summer."

She shot off with the bag with one glance over her shoulder and a quick wave before disappearing through the glass doors and off to her check in line.

I jumped at the presence and voice in my left ear. "She's gone, Romeo. Now move your damn car."

Fumbling for my keys, I hopped back into my car and joined the rest of the people leaving departures.

What if she met a smooth Italian guy and decided she was going to stay? What if she ran off to Paris with someone from her internship for a romantic vacation and decided to elope? What if she came back and I'd lost my shot?

———

TO: FOOTBALLSFINEST11@GMAIL.COM
   FROM: I_love_ripley_foreva@gmail.com
   SUBJECT: Guess what?
   Hi LJ,

I'm finally here!!! And guess what? I got bumped up to business class! Beat you to it. In a year, you'll probably be flying private. They handed out cool towels and I had my first glass of champagne. The real deal, not sparkling wine. The poor guy beside me wasn't nearly as fun to joke around with as you are. I hope you're having fun. I saw the pool party pics. Don't have too much fun without me.

My internship starts on Monday. It gives me just enough time to find a place to eat near the apartment I'm living in. Sending pics of the apartment! Want to video chat later?

———

TO: I_LOVE_RIPLEY_FOREVA@GMAIL.COM
   FROM: footballsfinest11@gmail.com

SUBJECT: Re: Guess what?

Hey Marisa, the apartment looks great! Business class!! You know you suck, right? The pool party was a last minute thing. It wasn't too bad, until Keyton had to drag Chris Farrell out of the deep end. Chris almost flunked out and got cut from the team and was drowning his sorrows in half a keg of beer. Other than that, things are quiet. My dad has his six-month doctor's visit in August. We're all holding our breath until then, but I'm sure that Magic Marisa bone marrow will keep on working. I'm good to video chat whenever.

———

TO: FOOTBALLSFINEST11@GMAIL.COM
FROM: I_love_ripley_foreva@gmail.com
SUBJECT: Re: Re: Guess what?
Hi LJ,

Of course, Chris ended up almost drowning. Sucks he got cut.

You didn't have to repaint my room, but I love the color. The food situation is precarious. I didn't think about how being in the museum would mean being so close to the tourist spots with insane restaurant prices. One thing I'll say is the bread and cheese are delicious—throw some ham on it and I'm good to go. A sandwich summer spectacular for me.

The house party looked like fun. Christmas in July was a great theme! Were you pretending to be Santa or something? There was a lot of lap sitting, LOL!

I hope your dad's visit goes well. Fingers and toes crossed. Video chat soon?

———

TO: I_LOVE_RIPLEY_FOREVA@GMAIL.COM
FROM: footballsfinest11@gmail.com

SUBJECT: Re: Re: Re: Guess what?

Hey Marisa,

Santa, haha. Good one. No Santa sessions. Just everyone trying to crowd into the pic. Is the guy you went to lunch with from your program? Looked like you two were having fun at the restaurant. Glad you're finally getting some hot food.

The date keeps changing for the doctor's visit. With our luck it'll end up being when you land. If it is, I'll see if Liv can pick you up.

———

TO: FOOTBALLSFINEST11@GMAIL.COM
FROM: I_love_ripley_foreva@gmail.com
SUBJECT: Time zones suck!
Hi LJ,

Don't worry about it. I can always take a taxi. I missed your last video call. Time differences are a thing. The meal was awesome. Pasta tastes so different here. Maybe because it's fresh. Henri is in my internship program. He's French and also speaks Italian. It's made getting around a lot easier, hanging out with him.

I can't believe you had a Nerf Battle without me! Who was the new girl? You haven't replaced me already, have you?

———

TO: I_LOVE_RIPLEY_FOREVA@GMAIL.COM
FROM: footballsfinest11@gmail.com
SUBJECT: Re: Time zones suck!
Hey Marisa,

Looks like you're hanging out a lot. Glad he's helping you get around. I talked to Liv. She's good to cover your pick up, if the doctor's visit runs late. Reece finished training camp last week, so he and Nix stopped by for one last game. The new girl is Elle's roommate, Jules. She's nice and lives across the street. She made some of the best brownies I've ever had in my life. She keeps giving us her baking experiments and we're all more than happy to be guinea pigs.

————

TO: FOOTBALLSFINEST11@GMAIL.COM
FROM: I_love_ripley_foreva@gmail.com
SUBJECT: I totally touched it!

LJ, Wow! A baker and right across the street. That's super close and convenient. She seems nice. Really cute too. You won't have to worry about satisfying that sweet tooth with her around.

And don't worry about the airport. It's fine. Seriously! I can get to the house on my own. How is this summer almost over? I'm going to be sad to leave. This had been the best summer. I got to touch a Picasso! Well, not with my bare hands. They were moving it and I slapped on my nitrile gloves and pitched in. It was surreal.

————

TO: FOOTBALLSFINEST11@GMAIL.COM
FROM: I_love_ripley_foreva@gmail.com
SUBJECT: Hello???

LJ, how are things going?

————

TO: I_LOVE_RIPLEY_FOREVA@GMAIL.COM
FROM: footballsfinest11@gmail.com
SUBJECT: Re: Hello???

Hey Marisa, it sounds like you're having a blast. Sorry it

took me so long to reply. Summer workouts are kicking my ass and I picked up two summer classes to lighten my load during the semester. Both had finals at the same time. I fell asleep most nights at my desk and my neck is killing me.

———

TO: FOOTBALLSFINEST11@GMAIL.COM
FROM: I_love_ripley_foreva@gmail.com
SUBJECT: Whenever you get to this…

Hi LJ, no problem. I figured you were busy. I'm sure Jules can give you something to help with the pain or any of the other people stopping by the house. Seems like things are pretty busy there. Lots of hanging out. I didn't know you were taking summer classes. I guess we don't have to tell each other everything, right?

I can't believe my flight lands in a day and a half. I feel like we were just saying bye at the airport.

———

TO: I_LOVE_RIPLEY_FOREVA@GMAIL.COM
FROM: footballsfinest11@gmail.com
SUBJECT: Re: Whenever you get to this…

Hey Marisa, the summer flew by. I'll see you when you get here. Have a safe trip!

CHAPTER 7
MARISA

AUGUST

Everyone around me stood up the second the glowing seatbelt sign flicked off. From my window seat, I was shielded from the overhead bin tug-of-war and aisle jockeying going on. Apparently, unlike everyone else, I wasn't chomping at the bit to step in the Philadelphia International Airport concourse.

They probably had flight connections to make or family and friends waiting for them at baggage claim. I'd been dreading coming back since LJ's emails dropped off. For the first week every email or text had gotten a same day reply—sometimes same hour. And then the gaps got bigger. A full day, then two days, and once, a whole week.

A sign of things to come. I'd better get used to it, right? After nearly fifteen years of seeing, talking, or texting each other daily, even when I was in New York, we had nine months left before we went our different ways.

Before I'd left, Matteo, the museum director, had dropped more than a few hints about a fellowship in museum curation they ran at the Guggenheim. It would mean two years in

Venice while working on my master's. I'd told him to let me know when the application period opened.

The people in the aisle moved toward the front of the plane. Jammed together and resting carry-on bags on the tops of the seats, they ambled past, banging into each row.

Maybe it was an omen that I hadn't gotten the bump up to business class on the way back. The flight in had been perfection: sunny skies when I arrived in Venice, and an easy transfer arranged by the business class lounge in the arrivals terminal.

Raindrops streaked down the window beside me. Cloudy skies were letting me know exactly what was in store for me on my return. Was LJ going to make it? Should I take a taxi? Was Liv going to show up?

A tap on my shoulder jolted me in my seat. "Are you okay?" The flight attendant peered down at me. The last person from my section in the back of the plane disappeared down the aisle past the bulkhead.

"Sorry." I unbuckled my seatbelt and slid out of my seat. I grabbed my bag from the overhead bin and thanked the flight attendants standing at the doors as I stepped onto the gangway. There was no one in front of me and only the flight attendants behind me waiting for the final passenger to disembark.

Senior year, here I come. The summer had been an escape I hadn't realized I'd needed. Other than a couple calls from my mom and dodged emails from Ron, it had been what I'd always imagined it would be like after I graduated. Spending time in the museum. Sightseeing. Train rides. Holding up the Leaning Tower of Pisa. But there had been a piece missing.

I didn't want to think about that piece. One I'd seen in social media pics surrounded by women fawning all over him. One I'd be rooming with for the next nine months.

It was a long walk through the concourse to immigration. I waited at the baggage carousel. And waited. And waited. As if my return weren't cursed enough already, my bag never turned up. Instead, I spent twenty minutes filling out the forms to have it delivered to me, if it was located. IF!

All the possessions I had were in that bag and my carry-on. When the check from the insurance arrived, I'd set most of it aside for this year. With my financial aid, I'd be able to pay for my last semester on my own or I could sit through one last semester of bullshit dinners with Ron and have a chunk of change to start my new adult life. Either way, I didn't have cash to spare buying new clothes again.

I headed toward the exit signs. After the final immigration check, I turned my phone on.

Messages rolled in. Every cell connection I'd made while flying over the Atlantic welcomed me to their country before the final one popped up for the US.

LJ: Liv should be on her way. We're at the doctor's office now.

Liv: Did you land yet?

Liv: The announcement board thing said you landed.

Liv: It says everyone has arrived. Are you here? Did you miss your plane?

Liv: Ford's here with me. He'll be easier to spot than me.

Liv: We're by the Terminal C doors.

I smiled, looking up from my phone. Even though I'd said I'd get back on my own, knowing Liv was willing to battle the airport traffic to come get me didn't suck at all.

She stood on the metal seats just inside the sliding doors leading to the humid August evening air, which flooded into the domestic baggage claim area with each exit.

"Marisa!" she shouted so loudly more than a few heads turned. "You're here." She squeezed me tightly, like she was overcompensating for her vertically-challenged state and channeling it into bone crushing.

"How was it? Tell me everything. Where's your bag?" She

glanced at my hands which were empty. My backpack was hefted on my back.

"They didn't." Her eyes widened before I could say a word. "And you just replaced everything."

"They think it's still in Venice and someone should deliver it after it gets here on the flight tomorrow."

"I'm sure you can borrow something from LJ until then. It'll be like old times." We walked toward the exit. The old times when we shared a bed, sleeping beside one another and I'd almost given him a handy. My chest flushed.

Ford stood with his hands in his pockets, eyes darting everywhere like he was a Secret Service agent waiting for trouble.

Liv had her hands full with him, of that I was absolutely sure.

"Hey, Ford."

"Hey, Marisa." His smile beneath the beard was totally teddy-bear cute. How Liv hadn't fallen for him earlier was the only mystery there. "Where's your bag?"

"They lost it." Liv butted in, anger dripping from every word.

"We can pick you up some clothes on the way to your place."

Over his shoulder, an obnoxious cloud of multicolored balloons walked through the door, the person holding them completely obscured by the colorful latex.

"Who is this asshole?" Liv mumbled under her breath.

All heads turned in the direction of the walking version of Up. How their feet weren't lifted off the ground was a miracle. The movements of the person behind the balloons were frantic before they whirled around and I got the full view, but I didn't need to see the maniac to know exactly who would show up at the airport with a circus's worth of balloons.

LJ's face lit up the second he spotted me and he ran toward me like he was headed into the end zone.

Lifted off my feet, I yelped, laughing and holding onto him. The latex and helium bomb masked his evergreen smell, but it was still there.

"Magician Marisa does it again." He dropped me, grinning so wide *my* cheeks hurt.

"What exactly did I do?"

"My dad's got the all clear again for another six months." He picked me up and spun me around. Staring into his eyes, the joy he radiated was contagious.

Relief for him, Charlie, and the rest of the family flooded through me. They deserved to have one another for as long as possible. But there was also a part of me that feared a day where the cancer came back. Would I stop being Magician Marisa? Would he still look at me and tuck a strand from my unkempt ponytail behind my ear, before tugging on it like we were eight again.

He glanced around behind me, his gaze sweeping over the floor. "Where's your bag?"

I explained again, and the four of us walked across the sky bridge connecting to the parking garage, Liv and Ford hand in hand and me with half of a ridiculous bunch of balloons. Down below, people were running across the drop off area with umbrellas, or just going for it and avoiding puddles while dragging their bags behind them.

"Thanks for coming. I figured by the time I got here, you guys would be gone and I'd have to race back to the house to meet her." LJ's cheek-aching smile hadn't let up since we'd left baggage claim.

"We're glad you made it. Is there any helium left on the planet though?" Liv smirked and Ford swallowed a laugh behind the beard, his chest rumbling.

"How could I not welcome Marisa back properly? It's been forever since I've seen her. I wanted her to know without a doubt how much she was missed."

The leaping heart feelings had to stop or I'd trip over my

own feet—although holding onto these balloons, I probably wouldn't hit the ground.

We handed at least fifty balloons out to people waiting for their loved ones, but I still felt seconds from being lifted off my feet by the time we made it to the parking garage.

Shoving the balloons into the trunk, we slammed it against a popping that sounded like a small war taking place inside.

"How did you even get these here?" I slid into the passenger's side seat.

LJ closed the door and ran around to his side. "Some in the trunk, I used trash bags to keep them anchored in the back of the car. Everyone at Party City hated me when I went before the doctor's appointment."

"I'm sure they did."

He turned on the car and we pulled out of the parking garage into the steady downpour. The beads of rain drummed on the roof and streaked down the windshield.

Streaks of lightning crisscrossed the sky and claps of thunder rumbled in the distance, but inside the car there was nothing but sunshine.

"I tracked your flight, and I swear there were clear, bright skies up until fifteen minutes before you landed."

"Looks like Philly is happy to have me back."

"I know I am." He reached over and patted my knee.

My heart leapt, centering everything on those five fingers wrapped around my leg. "You just need me to do your laundry don't you."

He let go making an exaggerated offended scoff. "All my laundry fits in the baskets in my closet." The dropped 's' covered by a cough didn't fool me.

"How many baskets did you buy? It's a Jenga tower of dirty clothes, isn't it?" I poked his shoulder. Laundry had always been my forte when it came to the home up-keep arts. Something about the fresh clean smell comforted me.

Also because I used to run the washer and dryer when I was home alone growing up, so I didn't hear every bump and creak.

LJ acted like his skin would burn off at the touch of a dryer sheet. For me, it was the thing that gave me comfort on cold, lonely nights.

"I might've picked up a couple extra from people who left them out on the curb after move out before the summer."

"And here I thought you just missed my sparkling personality." I tucked my hands under my chin.

"It's been boring without you here being the eternal pain in my ass, and workouts were less entertaining."

I laughed, forcing the air through my tight vocal chords. "Just getting you used to how things will go next year."

He drummed his fingers along the steering wheel and pulled onto the highway. "If I get drafted."

"Of course you will. You've been talking about this since we were seventeen. Don't tell me you're losing faith in the last quarter."

The worry line around the faint scar from his eyebrow to his hairline crinkled.

"LJ, in the worst draft possible, you'll go in the second round, maybe." I leaned back and slid my feet out of my sneakers, propping them up on the dashboard.

"Yeah, you're probably—" His eyes flicked to my feet and he swatted at them, while snapping his gaze back to the road. "Are you seriously putting your eight-hour plane feet all over my car?"

I clutched my sides, laughing and shifting my legs to evade his fingers.

At a light, he threw the car into park and mounted a tickle attack that left me in tears and out of breath. "I give. I give!" I shouted, scooting to the far edge of my seat with my back pressed against the door and my feet firmly on the floor.

"Did I say I missed you? I take it back." He shifted back

into drive and we drove the rest of the way while filling each other in on our summers. His worry line was gone.

By the time we made it through the city and back to campus, my eyelids were harder to keep open. The rain had let up, leaving only a spitting spray as we drove through the streets of off-campus housing.

I yawned as we pulled up to the front of The Brothel. "How can I be tired when I've been sitting on my ass for ten hours, if you include how early I had to get to the airport to check in?"

"Because you need to sleep in a bed, not propped up like a store mannequin with someone's head reclined three inches in front of your face."

LJ hopped out of the car and I grabbed my backpack from the back seat and opened my door.

Staring up at the house I'd stayed in for nearly a month last semester, I braced myself for what was to come. We were roommates now.

He stood at the bottom of the steps leading up to the gray and white porch.

The front door opened and Berk and Keyton burst past the door frame holding a cookie cake.

I grinned and laughed, walking up the porch steps past LJ, who stood leaning against the railing.

"You're here!" Berk jumped up and down while Keyton tried to steady the chocolate chip cookie cake with chocolate writing so it didn't splat onto the porch. He rushed toward me in full drama mode and wrapped his arms around me, spinning me in circles and nearly taking out Keyton, who balanced the cake in his hands.

"What the hell?" Keyton grumbled.

Berk set me down and ruffled my hair like I was a four-year-old.

I glowered and crossed my arms over my chest. "What the hell?"

"I'm just glad you're here." Berk jerked his thumb in LJ's direction. "Maybe Mr. Mopey will lighten the hell up."

"Fuck you." LJ's gaze narrowed at Berk before softening and turning to me. "He's been a pain in the ass all summer. We're happy you're here."

I fought against my yawn and kept my hands over my mouth. "Me too."

"Let's get you inside." LJ slipped my backpack off my shoulder. "You can borrow some of my clothes until your suitcase gets here." He pushed past Berk, who winked at me as I followed LJ into the house.

"Just like old times." I trudged up the stairs behind him.

By the time I made it to the last step, LJ had disappeared into his room.

I walked down the hall to the second door, the one that shared a wall with him and had been Reece's old room. On the bed were my favorite shampoo, conditioner, body wash and lotion.

My bag hit the floor with a thud.

Turning, I slammed straight into LJ's chest, pinning his arms between us. "You got my stuff."

The tips of his ears pinked up. "I figured they didn't have it in Italy and you'd probably run out while you were away. Here are your PJs and a towel."

I hadn't turned on the light and I was happy I hadn't. Tears prickled in the corners of my eyes and I threw my arms around him.

Sometimes it felt like I could disappear and no one would really care. It felt like I was a temporary fixture in someone's life until they moved on. But with LJ I felt like I mattered —always.

Dropping my arms, I rubbed my nose with my long sleeves and took the clothes from his hands. "Thanks, LJ."

"The bathroom's all yours. We'll stay out of your way. I know you're tired." He stepped back and walked out of the room before popping his head back in. "I missed you, Marisa."

I'd have said it back, but my throat was too tight to speak. I nodded and closed the door after he disappeared from the doorway.

How was I supposed to make it through this whole year without making a fool of myself—again?

CHAPTER 8
MARISA

SENIOR YEAR - HIGH SCHOOL

Standing at the bottom of the porch steps, I got my answer to how the hell he pulled this off.

One of the freshman football players had been squeezed into a Tinkerbell costume, complete with blonde bun, wings and a wand. His legs in those tights made me the slightest bit jealous.

"Welcome to the wonderful world of adventure. We hope you have a magical day." His falsetto voice, pouty smile and curtsy almost burst the dam, but I kept my laughter contained. They could probably have heard me from four blocks away. I bent over, holding my stomach.

My sides hurt as we stepped inside the house, which had been transformed. String lights were attached to the ceiling flowing out from the square columns, which made for perfect shielding during sock wars.

There was a popcorn machine in one corner. A cotton candy machine. A VR headset hooked up to the TV. Face paints on the dining room table complete with glitter.

"I know it's more like a carnival than Disney…" He shrugged.

"Are you serious? This is amazing. How did you get all this put together?"

"A little bit of raiding the concession stand supplies, bribing the underclassmen with a couple cases of beer and pulling the cancer card to get people to help out. Plus, after telling them why you were missing the senior trip, people were more than happy to pitch in."

"I can't believe you did this for me."

He peered over at me and my stomach flipped like there was a wacky-waving-inflatable-arm-flailing tube man going bonkers inside. "When are you going to get it? I'd do anything for you."

All those achy feelings came rushing back. The ones I felt when we were up late at night playing video games. The ones where I looked at him and wondered what his lips would feel like on mine. Not in a preteen or playground kiss, but a real kiss.

"Wait until you see the back yard." He grabbed my hand and I let him drag me through the house at a moderate pace to the back yard.

I walked out back, shielding my eyes from the glare of the sun.

It was complete with a treehouse we hadn't slept in since we were eleven. A wooden swing set where we'd both gotten more than our fair share of splinters had been out of commission for more than a few years.

There were plastic tubs filled with balloons and water guns set up like an arsenal on plastic folding tables ten feet apart, with chairs behind each one.

"I know you can't really run around and stuff, but I figured we could have a sitting water battle, if you're up for it."

We spent the day with off-brand cartoon characters

popping into the house. I had my fill of every carnival food I could think of, including hot dogs, so I wasn't in a sugar-induced coma by the end of the day. I changed into the spare clothes tucked into my drawer in LJ's room.

With soaking wet hair, I turned off the VR headset recreating some of the biggest rollercoasters in the world, complete with a fan blowing my drenched strands.

The sun had set a couple hours ago.

LJ handed off the cases of beer he'd acquired to the underclassmen. It would definitely require some prodding to find out how he'd broken his straight-arrow code to come up with that bribe.

He sat on the edge of the couch.

"That was the best day I've ever had in my life." I rested my hands over my stomach, which wouldn't rumble for another decade.

"I have one other thing to show you." He held out his hand.

Stuffed, sore and sleepy, I took his hand and followed him down to the basement. A disco ball spun from the ceiling and a multicolored ball light bathed the ceiling and walls in different colors.

He walked over to the tablet beside the speakers and tapped the screen.

An early-2000s hit filled the large space. "It wouldn't be a senior trip without a dance party." He waved his hands over his head, showing off his moves, which had gotten a lot better over the years.

I laughed and moved right along with him.

Anyone who thought a dance party of two didn't sound like a fun time hadn't met me and LJ. Bringing back old dance moves long since retired, we moved through the playlist he'd made and sang along to every song, screaming up to the ceiling and right beside each other.

Sweaty and filled with more joy than I'd ever been, I

dropped my hands to my sides when the last song ended and the next one came on.

It was a slow song.

LJ had one hand behind his back and held the other out to me. "May I have this dance?"

"Why, yes, kind sir." I laughed and attempted a restrained curtsey.

We went old school—middle school. He slid his hands on either side of my waist.

I'd popped another round of pain meds, so there wasn't more than a distant throb, even after all the running around today. I held onto his shoulders. Rocking back and forth, I felt like we'd been transported back to the seventh-grade dance. The same one where our mouths had been almost welded together. Neither of us were sporting braces anymore.

"How are you going to get all this cleaned up by tomorrow?"

"The underclassmen are coming by in the morning to take everything away and put it all back the way it was."

I rolled my eyes. "Football player perks."

A chuckle rumbled through his chest. "If you hadn't helped me with Quinn, I'd never have even been able to play football for the past two seasons."

"I did what anyone else would've done." And hanging out with his sister had given me a reason to be at his house. It hadn't only been for selfish reasons—LJ needed to focus on football, and Jill had a lot to handle with Charlie. I helped out where I could.

"No, they wouldn't have. A lot of people acted like I had the plague once my dad got sick last year, but you didn't." His gaze held an intensity that sent a flush flooding through my body.

Staring at him, I knew then that my feelings for LJ were real. But in a matter of months I'd be going to New York and he'd be going to Fulton U.

The level of attention for him would be even higher, especially female attention. Not to say there weren't girls who flirted with him now, but he mostly didn't pay any attention. But his college games would be on national TV. There would be coeds from all over the US—and some from outside— vying for his attention. And he wouldn't have me there as the plucky tagalong cock-blocking him with my presence alone.

His fingers inched closer to my back and I let my arms soften, the joke of our middle school dancing fading with each repeat of the chorus.

Soon my arms were draped over his shoulders and his hands were locked around me, resting on the small of my back.

His lips were inches from mine.

The light from his glow stick glasses shone off his tropical ocean blue eyes.

"This was the best senior trip ever." I interlaced my fingers against the back of his neck, letting them rub the short, smooth hairs.

"It really was." His lopsided grin made my heart do cartwheels inside of my chest.

Third time was the charm, right?

Pushing up on my tiptoes, I pressed my lips against his. He tasted like cinnamon sugar and root beer.

His eyes widened before he returned the kiss—tentatively at first, before seeming to give in. His tongue demanded entrance to my mouth that I was all too happy to give. He groaned and I closed my eyes, sinking into this moment I'd never thought would happen.

For so long, I'd wondered how it would feel for him to touch me like this. To make me feel like this.

His arm tightened around my waist, tugging me closer against him.

I yelped, the bruised extraction points grinding against the hard denim of his jeans.

"Shit, sorry, I forgot." He dropped his arms and took a step back, staring down at the floor.

I rubbed my hand over the throbbing spot on my hip and tried to catch his eye. "It's okay. I'm just still a little sore."

"I shouldn't have…" He reached out, his touch skimming along the edge of my t-shirt.

I peered up at him, my cheeks heating as he kept his hands on me. "Really, LJ. It's okay. And thank you for everything."

His head shot up. "Of course. I owe you." His smile sobered and he swallowed, his Adam's apple bobbing up and down. "You saved my dad's life. The debt doesn't get any bigger than that."

And with his words a chill ran through my body. My hand shot to my lips. His hesitancy came back to me. How much of this was because he wanted me too, and how much of it was because he'd written me a blank check for what he'd do to repay me for something I'd never had any intention of cashing in on?

What happened if the transplant didn't work? What happened if his dad got sick again and the Marisa Magic ended? How would they look at me then? How could I face him or his family?

My throat tightened and I took a step back, letting his hand drop. "This—" I cleared my throat and blinked back the tears making it hard to see. "This was really sweet of you, LJ."

His eyebrows dipped. "What's wrong?"

I shook my head. "Nothing, I'm just tired. The doctors said I should take it easy."

His face fell. "Shit, you're right. I'm sorry." He rushed toward me.

Stepping back again, I dropped my gaze as his searched my face. "Can you give me a ride home?"

"Why don't you stay here? Is your mom back yet? Did she message you?"

My lips trembled before I slammed them together to keep in the sound trying to claw its way out of my throat. With a strained smile, I shook my head.

I didn't need to check. She'd turn up when she wanted, just like she always did.

Staying here would hurt. It would shred my heart to be in the four walls with my best friend who gave in to what I wanted because of what I'd done for his family. I refused to use his gratitude to manipulate him into getting what I wanted. I wouldn't be like my mother.

But leaving and going back to my empty house would hurt more.

"Do you want the bottom bunk tonight? Can you climb?"

I forced the words out and mustered a pitiful smile. "I'll be good. Then I'll be out of your way."

His mouth opened and snapped shut.

We walked up the basement stairs and through the indoor carnival he'd put together for me. On the second floor, I walked into his bedroom.

It was huge compared to mine, big enough to fit the double bunk bed along with his desk, dresser, TV and two bean bag chairs.

I went straight to the ladder and climbed up, crawling under the blankets.

His head popped up at the top of the ladder. "Do you want to change? There's pajamas in your drawer."

I curled the blanket tighter around myself. "I'm good. Just so sleepy all the sudden, kind of like I'm drunk." Although I'd never been drunk. Other kids snuck into their parents' liquor cabinet; I got in trouble for hiding my mom's booze.

"I'll bring you up some water. Do you need anything else?"

The concern in his voice turned my embarrassment into guilt.

"No, just let me sleep it off, and tomorrow everything will

be back to normal." And we can forget all about our kiss. We can forget how I thought this would change everything. We can forget about ever being more than friends.

CHAPTER 9
LJ

PRESENT

Laying in my bed, I stared up at the ceiling. Marisa had been back for three weeks. I'd played three games—well, not exactly played, but suited up for and bench-warmed. We edged closer to the end of September and the season was already a quarter over.

Brutal would be the only word to describe this semester. If Coach Saunders's sidelining me and Monday dinners didn't kill me, Marisa would. There had been a Monday dinner reprieve for the last two weeks with all the beginning-of-the-season work Coach had going on, but this week, I wasn't so lucky.

My arms and legs were tight and climbing out of bed in the morning would take a solid ten minutes of psyching myself up for my screaming muscles. Working out in the gym seemed to be the only way to expend all the excess energy, since I wasn't on the field. At least we were winning. It was tighter than last season, but we were pulling out wins, which didn't make me feel any better about my chances of getting off the bench.

If we could win without me on the field, he'd keep me out for the rest of the season.

There was a knock at my door and it opened before I could say come in. Only one person would do that.

"LJ, Ron messaged to say dinner is at four on Monday. Of course he doesn't give a damn what I might have going on, but it is what it is. You know you don't have to come, right?" Marisa walked in wearing her pajamas. The long sleeve t-shirt and shorts combo had always been killer, but it was even worse now. She'd fling her legs up over the side of the couch while studying or hop up on the counter while I was cooking, swinging her legs back and forth. Or, worst of all, she'd burrow her feet under the side of my leg when we watched TV.

That usually meant I spent the rest of the show with a pillow welded to my lap, or I'd find a reason—any reason—to head upstairs straight into a cold shower.

Bed head Marisa. Falling asleep on my shoulder on the couch Marisa. Studying intently at the kitchen table Marisa. They were all driving me crazy.

"That's fine. My last class finishes at 3:45, so I'll meet you there."

She sat on the edge of my bed in her pajama shorts and long sleeved t-shirt. "There's a new application up for the Guggenheim Fellowship in Venice."

Her luggage had arrived a couple days after she landed. Her wearing my clothes while we waited for her bags to be delivered to the house had stirred up all kinds of feelings I'd worked too hard to smother. It hadn't worked. The shorts inched up higher as she shifted her legs. Her smooth legs that had been all tangled up with mine under the blankets last year. The ones I wanted to run my hands over and finally show her how much I'd missed her.

She drew her legs up to her chest, wrapping her arms around them and dropping her head to her knees. "What do you think? Should I go for it?" She nibbled on the inside edge of her bottom lip.

Shit. She'd been talking the whole time and I'd been fixated on her legs.

"You loved Venice, right? Spending more time there would be a lot of fun. You could explore even more old paintings and sculptures."

Her breath hitched and she stared at me intently like she wasn't sure she'd heard me right.

"Every time we talked you kept bringing up how hard it was to leave. Going back seems like a great opportunity."

We'd have the spring semester after the Combine in April after I'd signed with a team, if I ended up getting drafted at all. A month and then the summer off and as long as I needed to convince her how much she meant to me.

Once her Italian summer was over she'd come back in time for my first pro season to start. With her away in Venice, focusing on training camp would be my sole focus.

"And you'd be fine with me going?"

"Why wouldn't I be? It's not like I'm not going to be busy. A new season. A new team. A new city. Who the hell knows where I'll end up? We probably wouldn't get to see each other much anyway."

She slid off the bed and kept her back to me. "You're right. It was stupid to second guess it. It's an amazing opportunity" Folding her arms over her chest, she cupped her elbows and glanced over her shoulder at me. "Night, LJ."

"Night."

As I lay in bed, a new set of implanted Marisa-centered images filled my head. Marisa's new sleep shorts. That birthmark high up on her thigh that I hadn't seen since the summer between seventh and eighth grade when she swapped from her one piece bathing suit to swimming trunks and a bikini top with a rash guard shirt.

The summer she jumped from 'is Marisa getting boobs' to

'holy shit, guys are literally tripping over themselves in the hallway to watch her walk toward them'.

Maybe we could take a trip after graduation. A slow meandering few weeks before she went to Venice for the summer and my workouts intensified. She could show me all the spots she'd explored this summer and I could set up some surprises along the way. I could make it a trip we'd both never forget.

———

"I NEED MORE FOOTAGE IF WE'RE GOING TO GET YOU THE INVITE to the Draft Combine in April. You were only on the field for one play in the last game." My agent—it still felt weird knowing I had an agent—sounded even more upset by the one play I'd been on the field for in my last game.

Inside the darkened interior of my car, parked in front of a white, two-story house with a Fulton U football flag staked in the front yard by the steps, I tried to calm him and myself down.

These streets were quiet. It was mainly professors and other college staff here; no students streaking down the sidewalks or the low thump of bass rattling windows. I'd parked on a tree-lined road with manicured lawns and two-story houses with blue-and-white shutters.

"I know." I rested my head against the headrest, trying not to think about how just by being here, I was shoveling even more dirt for my own grave. But the couple dinners I hadn't shown up at had required a double s'more recovery with Marisa after she swore her dad was going to pull her tuition waiver. It's why I'd started coming. It's why I had to keep coming until she got the final one for her last semester, which was also at the end of the season.

"Are your workouts going well? What's the friction you have going on with the Coach?"

"There's no friction. Everything is fine. I'm actually…" I stared up at the house. "I'm heading to dinner with him right now." Our first in three weeks.

Every dinner Coach seemed to say the wrong thing. Remembering the wrong major. Mixing up her time in Venice with Rome or Florence. Not to mention the times he'd had to cancel. But the two of them were locked in a battle of the wills on who could outlast who in the not moving an inch department.

"Good, maybe you can ask him why he's not playing the best inside linebacker in Fulton U history and why he hates shutting down offenses by not putting you on the field."

"I'll get right on that."

A message came into my phone.

Marisa: At the end of the block. Are you here?

I swapped the phone to speaker.

Me: Yes, I'm parked out front, just finishing up a call with my agent.

"Are you listening, LJ?"

"Sorry, yes, I'm listening."

"Do I need to send a bottle of whiskey or scotch for you to give to your coach?"

"I don't think he's much of a drinker." He hadn't even taken a sip of the celebratory champagne after a championship win. If he got drunk, it would probably involve unbuttoning the top button of his polo and scribbling football plays on the windows with grease pencil. A regular party animal.

A Marisa-shaped shadow walked past the back windows of my car and toward the mini-lantern-lit walkway to the house.

"I've got to go. I'll talk to you later."

I ended the call and jogged up the walkway, following Marisa.

The front door opened.

Coach Saunders's face softened. "You're here."

She nodded. From the tightness in her neck and shoulders, the frown she wore had to be as deep as the Grand Canyon.

He pushed the door open wider, his reed-thin smile staying in place until my foot hit the bottom step leading up to his house.

"And LJ." He stared at me like I'd brought a casserole of dog shit to his front door, so exactly what I expected. After the first couple Monday dinners, it had sunk in that Marisa planned for me to come along to all of them, and that's when things had gone south on my playing time.

"Coach."

We walked inside. The second hand of the clock in the living room echoed in the silence of our steps.

Marisa unzipped her coat, but kept it on, shoving her hat into her pocket and sitting in the chair beside the one at the head of the table. There were only three place settings.

I took my coat off and hung it up on the back of the chair facing hers.

Coach went into the kitchen and brought out a pan of lasagna in a foil tray from the straight-to-oven section of the supermarket, along with a loaf of garlic bread. There was a pitcher of water and iced tea at the center of the table.

He sat down and slid the napkin off the table and onto his lap before jumping back up and rocking the tea out of the pitcher. "Damnit." He grabbed the napkin and mopped up the spill. "Marisa, do you want some parmesan cheese? I've got some of that too."

Leaving before she could answer, the kitchen door swung shut behind him.

"Can we try this time to be a little conversational?" I sliced into the lasagna and served out a chunk of the barely-bubbling block of pasta, sauce and cheese to Marisa and myself.

"That's why you're here. What the hell am I supposed to

talk to him about? At least you two can talk football." Her whisper-hiss turned into mild hysterics.

"You know just as much about football as I do."

The kitchen door swung open and Coach walked out with a block of parmesan cheese and a grater. "Cheese?" He held it out to Marisa.

"No, thanks."

I kicked her under the table.

She glared and lifted her plate. "Sure, I'll take some."

Coach grated cheese over her food and took his seat again.

"Smells good, Coach Saunders."

He cleared his throat and turned to Marisa. "How's the semester going?"

My fork scraped against the plate. The second hand of the clock in the other room blared.

Marisa's hands tightened around her fork and knife. "It's fine."

"How was Venice? It looked like you had a lot of fun."

Her teeth clicked together. "How would you know?"

He reached for the brim of the hat that wasn't there. "Your social media." With a pained smile, he speared a chunk of his lasagna. "I looked through some of your pictures."

Beside me, Coach Saunders sawed across his lasagna like he was imagining my throat served up on his plate.

"Why are you snooping?"

My head dropped slightly. Every question he asked was always met with the same defensive snap. She swore she wasn't doing it, but I had ears and eyes. That's how I knew that mentioning anything about my game play would burn up even the smallest ground gained over the last two years, At least now she responded to him when he spoke to her.

"Sorry, I didn't realize posting something on a public website meant you didn't want anyone to see it."

The silence suffocated. Outside, people walked past talking and laughing. Maybe I could blink out a message in

Morse code and they'd send reinforcements. Maybe a face painter or a pony to break up some of the Titanic-sized icebergs floating through the dining room.

"We'll have to cancel next week's dinner. We'll be on our way back from Michigan late afternoon on Monday."

"Oh no, I'm so upset."

His silverware clinked and clattered against the plate. "I'm trying, Marisa. I'm trying with you."

"Fourteen years too late, *Coach Saunders*. I'm graduating from college in eight months. And I just turned in my application for the two-year Guggenheim fellowship in Venice."

I choked on my iced tea, shooting out of my chair. My chair flipped back, clattering to the floor.

When the hell had she mentioned two years? That wasn't part of the plan.

The sweet liquid burned my nostrils. I grabbed my napkin and covered my mouth and nose, staring at Marisa across the table. "Two years?"

My lips went numb.

"Yeah, we talked about it last week. You said I should go for it."

Someone had slammed their foot down on the accelerator and I was careening toward a brick wall.

"I thought it was for the summer." Picking up my chair, the tips of my fingers tingling like I was winded from a 50-yard sprint.

"No, I told you they liked me so much after the internship, they invited me to apply for the fellowship. It's two years, and I'd get my master's from the University of Bologna in the summers."

A firm grip tightened around my heart. I rubbed my fist along the center of my chest to ease the ache. My hand shot out and I grabbed my glass, chugging the water, trying to keep the sawdust feeling from making its way to my throat.

I slammed the glass down, still trying to make sense of

what she said. "I must've missed that part."

"I was talking to you about one of the biggest decisions of my life and you blanked out." She flung her hands up into the air and glanced up at the ceiling.

"Two years." I sunk back into my chair, dazed, trying to picture my life without Marisa for 730 days.

Her gaze skirted to her dad like we were a married couple fighting in front of company. "Two years. You don't think I should go?" Her hurried whisper was a splash of water snapping me from my stunned stupor.

Two years.

My heart skipped triple time, like ladder drills at noon in August.

"Marisa, tell me more about the program. It sounds important to you." Coach leaned in, resting his chin on his fist.

"Now you care? Just in time to disappear for another week. How about I save you some time? Awesome dinner as always." She got up, glaring at both of us, re-buttoned the coat she hadn't taken off and stormed out of the house.

The door slammed shut behind her. We were left in the dead silence.

I slid my chair away from the table. "Thank you for dinner, Coach." I grabbed my coat and took off after her.

"Marisa!" I called out to her from half a block away.

She stopped for a second before charging ahead.

I jogged after her and jumped in front of her, blocking her path. "Wait. I'm sorry, okay? I'm sorry."

Her lips pinched tight and then her shoulders dropped. She stared into my eyes, worry swimming in them. "You really don't think I should go?"

"I never said that."

"Then why did you freak and go so quiet?"

"I was caught off guard. When you were talking." I scrubbed my hands over my chin. "I missed the two years part." I held onto her arm and guided her back toward my car.

She rubbed her hands together, fishing under her coat sleeves for her long-sleeved ones. "Yeah, two years. It's an amazing opportunity. They only give out one fellowship a year. Henri's finishing up his first year."

"Henri—awesome. Great." It landed flat with a splat.

Her eyebrows dipped, staring back at me over the roof of my car.

"I mean, great!" I threw more enthusiasm into my voice. "You'll have someone who can show you the ropes and you'll be working with him for a whole year." An art history guy with an accent, who'd already been showing her around Europe. I could see the social media post of the two of them making out under the Eiffel Tower with a tasteful, antique diamond ring on her finger.

I peeled away from the curb and swung a U-turn, heading toward our house.

"Why are you so upset?"

"No reason, just my best friend leaving for Italy for half a decade."

"Math much? It's two years. I was in New York for a year and you barely noticed I was missing."

"I noticed." The brutal freshman football season and practices, as well as a full course load of classes, had been the only things that kept me from taking the train up to visit her every other weekend.

"With all the partying you'll be doing, it'll fly by. Champagne. Strippers. Trashing hotel rooms. And then I'll be back."

"Why are you saying this shit?" My annoyance amped up —at her and myself. I'd been so fixated on her legs I'd blanked the whole "moving an ocean away" part of the conversation, but she was talking like she didn't even know me.

"It's the truth."

"Rock stars trash hotel rooms, not football players. Reece isn't partying like a maniac."

"Reece and Seph are practically married. Of course he's not out living it up and making it rain."

"And what makes you think I'd be doing that?"

She shrugged.

I pulled up to the front of the house. "You think I'm going to turn into a different person? This isn't my chance to transform into some Grade A asshole. I'm digging my parents out from under their bills, helping Quinn with college. That's what it means for me."

"I forgot. You're the saint and I'm the jerk." She grabbed the handle.

I jammed my finger into the door lock button. "Why would you say that? You saved my dad's life, stop trying to pretend anyone thinks you're a jerk."

Her shoulders stiffened. "Let me out."

"No, we're going to talk."

She flicked the button and I hit mine again.

"Are you holding me prisoner?"

"Hardly."

"I'm the one who should be upset. You weren't even listening when I asked you about Italy."

"I'm sorry. I screwed up. I was…distracted. Now tell me why you don't think I should be upset about you leaving for two years."

"All I'm doing is leaving first." She jerked the handle and flung the door open, slamming it shut, abandoning me in the slowly-fading glow of the overhead light.

After graduation we were supposed to have all the time in the world. After graduation we were supposed to finally have our chance. But after graduation she was running to Europe and ready to say goodbye.

CHAPTER 10
MARISA

The crowd at Archer's was heavy for a Tuesday night. Techno Tuesday came with $2 rail drinks and music loud enough to drown out most conversations until the happy hour ended at nine. After dinner at Ron's last week, I'd successfully avoided LJ. It helped that I'd only had to do it for three days, and I'd taken a tutoring session on Thursday instead of our traditional movie night. After that, he'd been gone from Friday morning until yesterday afternoon.

But I wasn't here to drink. I was here to dance and hang out with Liv. I'd had enough experience to know that drinking to dull the pain or numb myself would lead to a shitstorm of epic proportions. It didn't mean I never drank. But never alone, never enough to get more than a little tipsy, and never to escape what was happening in my life.

She tapped out a message on her phone and slipped it back into her bra. "Ford says he'll stop by after he's finished at the rink."

"Awesome, we can party all night."

"Are you sure you want to be here tonight?" Liv shouted in my ear and took a sip of her drink.

"Why wouldn't I want to be here?" I threw my arms up over my head and jumped around to the music.

"Because you look like you're trying so hard to have fun."

"I'm having fun. I've got my water. I've got great music. I've got my best friend." I flung my arm around her and tugged her close and planted a kiss on her cheek.

"Now I know something's wrong. What the hell did LJ do to piss you off?"

"Why do you think this has anything to do with him?" I laughed at her out-of-nowhere question. I hadn't talked about him the whole night.

"Because you haven't mentioned him once. Not the first three games of the season. Not what movie you watched on Thursday. Not something he's done to annoy you."

Dammit. Did I really talk about him that much? Stupid LJ. "So what?"

"And you just called me your best friend."

"You are."

She leveled her gaze at me like a disappointed coach. "Plus, he and Keyton got here about twenty minutes ago and he hasn't come over here and jumped onto your back or anything, but he's checked you out at least fifty times."

I whipped around, putting ballerina Liv to shame—well, probably not even close, but a girl could dream. Good thing I hadn't had a sip of booze or I'd have had the spins for the rest of the night.

Sure enough, the two of them were at the bar. Of course, they were gaining the attention of more than one of the groups of women over there.

In full T-Rex mode, I made it to LJ and leaned my back against the bar, resting my elbow beside his beer. "What are you doing here, LJ?"

Liv popped up beside me.

He whirled around like a contestant in a beauty competition with big, Barbie eyes. "Marisa? What are *you* doing here?

We had no idea you were here." He slapped the back of his hand against Keyton's shoulder. "Did you know Marisa was here?"

Keyton shook his head and sipped his beer, evading my gaze.

"You had no idea I was here? Cut the crap."

"I can't go out?" LJ clinked a beer with Keyton who looked uncomfortably bored. "Archer's is the closest bar to the house with good music, why wouldn't we come here? It's not like I decided to come because I knew you were here."

Least convincing acting ever. Almost as bad as our seventh-grade class performance of Peter Pan. "Then why'd Liv say you were watching me?"

"What? Me? Never. I maybe saw someone out on the dance floor who maybe looked like you and squinted a few times to see if maybe it was you, but I couldn't tell with all the spinning and arm flailing. Just here to have a beer and hang out with my roomie. Right, Keyton?"

I lasered in on Keyton, who set his beer down without looking my way. "Yup, just like he said."

"Fine, as long as you're not in watchdog mode, I'm going to go have some more fun with my bestie. Let's go, Liv."

Linking my arm through hers, I turned us back toward the dance floor.

"That was cold." She checked over her shoulder. "He looks like you just told him there's no Santa."

A rumble of regret raced through me. "Don't take his side. I sat down for a heart-to-heart with him about the next two years of my life and apparently he was running through foot-ball plays in his head. And then he made me second guess the whole thing while I was sitting in front of Ron. He's supposed to be there as part of my united front."

The sea of people on the dance floor was more of a pond, so it wasn't like I could avoid seeing LJ.

"Shouldn't you be the least bit happy he's worried or sad you're planning on leaving?"

"Why is he so shocked? He's leaving at the end of this year. Am I supposed to stay behind as the girl pining— waiting around for him to call me or throw me a few free tickets for his next game?" I wasn't going to be the pathetic person chasing after him, vying for a crumb of his attention when he'd moved on. I'd seen my mom go on that path over the years with guys whose faces I couldn't even remember, let alone their names, and all it led to was her crawling deep inside a bottle.

"No, but…" Her gaze drifted to where the two of them sat at the bar.

I followed it and LJ snapped forward. "It hurts to think about losing my best friend." All the convincing, all the preparation, all the reminders wouldn't lessen that hurt.

She clutched her hand to her chest. Her mouth hung open with mock outrage and she shouted into my ear. "I thought I was your best friend."

I rolled my eyes and swatted at her shoulder.

Bracing her hands on my arms, she stopped our barely-dancing and looked from me to LJ. "Then maybe you should stop pushing him away and enjoy what time you have left."

My heart tripped like I'd knocked into a priceless statue at the museum, and could only watch as it smashed to the floor. Eight months left.

Without saying a word, I left the floor and headed to the spot LJ and Keyton had been hanging. Probably slid into a table to talk to a fan or out on the dance floor to make me jealous. Not that he'd want to make me jealous. Not that I would be.

I leaned over the bar. "Did you see where the two guys who were sitting here went?"

The bartender gestured in the general direction of the bathrooms.

"Figures, they'd go together like two gossipy chicks." I wove my way through the tables and past the people crossing in front of me on the way to dance.

The hallway with the bathrooms was empty. I'd camp out and wait for them to come out. A step into the hall, someone slammed into my back, nearly knocking me off my feet.

Catching myself against the wall, I glanced over my shoulder prepared to lay into the asshole who'd bumped into me. Instead, the words caught in my throat.

Blocking my exit was the six-foot-four, three-hundred-pound offensive tackle who was no longer my tutoring problem. He was a different problem. A much angrier, drunker problem.

"You stupid bitch. All I asked you to do was take a fucking test for me." Chris staggered and breathed on me with drunk dragon breath.

I jammed my back against the painted brick wall behind me. My exits were all behind him. Dealing with drunks wasn't anything new for me, but I was used to the ones who landed their blows with words.

"Hey, Chris, long time no see. How was your summer?" I tried to keep it light to buy some time.

Of course this would be the one night there wasn't a line out both bathrooms. It's what I got for coming on Techno Tuesday.

"Fuck you." Spittle clung to his lip.

"You seem like you've had enough, maybe you should get some sleep." I looked over his shoulder to the light at the end of the darkened hallway with people milling around, laughing and drinking, the music drowning out even my own thoughts.

"You think you're hot shit living with Berk, LJ, and Keyton. I bet you do all their work for them. Probably blow them all too."

Stepping back, I clenched my fists at my sides, waiting for

someone to see what was going on, so I could get past this drunk idiot.

"Don't be a dick, Chris. You're drunk; let me get past." I tried to walk around him, but despite how drunk he was, he was faster and blocked the sliver of space that had been my exit plan.

"Hey!" I waved my hands over my head, trying to get someone's attention.

I shouldn't have taken my eyes off him.

One push from his palm and I went flying, slamming straight into the dead-end wall behind me. It wasn't far, but it crushed the air from my lungs like an empty soda can underfoot.

I bent at the waist, heaving to suck in a complete breath. "You're right. I was an asshole and I'm sorry." My words were wheezes, barely audible even to my own ears. Apologies were sometimes the only way to get people that drunk to back down. Giving them the satisfaction of being right and backing off could give you an escape from their alcohol-enhanced need for recognition.

His droopy gaze narrowed. "I don't want your fucking apology." He leaned in closer, the biting stench of his breath flooded my nostrils and bile raced for my throat.

I jerked back, nearly slamming my head into the bricks.

His hands tightened around my upper arms, gripping them in a bruising hold.

I opened my mouth to scream at the same moment the bathroom door opened. The light from inside, blinded me. Two forms stood in the lighted doorway. "Help." Frantic whisper eeked out of my closing throat.

Before I could say another word, the pressure on my arms was gone, and so was Chris.

A fist connected with his nose.

LJ rushed in and cupped my cheeks in his hands, searching my face with wild eyes.

Absolute and complete relief swamped me. Only then could I let a fragment of fear invade my brain flashing through what could've happened.

"Are you okay? Did he hurt you?" His nostrils flared, but he kept his attention on me and his back to the shouts breaking through the thumping beat.

Stunned, I stared over his shoulder at the fight unfolding. Another hit was so hard, Chris's head bounced off the wall. The barrage kept coming. The sounds of wet hits turned my stomach.

A flash of recognition stole over me. I tried to process everything happening in front of me and what had almost happened to me.

Keyton. It was Keyton. Keyton, who looked seconds from ending Chris in the bathroom hallway.

"Stop him." I grabbed at LJ's shirt.

He ripped his gaze from me and turned, keeping me behind him.

"Keyton." I screamed his name, trying to get him to stop.

His words traveled over the booming music far better than mine had. "You put your hands on her like that? You think you can touch her, you piece of shit? Why don't you hit me?"

I shoved at LJ, trying to get past. My fear changed course in a matter of seconds. The panic wasn't for me, but what was being done on my behalf.

"He could kill him." I squeezed LJ's arm, trying to force past him.

The muscles in LJ's jaw worked before he stepped in, grabbing Keyton's arm, stopping him from landing another blow.

Keyton whirled on LJ pulling his punch at the last second. His gaze clouded by a rage I'd never seen before.

I rocked back, still keeping myself upright against the onslaught of adrenaline hammering in my veins. He'd almost hit LJ, almost taken him out like he expected to get piled on.

His eyes cleared and he looked to the sniveling Chris, bloodied and beaten on the ground. Hands clenched at his sides, his chest heaved and his gaze flicked from Chris to us. The thunderous expression clouding his face gave way to horror and embarrassment.

Without saying a word, Keyton backed up, racing from the hall before disappearing out into the club. I didn't even get to tell him thank you.

Chris picked himself up off the floor and wiped his bloodied nose with the back of his hand, glaring before running off.

The muscles in LJ's neck strained. With his gaze red with rage, he stepped toward the direction of Chris's retreating figure.

I tightened my fingers around his arm. "Take me home, L."

He jolted and glanced over at me.

Staring into his eyes, I begged him with mine to get me out of there.

I needed to get back to the house, get under the blankets. "Shit, Liv! She's still here."

LJ glanced around and waved his hand in the air and pointed to me and the front of the bar.

Glancing past him, I spotted Liv at the bar with Ford.

She shot up off her stool.

I waved her off and patted LJ's chest, tucking myself against him.

Ford glanced from us to Liv. She lowered herself back to her stool.

With his arm around my shoulder, LJ guided me out of the bar watching everyone's movements like he was my own personal bodyguard.

My phone vibrated in my front pocket.

Liv's messages were probably rolling in five at a time.

The ten-block walk was silent beside my sentry. A shudder raced through me, and I tried to push away how badly things could've gone tonight.

He tightened his arm around me, his head whipping from side to side to take on anyone.

I squeezed him for the last half block. Holding on kept me from thinking too much, from digging too deep into what could've happened, from being too scared.

Back at the house, he led me to my room like I'd forget the way without his arm around me. Not that I was complaining.

"Are you sure you're okay?" He hovered.

I grabbed a long-sleeve shirt from the pile in the laundry basket by my desk. A quick sniff—clean. For some reason my clothes went from the dryer straight into the basket to be used later, but I folded LJ's. It was how he liked it, even if he hated doing it himself. At least there was one thing I could do for him.

I jerked my shirt off, leaving me in my camisole and bra.

LJ hissed. A high, ragey hiss.

"Risa." He turned me and ran his hands, feather light, down my shoulders.

Goosebumps jumped up like the ROTC cadets marching across campus.

"LJ?"

"I should've let Keyton kill him. Better yet, I should've joined in." His fingers moved in small, slow circles on my arms.

Dropping my head, I cringed. Four distinct finger patterns wrapped around both arms. "It's okay." I held onto the back of his hand.

"It's not okay." His words shot from his mouth.

"I didn't mean what he did was okay. I meant I'm okay. They don't hurt."

"Should've never happened."

"We could say that about a lot of things." I nudged him with my elbow.

"We should call campus security."

"No, we shouldn't. Keyton was involved in that fight. From the looks of Chris's face, they'd ask questions, and I don't want Keyton getting suspended or kicked off the team because of that asshole."

"But—"

"I'll steer clear of Chris and make sure I don't wander down any dark hallways on my own from now on. I'm fine. Now get out of my room, so I can change."

The fire in his eyes cranked down a notch from angry inferno to campfire. "Why? We used to change in front of each other all the time." He dropped his hand, lips twitching.

"When we were nine." And from our sleepovers last year, I'd probably need an industrial sized fan to cool me off if he dropped his pants right now. "Get out already." I grabbed his shoulders and shoved him out the door.

After changing, I slipped into my bed, tossing and turning. The uneasiness I'd tried to banish after my run-in with Chris still ran rampant in my brain.

Slamming my hands into the mattress, I flung off the covers and peered out my door.

The house was quiet. I tiptoed down the hallway to LJ's door beside mine.

Keyton's door was open, but his room was empty.

Gently knocking my knuckles against LJ's door, I opened it.

He lay in bed on his back and turned to face me.

The creases in his forehead deepened. He had probably been grinding his gears about me not letting him fix the Chris problem.

"Couldn't sleep?" I walked further into the room, floorboards creaking under my bare feet.

"No. I want to get dressed and go beat the shit out of him." Ding. Ding. Ding.

"Can we not talk about him?"

He propped his head up on his hand and lifted the blankets.

I dove for the invitation, laying on my back beside him, staring up at the ceiling.

"Thanks."

"Anytime, Risa. Night." The bed dipped. He scooted away, but laid on his side facing me.

"Night." I closed my eyes and let his steady breaths ease the tension from my body.

Only for tonight.

This was the last time we'd share a bed.

CHAPTER 11
LJ

t had only taken me forty-eight hours of snapping at everyone and pacing in my room to finally storm across campus to the on-campus senior apartments. We had a game this week, so Marisa would be home alone.

Marisa hadn't slept in my bed last night, but she'd stayed up late and had left her light on.

It made me feel like a rampaging beast was trying to gnaw its way out of my chest.

I pounded my fist against the door. The metal rattled against the frame.

The door opened. In the gap, the bruised and scabbed face of Chris stared straight back at me. "What the hell are you doing here?"

I slammed into the door, pushing myself inside. "What do you think I'm doing here?" The debate had raged in my head on the way over.

Marisa would kick my ass for doing this, but it needed to be done. It wasn't like getting suspended from the team would cut back on my playing time anyway.

The blood leeched from his face, showing off the yellowing of the edges of the bruises.

"It was a mistake. I was drunk." He licked his lips, wincing when he hit the patches of broken skin.

"You think getting shit-faced is an excuse for hurting Marisa? She's got finger bruises on her arms thanks to you."

"I was just messing around, trying to scare her." His voice was pitched up and squeaky with a tremble. Good, he should be scared.

I closed the gap between us so quickly, he stumbled back and fell onto the couch. "And you think that's better? You think it makes you tough?"

Looming over him, I reigned in my anger, leashing it and holding on tight. The last thing I wanted was to knock him out and for Marisa to take it on as her fault. "You don't come near her. You don't breathe near her. You don't even be in the same building as her."

His head bounced up and down like a bobblehead on a dashboard.

"If she shows up to a party, coffee shop, library, whatever, you leave. Don't even take time to gather up your shit. You walk out the door without a word or a look."

"I…I will. I promise."

"You'd better." I wanted to rip his fucking head off. Instead, I backed up and left his apartment without even closing the door. Maybe I shouldn't have stopped Keyton. Maybe I should've piled right on.

Knowing he was on campus would keep me on edge, but Marisa was adamant about not going to campus security.

Crossing campus, I got to the locker rooms early to change for practice. We had a game this weekend. Not that I'd be playing.

The room was quiet—at least as quiet as a locker room ever got on a practice day. A few coaching staff went over their clipboards and binders like they held a treasure map to the Holy Grail. The lingering scent of muscle rubs, athletic tape and sweat permeated every inch of the place.

By the time I got into full pads, more guys had filled the room.

Keyton followed behind a group of defensive linemen and froze when he spotted me. His door had been open the night Marisa crawled into bed with me, but closed in the morning and in the two days since, like he'd been waiting for everyone to clear out before leaving.

Instead of avoiding me, he clenched his jaw and made a beeline straight for me. "Sorry for losing it the other night. How's Marisa?" It all *wooshed* out like a single word.

"She's good, a few bruises from where he grabbed her. And you have nothing to apologize for. I was so fixated on making sure Marisa was okay, that piece of crap probably would've scurried away if you hadn't been there."

He swiped his chin back and forth, his nostrils flared and he squeezed the back of his neck. "It's been a long time…" His lips tightened. "I'm glad Marisa's okay. I fucking hate that she's got bruises at all."

"I know. But I paid Chris a visit, so he won't come anywhere near her again."

Keyton's shoulders relaxed like he'd been on edge since Tuesday night. "Let me know if he does and I'll go with you to kick his ass all over again."

I laughed and punched him in the shoulder. "We're good, man. You don't have to go into hiding over something like this."

The breath he let out felt like he'd been holding it for days. "I know. I just…I don't like losing control like that and I didn't want you guys to think I was a loose cannon."

"You're the most even-keeled guy out of all of us. If there was a time to lose your cool, it was on Tuesday."

The door to the locker room flew open. Coach Saunders marched in. "You've got twelve minutes to get out on the field. The bus to the airport leaves at three tomorrow. If you miss it, you're buying your own ticket to Michigan. I'd suggest everyone gets here on time.

"Today we're running the three new defensive line plays and we need you all to know these and be able to run them in your sleep. Offense, there were two turnovers in the last game, so you're going to drill those passing plays until they're branded on your brains. Let's get a move on." He clapped his hands against his clipboard and disappeared back out the door.

Keyton rushed off to get changed and I left the locker room, following Coach out to the field and taking my spot on the bench.

First one suited up. First one ready for practice. First one to ride the bench all season.

Guys slowly made it to the side of the field, breaking off as the defensive and offensive coaches called their squads over.

I joined the defensive coach on the sidelines. Sixty guys stood around him, all itching to get out on the field and prove themselves in the ten games we had left this season.

"I want my seniors out there to start. We'll be taping to add to your reels, so don't fuck it up." His words ignited a flame in my chest. Practice tape wasn't as good as the real thing, but I'd take what I could get and push it to the max.

Keyton jogged beside me, smiling, headed to the offensive line. "How encouraging."

We stood in the center of the field, finding our spots for the play.

I glanced at the sideline against my better judgement. Coach Saunders walked up and down a six-foot track with his headset on and clipboard in hand.

The second string QB made the call and the snap kicked in.

We broke off, covering our players on the other team, but I spotted a gap in the defense. Slipping into the pocket, I took down the receiver before they made it ten yards.

The next play, I spotted my opening, smacking the ball from the air and swatting it to one of the cornerbacks who ran it in for a touchdown.

On the next, I blocked, giving an outside lineman the opening to sack the quarterback.

Running to the sidelines, it felt like I was riding through a car wash with the top down from all the knocks and nudges to my helmet. My grin was 50 yards wide, satisfaction settling deep into my bones. I wanted to show the guys I hadn't been benched because I didn't have it in me. I still had all the same skills and wanted to use them to get us our next W.

Coach Saunders's stare was the pinprick to my helium-balloon feeling once I left the field.

The whole team huddled around, some standing, some taking a knee.

"Good hustle out there. Those plays looked sharp. Keep them that way and you'll make everyone proud this season. Don't let your heads get too big. We've got a lot to prove and even more people coming for our necks. STFU is ready to end our streak and we're not going to let them, are we?"

"No, Coach." Everyone shouted at once, as one. And the vibrations rumbled in my chest.

"Are we going to get complacent?" His voice rose, higher above the team shout.

"No, Coach!"

"Are we going to give them a chance?"

"No, Coach!"

"That's what I like to hear. Hit the showers and be ready for our trip tomorrow. We're going to break Michigan's streak and show them how we do things at Fulton U." His words energized the guys and everyone got up, charging toward the locker room.

Sweat, steam and the steady beat of the showers filled the locker room with chaos.

Berk found me after I'd gotten my shower, still standing in my towel, fishing my clothes out of my locker.

He panted, shower sweat breaking out on his forehead. "Do you need a ride home?" His shirt still clung to his body.

"You're in a rush."

"Jules is baking something new today and she told me to swing by after practice to pick it up."

"I can't blame you then. No, I've got my car. And I'll see if Keyton needs a ride."

"Cool, awesome." He was already jogging backwards. "Thanks!"

Everyone was amped up for Saturday, like an electric current running through the humidity in the air.

Ten games were left in the regular season for the under-classmen to prove themselves and get their spot on the starting line-up.

Ten more games for all the seniors to get enough solid plays in to boost their draft prospects.

Ten more games until I might be relegated to playing pick-up football in a local park.

———

"ALIEN OR ALIENS?" MARISA CALLED OUT FROM THE LIVING room finishing up folding my clothes.

I didn't hate how she'd come right in and trudge out with my baskets of clothes grumbling about one day setting it all on fire in the backyard. But she'd also wrestle the pile of clothes away from me muttering about how I couldn't do it right if I tried. Although I only usually tried to get her to spring into action to do it.

The microwave counted down and I waited for the popping to slow, counting the seconds between each one. A charred bag sat in the sink—Marisa's handiwork.

I shoved the zipper up on my hoodie even higher. The

breeze raced through the house from the open back door straight through the windows at the front of the house to purge the charred popcorn smell from the air.

"What about Terminator?"

"Terminator, T2, T3: Rise of the Machines, Salvation, Genisys, Dark Fate?"

"I only recognize those first two as actual movies for my own sanity. Maybe Salvation, if I've had enough to drink. Maybe." I filled the bowl with popcorn.

"You're such a movie snob." She grabbed cups and poured us some soda.

"Protecting my brain from the plot holey-est terrible movies that tried to ruin two of the best movies ever doesn't make me a snob. You're into 18th Century paintings and Greek statues. You're telling me you'd choose T3 over T2?"

"No, but I love to see how worked up you get when it comes to crappy movies." I kicked her butt on her way out of the kitchen.

"Jerkface. You almost made me spill our drinks."

I stopped as she disappeared into the living room, my heart leaping high like it had hurtled over an offensive lineman headed for the sack. These easy, fun moments made it hard to imagine my life without her. The thought of losing our Thursday movie nights was like a spike to my brain.

I sat beside her on the couch with the bowl overflowing with popcorn. "How about Aliens?"

She picked up the spilled popcorn from my legs and the couch. "I see someone doesn't want my nails embedded in their arm tonight."

"I'd like to be able to block properly at the game on Saturday."

"Oh, do you have a game coming up? I hadn't noticed."

"Are you sure you're going to be okay here with all of us gone?" Worries drummed inside my head. Chris. Her being alone. Her deciding to cook.

She shoved her hand into the bowl of popcorn on my lap. "It's no big deal. Nix brought over that giant catering tray of chicken fettuccini, so I'm good with food."

"Didn't he bring that a week ago?"

"Yeah, what's the problem?" She shoveled the popcorn into her mouth.

"Iron Stomach Marisa."

"The pasta will be two weeks old, max. It's fine."

"Please don't end up in the hospital with food poisoning."

"When have I ever?"

True, she'd only nearly sent everyone in the house to the hospital. She could choke down anything. I'd pick up some lunch meat before I left, or ask Nix if he could drop off some more food for her.

"Enough talking, let's watch!" She jammed her finger into the remote and the dreary, dark mining vessel holding one of the most badass action heroines in history—Ellen Ripley—came on the screen.

Marisa hid behind my arm when the aliens crawled through the vents toward our totally screwed main characters. She linked her arm through mine when Newt fell into the water, completely surrounded by aliens.

The front door banged open at the exact moment the queen popped back up on screen. Marisa screamed and flung her empty cup in the direction of the noise.

Keyton popped his head in.

She clutched the front of her shirt and I paused the movie, laughing hard until she shoved my arm.

"How many times have you seen this movie? Did you think the queen alien was here?"

"Shut up, I was into the movie."

Keyton chuckled and walked over, handing her the cup.

"Did you want to stay for Thursday movie night?"

"I'm good. It's almost over anyway. I'll let you guys finish your movie." He offered up a weak smile, picked up a bag from beside the front door, and took off up the stairs.

Marisa ducked her head. "Was that a guitar case?"

"I think so."

She dropped her hand into the empty bowl and it sent the vibrations straight to my dick. "One day you're going to have to ask him what the hell that's about, because as far as I can tell, he doesn't even play."

I willed my semi to deflate. "Maybe. Let's finish the movie."

She relocked her arm with her feet curled beside her on the couch.

When the credits rolled, I didn't want our movie night to end.

She yawned covering her mouth and shook out the last bits of popcorn into her hand.

"Do you want to watch another one?"

Rubbing her eyes and stifling another yawn, she nodded. "Sure, let's do this."

"Do you want to pick?"

"You go. I won't make you suffer through one of my picks."

"Who are you and what's gotten into you?"

She shot me a sleepy smile. "You'll be gone for four days. I'll have plenty of time to binge on all my terrible faves while you're gone."

I popped another bag of popcorn and Marisa got the drinks. We sat back and the metal cadence of the Terminator theme accompanied us into a desolate dystopian future.

Her yawns got closer together.

"We can stop."

She shook her head and opened her eyes horror-movie wide. "No, I'm good. It's a great movie." Another yawn.

Not wanting to move either, I propped my feet up on the coffee table.

Her head drooped throughout the movie, until it rested on my shoulder.

I may or may not have wiped away a tear as Arnold lowered himself into the vat of molten metal. At least no one else was around to witness it.

"Risa." I lifted my shoulder, nudging her head.

She made a sound between a growl and a grumble and burrowed deeper against me.

"Marisa, we need to go upstairs."

"Don't want to. Carry me." She kept her eyes closed, her voice soaked in a sleepy half-yawn. Her fingers brushed across my stomach and I sucked in a sharp breath.

She wouldn't remember a thing in the morning. I'd had more than a few full conversations with her sleep talking so convincingly, I'd thought she was faking it. Mostly, they'd been about needing to buy sprinkles in the morning or finding a badger in the washing machine. Tomorrow, whatever was said between us would be met with a blank stare.

I would take a moment, just one, to admire her. I brushed her wavy black strands away from her face. The curve of her nose had long ago been committed to my memory. It was so burnt into my brain that, from halfway across campus, I could pick out the slight upturn at the end and small dent in the side from when she was eight and fell out of a tree in my backyard.

Standing, I draped her arm over my shoulder and shifted mine behind her back and under her legs. I lifted her off the couch and took care of her head, while walking up the stairs.

"I'm going to miss you when I go to Michigan. I wish you could come with me, but it's going to be cold as balls. The time is slipping away so quickly, and I don't know what I'll do if you go to Venice for two years. I'll miss you even more."

I set her down on her bed and dragged the blankets down, tucking her under.

She grumbled and hugged her pillow to her chest.

"Night, Marisa." I flicked off the light and walked to my room next door. Dragging my fingers through my hair, I sat on the edge of my bed.

If she got accepted for her Venice fellowship, I'd hate myself for losing this time with her. Her dad would probably murder me if we started dating. She'd probably scream it from the rooftops just to piss him off.

I punched my pillow and slammed my head back onto it. The path to my future was diverging and I was holding onto both possibilities, trying to stop the passing of time through sheer will alone.

CHAPTER 12
MARISA

The intern office in the museum was an alcove of a space off the larger curation offices. Temperature controlled, the air carried the perfect blend of humidity, hundred-year-old canvases, and paper, right along with the French press coffee blend everyone nursed throughout the day.

Everyone else had gone to lunch, almost like they'd sensed the incoming storm and had run without giving me a heads-up.

Usually within these walls I felt part of something bigger. I felt a part of history. Now I felt like I'd rather gnaw my own arm off than stay on the phone a minute longer.

"This is the third time you've asked me to come to dinner this week. Why?" I set down the palm-sized framed painting and tapped a few keys to add it to the donation inventory.

"I can't want to see my daughter?" Anyone else would've thought she was sad her daughter was graduating from college and would be moving away. Anyone else would've thought I was an asshole for blowing off my dear mom. Anyone else didn't know there wasn't a loving bone in her body.

"Mom."

She huffed and I could feel her eye roll.

Yes, difficult Marisa wanting to know exactly why she should walk straight into the lion's den and serve herself up on a silver platter.

Her voice was muffled and a door closed on her end of the line.

"I'm dating someone new."

"I don't—"

"He's nice. A nice, boring guy who treats me well. And he has daughters your age. A little older, and we've had dinner with them twice, and he keeps asking to meet you."

Once again, this had nothing to do with me. "So you're trying to pretend you're a doting, loving mother, and you want me to help."

"I was a damn good mother. I never expected your dad to split on us like that. Sorry, I still wanted to enjoy my life after having a kid."

"There's having a life and there's leaving me to fend for myself." What other kid developed a taste for tuna fish and frosted flake sandwiches? It wasn't half bad, if salty-sweet fish was your thing.

"Looks to me like you've ended up all right. Even landed yourself a football player too. I'm sure LJ'll last longer in the pros than your father did."

"LJ has nothing to do with this." They were nothing alike. Her talking about them as if her relationship with my dad was anything like my friendship with LJ pissed me off even more. LJ could never do what Ron had done.

He'd never have a kid, cut and run, then extort them into weekly dinners to prove a point. What that point was, I'd never know—and I wasn't digging deeper to find out.

"Of course he does. You should've locked him down in high school. You did save his dad's life."

"There's no locking down. We're friends—for the thousandth time."

"But he's going to get drafted, right?"

If there was any fairness in the universe. "Yes, he should."

"You'd better jump on him now then, if he's not already in the crosshairs of the football groupies."

I squeezed the bridge of my nose. "I'm not jumping on anything. And he's not like that."

Her scoff grated my nerves like a cheese grater against a ball of steel wool. "They're all like that."

"Why are we having this conversation?"

"All I'm saying is even if you don't want to be with him long term—God knows fidelity isn't a trait of pro athletes—you could always slip in before graduation and get a parting gift to remember him by. And keep those checks coming once he leaves you behind."

A mental slap reverberated in my head. There wasn't a hint of a joke or irony to her words. She was one hundred percent serious. When I thought she couldn't keep proving to me that redemption was a mile-long road of broken glass, she added another dump truck of shattered vodka bottles to the mess.

"Did you just try to friendly-advise me into trying to get pregnant by my best friend to weasel child support money out of him?"

"Stop being so dramatic, Marisa. It's not like you both wouldn't get what you want out of the deal. It's the least he could do for you." Bottles clinked in the background. "So dinner? Next week?"

Rage waged a battle in my chest against the fear that I might have even the smallest part of her manipulation and deception flowing through my veins.

I ended the call, throwing down my phone like my hands had been scalded.

Once again, I'd fallen into the trap, walked straight into it like a cartoon character who never learned. For a nanosecond I'd thought she'd been trying to make amends. Maybe she'd realized I was an adult now and she'd missed out on so much.

Nope! She wanted to parade me in front of a new boyfriend as a testament to how shitty of a parent she was. I'd rather have a herd of hermit crabs shoved into my bathing suit.

I finished up my shift and hopped on the bus back to campus. My mother's words sat under my skin like a bad case of poison ivy. It scared me to know I might have even a trace of her in me—a piece I couldn't recognize, infecting me and turning me into what I never wanted to be.

How the hell did I even know how to have a real relationship when my models were an absentee father and a narcissistic mother who only cared about herself?

———

BACK AT THE BROTHEL, I JOGGED HALFWAY UP THE STAIRS BEFORE the movement from the living room stopped me.

"Keyton."

Sitting on the couch, his muscles unlocked like he'd thought if he didn't move I wouldn't see him.

"Hey, Marisa." He gathered up his notebook and textbook from the couch, holding them both in one hand.

I walked back downstairs and faced him trying to get him to meet my eyes. "Have you been avoiding me?"

The tendons in his neck tightened. "Possibly."

Who could blame him for not wanting to get caught up in any more problems? "Listen, I'm sorry about the other night." I cringed and ran my fingers over the collar to my shirt. The regret and guilt over him needing to jump in to save me sandbagged in my chest.

His head snapped back like I'd flung a barbed-wire-wrapped salmon in his direction. "What the hell do you have to be sorry about?"

I bit my chapped bottom lip. "Just sorry you had to come to my rescue like that. I know fighting can get you guys in a lot of trouble."

"You have nothing to be sorry about. When I saw what happened, I just blanked. Lost control."

Understatement of the year. I'd have been less shocked if Liv turned out to be a badass blackbelt blasting her way down the hall to come to my rescue.

"Sure as shit surprised me and LJ. But you know what they say? It's always the quiet ones." I peered over at him wondering what other secrets he was hiding.

The corner of his mouth twitched.

Resting my hand on his arm, I gently squeezed. "But I do want to say thank you for the other night. Really." I stopped short of a hug because he was giving off all kinds of super uncomfortable vibes right now and I didn't want to make any of this worse for him.

"Don't worry about it." He ducked his head. "I'm glad LJ was there."

He was probably the only thing that had kept me upright and not freaking out. Just like after the fire. He'd been the first number on my speed dial. He was my rock. The one I could always count on. And his life was about to get a lot more complicated with a lot more demands on his time. More worthy demands.

"Me too." He'd been there for me, and in his arms, the scary what-ifs stayed away.

He shoved his hands into his pockets. "LJ said you didn't want to go to campus security. You should make a report." His head tilted and he peered at me out of the corner of his eyes.

I'd wrestled with this one a lot, running over it in my head trying to figure out the best way to move past it. Campus security, honor council, the campus rumor mill—getting everyone caught up in that wasn't what any of us wanted or needed. Not in the middle of their season. Not when LJ needed to focus on the field, not on coming to my rescue. There was no doubt he'd stand up for me no matter what— even if it wasn't in his best interest. He was an annoyingly good best friend that way.

"You protected me. And I know what he did was fucked up, but I don't want you to get in trouble for fighting. I know they're strict about that. The bruises on my arms are almost gone. It's the middle of the season." I shrugged. "I don't want to jeopardize your chances this season."

"But—"

"I can only hope the ass kicking you laid on him--"

He flinched like I was making him relive it by bringing it up again. A bad memory he didn't want. It reaffirmed why I'd steer clear of Chris and keep Keyton and LJ out of the campus council.

The joking tone dried up from my voice. "I think now he knows he's not untouchable and he'd better not do anything like that ever again."

His frown deepened and the muscles in his neck strained, but he didn't say anything else. Time to direct this conversation elsewhere or I'd have him avoiding me for the rest of the year.

"You guys leave tonight, right?" How are you feeling about the season so far?"

"It's been down to the wire more than a few times."

"They've been hard to watch sometimes. But I know you'll kick some Michigan Wolverine ass."

He slipped on a sly grin. "You know we will. Hopefully LJ will get some time on the field."

"Yeah, what's up with that? He's not getting anywhere near the time he should be getting. He played—what? —two plays last game." It didn't make sense. Ron was all about the win. It's why he'd left to go on the road from college to college until he built the powerhouse program at Fulton U. It's why he made me come to Monday dinners. There had to be an on the field strategy where it made sense to save LJ up until he was most needed.

The door opened and LJ walked in with his backpack slung over his shoulder after this afternoon's classes.

"Hey, LJ. Marisa was just asking why the hell you're not playing much this season."

LJ's face fell like he was looking over a hundred-foot ledge. "Slacking on workouts and stuff. Just not putting in my all."

"You were always the first one in the gym and the last one to leave." I folded my arms and stalked across the living room. Slacking wasn't a word in his vocabulary.

"I've been distracted with graduation right around the corner." His voice trailed off and he wouldn't meet my eye.

Diversion. Evasion. Deflection. We might as well have been in the Philly Zoo for how cagey he was being.

"I have cookies!" He held up the massive plastic container. "Jules stopped me on the way in with these new ones. They're supposed to be for Berk, but he won't mind." He shot a look over my shoulder toward Keyton.

What was he up to? And why was he dragging Keyton into it like that night at the bar?

He rattled the container and popped off the lid. "Let's break these bad boys open. Marisa, you can make a pitcher of drinks to go with these."

"Yeah, but about what Keyt—" My words were cut off by a cookie shoved into my mouth.

The soft-baked cookie was a peanut butter and chocolate explosion of ecstasy. I moaned and took another bite. Something was up with LJ. But I didn't want to subject Keyton to even more uncomfortable conversations, and these cookies were first-in-line-at-a-new-exhibit phenomenal.

"Holy shit." I stared at LJ and grabbed another one from the box. "Keyton, you have to try these. They're insane." Devouring mine, I handed one to him.

"It would have to be…" He took a bite and his eyes widened. "Damn."

"Right?"

"So, Marisa, what drink do you think would go with this?" LJ herded me into the kitchen.

"Do you really want to drink tonight? You're on a plane early tomorrow."

"A couple won't hurt. We need to celebrate these cookies." He handed me another. "What would you make?"

I racked my volumes of alcohol knowledge. Liv tended to show off her boarding-school bartending skills most often, but I was a solid fallback when it came to getting creative. "Maybe a hazelnut liqueur with hot chocolate."

Keyton poked his head into the kitchen. "Did someone say hot chocolate?"

"Yeah, we could try that, it would be sweet enough to go with these cookies, but not too hard-hitting. Plus it'll be a nice fall drink." I grabbed another one from the box. "Berk better hurry up or these are going to be gone."

"Perfect. I'll go to the store and Keyton can come with me." LJ didn't wait for anyone to agree with anything. He took another cookie from the container and shoved it into Keyton's mouth and marched them both out the front door.

If he thought dessert, drinks and distractions would keep me from finding out why he was fumbling his last season, he'd clearly taken one too many hits in practice.

We couldn't have a dinner of cookies alone, although leaving them here with me by myself was a liability. The smell of them wafted to me like they were cartoon curls curving through the air and straight up my nose.

I slammed the lid down on the box and turned to the fridge.

Pizza boxes, leftover meal platters Nix had dropped by, old wings and beer.

I checked inside the freezer. There were a few packs of frozen chicken. I grabbed two and banged them against the counter. Frozen solid.

Eyeing the blocks of meat and the microwave, I formulated a plan. Both packs went into the microwave. I chucked them inside, hit defrost, put in the weight and hit start.

The timer flashed 25 minutes.

I went back upstairs and sat down at my computer to finalize my Venice Fellowship presentation. I'd made it to the final three applicants across twenty schools. When the email from Professor Morgan had landed in my inbox, I'd been afraid to open it, but I had.

She'd sent over the requirements to move forward with my application. It included designing a social media plan for a collection they currently had in-house and a one-day course for visitors to the museum.

LJ hadn't brought it up since the night we'd last talked about it. It felt like an undetonated landmine in our friendship. Easier to pretend it wasn't there—just like my attraction to him.

My nose itched and I grabbed some tissues. Next, my eyes watered. I looked at the window, which was closed. What the hell?

The front door banged open. "Holy shit!" Berk's voice boomed from below.

I flew from my desk down the stairs. Coughing, I was caught in the all-too-familiar feeling of dread.

Berk rushed from the back door he'd flung open and popped open the microwave. Grabbing a pair of oven mitts, he pulled his shirt up over his nose and shoved his hands into the opening. Out came a melted mess of plastic and Styrofoam.

He shot me a look split between 'what the fuck' and sympathy.

Something inside my stomach curdled like month old expired milk. I'd done it again. "Sorry."

I ran to the other windows and opened them, to help get rid of the smell of burning plastic.

He flung the melted mess into the backyard, came back in and dumped the oven mitts into the trash.

"I'm sorry. I got distracted. I thought it was on low. Sorry." I jammed the heels of my hands into the window over the sink, shoving at it. The freaking thing wouldn't budge.

Berk walked up beside me, flicked the latch and pushed it up with one hand.

"Show off." I grumbled stepping back.

"What were you trying to do exactly? Other than start a kitchen fire?"

I opened the front door to let in even more air. "I was going to make you guys dinner. Jules dropped off some cookies with LJ and—"

"Jules sent cookies." He was in a scrimmage line stance, head whipping around, dark hair whooshing as he searched for cookies. When he spotted the container on the table, it was like watching a bear go after honey.

"Why's the door—" LJ and Keyton coughed the second they stepped inside with a plastic liquor store bag.

"Marisa, what happened?" LJ's head tilted and he looked at me like a disappointed sitcom dad.

"She tried to defrost eight pounds of chicken in the microwave—all at once—still in the wrapper." Berk spoke around the cookies shoved in his face.

"Way to sell me out, Berk!" I cringed and met LJ's stare. "Whoops!"

CHAPTER 13

LJ

I slid on the oven mitt and took the tray of grilled chicken breasts out, sitting them on the stove. Marisa was banned from the kitchen without supervision. She'd accused me of calling her every hour while I was in Michigan. Maybe every other hour.

With Nix, our cooking extraordinaire, gone, we were left with a rotation of bulk cooking to keep everyone from gnawing on the baseboards and to keep Marisa from trying to help us out by pois—cooking for us.

Keyton wasn't too bad either. All three of us combined managed to at least keep ourselves full and geared up for practices. There were also the occasional stops at the dining hall to acquire large quantities of lunch meat.

We'd won against the Wildcats and our next two games. The season was halfway over, and I barely had enough tape to make it to a European football league, let alone the pros.

The reminder of why I needed to figure this situation out was blasted in my face while talking to my mom.

"Yes, I have my vitamin C powder." I switched my phone to the other ear.

"The air on those planes is so rough on you."

"I'll be okay, Mom. And I'll come home next Thursday for your birthday dinner."

"You don't have to do that. I know you're busy with the season and classes. Aren't you on a plane at dawn the next day?"

"I'm not going to miss your birthday."

"As long as you know you don't have to."

"Is dad making his brisket and lobster mac & cheese?"

"Of course."

"Then you can't keep me away."

"Just you? Is Marisa coming?"

"I'll ask her. They have a big new exhibition coming to the museum and she's been spending a lot of time there, and working on her presentation for her fellowship application, which I'm headed to after I get off the call with you."

"I hope she's not working too hard. What's this fellowship she's applying for?"

"She might be going to Venice for two years after graduation." My throat clenched. It was still hard to say the words, but I didn't freeze every time I thought about it now. Slowly, I'd work out how to keep all the pieces together when it felt like they were slipping away.

"Two years…"

"I know! I said the same thing."

"How do you feel about that?"

"I'm happy for her. She loved Venice and it seemed like Venice loved her." Every time we'd video chatted, she had a new exciting discovery to tell me about. A painting she'd finally seen up close. How the brush strokes weren't what she expected. The smell of the room sent her into a five-minute TED talk on temperature-controlled preservation.

As hard as it had been to have her gone for the whole summer, seeing the happiness pouring off her in waves had helped. She deserved that and more.

"That's it?"

"How else is there to feel about it?"

"You two have been nearly joined at the hip since third grade. And she's going to be moving to another country for two years."

"She was away all summer and we still talked loads." Not as much as I'd have liked. I'd hated not being able to experience it all with her. The Henri talk hadn't made it any easier. Now she might have a whole year with her art appreciation accomplice, dashing from one historical site to another.

"But you'll be so busy with football."

"That's a big if, Mom." Letting my family down was the last thing I wanted to do, but I'd rather under-promise and over-deliver. With the time I'd been playing this season and my agent squawking in my ear every chance he got, concern of not making the cut mounted every game. The Plan B of getting an office job didn't provide nearly the security my family needed or anything close to what I'd need for all my big plans for me and Marisa.

"Your father and I wanted to talk to you about it, but weren't sure how to bring it up. What is going on with your playing time this season? Are you hurt? Did something happen?"

I paced, squeezing the back of my neck. "The coach and I aren't seeing eye to eye."

"The coach as in Marisa's dad?"

Her short hmm came from her end of the line.

"What's that supposed to mean?"

"Nothing." Worry edged into her tone.

I'd figure it out. I'd figure something out, although the time was ticking down.

"Your sister has been working on her portfolio painting since September and she can't wait to show it to you."

Clinging to the subject change, I jumped to Quinn. "I can't wait to see it."

"She's entering it into a scholarship competition for RISD, but there are only so many spaces."

The Rhode Island School of Design had been the school Quinn set her sights on when she was eleven and I was fifteen. It was one of the best art schools in the country and had an annual price tag the size of a luxury car. And all bells and whistles of a luxury car.

"Does she have a backup plan?"

"Pratt. Cal Arts." The chuckle was barely stifled.

I groaned. Just like that, we were right back at how important this season was. Her dreams and mine were intertwined, and the whole family was looking to me for the way out, even if they said they weren't.

Quinn deserved to go. So much of her childhood had been being shuttled around to hospitals with dad or stuck at home with me, or even worse, brought to football practice with me. She and Marisa would hang out in the stands and split concessions during games.

Getting in was one part of the equation, but paying for it was the other. Even with financial aid, if I didn't sign a fat contract she'd never be able to go.

"Sensible, practical options."

"Honey, I know you're putting a lot of weight on your shoulders right now. You always did." Her voice got watery and my throat closed up.

Mom crying was in my top three worst sounds ever. There had been plenty of nights she'd do it behind closed doors when she thought everyone else was asleep when dad was sick. I'd heard and vowed there would only be happy tears from her once I got older. Older like I was right now.

"But I want you to know we're proud of you no matter what happens. You'll have graduated and played amazingly well all these years. You've been the rock long before your time, so I want you to promise me you'll have some fun for yourself before you graduate."

Flashes of fun blazed through my brain. Celebrating after a win. Nerf battles in the house. Marisa in my bed. I shook my head, trying to knock the last vision loose. Seven games left until playoffs. Keep it together.

"Don't worry, Mom."

Her lyrical laugh flooded the line. "It's what moms do. Tell Marisa I said good luck on her presentation and I can't wait to see her."

"I will. Love you, Mom."

"Love you too, honey. See you in two weeks, and have a great game on Saturday."

Our call ended. There wasn't time to heat my dinner up and get to Marisa's presentation on time. I scarfed down my now-lukewarm food, grabbed my coat with the surprise tucked inside, and headed for the door.

The Franklin Building was in the older part of campus. It hadn't yet been replaced by the steel-and-glass sleek renovations popping up from behind the construction barriers.

I followed the signs for the Art History Department and the sign taped on the door for the Guggenheim Fellowship presentations.

The door swung all the way open, banging into the chair of an older man sitting nearby. Inside the conference room, all heads turned in my direction.

"Sorry." I cringed.

On the other side of the room, Marisa slapped her hand over her forehead before straightening back up and directing her attention back to the front where the first applicant had begun their presentation. Marisa's gaze darted in my direction with a half-smothered smile twitching her lips.

Chairs were jammed into the conference room meant to hold eight people. The presentation screen up front was lit up with artwork Marisa had probably told me about twenty times, but I couldn't remember the names.

I climbed over three people in the second row, squeezing myself into the one empty chair.

The guy presenting spoke so excitedly about the sculptures on his slides, all of which seemed to be studies of the female form. I wasn't 100% sure this guy wouldn't be hauled away for attempting to bang one.

"As you can see, the lines are magnificent." There was an uncomfortable silence as he ran his finger along the curves of a sculpture of a headless woman. Not creepy at all.

"Thank you for that." Marisa's professor cleared her throat and stepped to the front of the room to slice through awkwardness so thick I was surprised we could still see each other. "Fascinating presentation. It's always wonderful to see people genuinely excited by the art."

So excited, he probably had a semi.

"Up next, we have Marisa Saunders. She spent this past summer at the museum and has focused her studies on preservation efforts with a dual degree in chemistry and art history. It's quite a unique combination, though I know it's a bit of home team bias on my part. Marisa." The professor held out her hand to welcome Marisa to the front. She was in her museum gear: a blue button-down shirt I'd ironed for her yesterday and a grey tweed skirt. All she was missing were glasses and a blazer with elbow patches, and she'd match half the people in the room.

I kept my seat. Learned that one the hard way, when I got up and cheered during a gallery presentation her sophomore year. She hadn't talked to me for a week afterward. The art crowd wasn't used to rowdy sidelines support. Who didn't love someone starting a chant spelling out each letter of their name? Apparently, art appreciators.

My fingers gripped the sides of my chair.

She didn't look half as nervous as I felt. This was worse than standing inside the tunnel waiting to run out onto the field, but there were no walls to bang into or jumping around knocking into other guys' helmets in this stuffy room.

Standing in front of a room of art buffs, she commanded everyone's attention and launched into her plans for the summer. She came alive, animated in a way that didn't signal she might start making out with an Andy Warhol or Kandinsky.

"Another community outreach project would be to get tour groups to work together to create their own Jackson Pollack. We could set the canvases out at the beginning of the tour. Smaller than Pollock's. I don't think many visitors would be able to find room for an eight-foot by twenty-foot painting in their luggage. Using quick drying water-based paints would allow the guide to provide them with the finished canvas at the end of their tour. There could be a designated photographer at the end to photograph them and provide them to the visitors to take as a keepsake." When she'd first told me about this idea, I'd been blown away. Not only would it show everyone how hard the 'easy' art truly was, but getting people involved in the art would take it from stuff on a wall to things created by insanely talented people.

A mumble rippled through the crowd jammed into the room. Whispers of what a great idea it was and how some might want to try it in other museums circulated around the room.

Pride did an end zone dance in my chest.

Marisa wrapped up her presentation and there was polite applause—not the chest-bumping, face-painted screams of a touchdown there should have been.

After a few more remarks from her professor, the group was invited for coffee and snacks in the department hallway.

I let everyone else filter out of the room, including the shady statue guy.

Marisa bounded over to me, grinning like a maniac.

"What did you think?" Her eyes glinted with a championship win light.

"You nailed it." I held up my hand and she did a jumping high five. Leaning in, I pulled her closer than I needed, but I'd take what I could get. "Was the first guy as creepy as the statue sicko?"

She wide-eyed whispered back. "That was seriously weird, right? I was wondering if it was just me."

"I hope no one breaks out a black light on any of the artwork he's been near."

Her face contorted with dread and disgust. "Gross, L."

I laughed, not even trying to hide it.

"No, the first guy was so dull, I had to jam my pencil into my hand to keep myself awake." She held up her hand.

Taking it, I traced my thumb over the barely-there indents between her thumb and pointer finger. Her skin was smooth and soft and it had been too long since I'd had an excuse to touch her like this.

"You really did kill that presentation." I offered up a watered-down lemonade of a smile. As proud as I was, a part of me didn't want her to be so passionate and excited about this trip. On the fifty yard line wearing the number one jersey, we have me, the total asshole. That I wanted them to—even in a small part of my mind—choose boring guy or way-too-into-art guy showed me how much of an ass I was.

Marisa had worked hard for this, and I'd support her in this like I did all things.

"Come on, let's raid the food set up and drink some terrible coffee and stuff ourselves on crumbly cookies."

"Sounds like a great plan."

Two years.

CHAPTER 14
MARISA

Every time I was a block away from Ron's house, my stomach knotted, twisting like a wrung-out cloth filled with dirty mop water. The need to graduate was the only thing that kept me coming. If I was lucky, he'd cancel more of these. Something always came up.

The nip in the air was more pronounced, and before long I'd be able to see my breath hanging in the air. In a couple weeks, those poor trick-or-treaters wouldn't be able to show off their costumes under all the layers.

I tugged my sleeves down from under my coat. Maybe we'd get some early excuse to bail on a dinner with Ron.

Not that I cared. I loved the days he cancelled. It shone the light on exactly where his priorities were. There were 28 Mondays between me and graduation. He'd cancel at least half, and I'd be scot-free. Hell, once he'd signed my tuition waiver for the spring in December, maybe I'd end up just as busy as he was and skip them entirely. Gratitude to a man I should hate, who'd caused me so much pain was a glass covered pill to swallow. The guilt came next at not being appreciative that I'd graduate college with almost no debt, which triggered all kinds of anger that he didn't deserve any of my gratefulness or appreciation after walking out on me.

When I'd contacted him about transferring to Fulton U after realizing where he'd ended up and where LJ went were one in the same, part of me thought he'd never even respond and I'd have to figure something else out, but he'd said yes. The deal came with a catch. The not-so-weekly dinners. And he still held onto those puppet strings for a few more months. Then I was done. None of these dinners had shown me he'd made more than the most basic effort. Always on his terms and at his convenience.

I stopped on the corner two blocks away from the house, waiting for LJ. Doing these dinners without him had sucked. But after the first few he'd insisted on coming with me. When the choice presented itself to do something with or without LJ, there was a hands down, no contest, clear winner.

He was my rock, and the one person I could count on to have my back—even if he apparently had a hard time listening. But he had a lot on his mind too.

I hated how much I needed him. I hated feeling needy. I hated feeling vulnerable.

He could slice me in two with a word without even realizing it. Our senior trip kiss and the day at the door with my dad. Completely oblivious, he'd reached into my chest, grabbed my heart, and dumped it straight into my hands.

This was the best time to think about my future. The one without him. I couldn't be the needy, annoying one in this relationship forever. I just needed a few more months.

I checked my phone.

No messages from LJ.

There were still fifteen minutes until dinner officially started, but I wasn't showing up early. I tapped my phone against my palm and paced the sidewalk.

An email notification popped up from my advisor with the subject line. "Congratulations! - You've been selected."

Had one of the art history professors opened another phishing email that threatened to take down the whole email server again? Last month, we'd been hit with a lottery winning notification.

Against all of IT's advice, I opened it.

And yelped, nearly dropping my phone to the sidewalk.

I snatched my phone off the ground and read through the email with my hand over my mouth.

"Marisa! You okay?" LJ called out his passenger side window.

"Great. Totally great." I kept my happy dance in check and hopped into his car, wanting to hang out the window and scream into the autumn air.

He rolled toward the house. "You looked like a clickbait YouTube thumbnail back there. What's going on?"

I wanted to tell him. I wanted to jump up and down and scream with excitement, but I reined it in. It was a big step. Huge.

I'd need to run through all the final financial aid information to be sure I could make it work. Without the insurance money from the fire, the living situation would've been tricky in Italy over the summer. Two full years where I'd only have the fellowship money to depend on might blow up in my face, if I didn't run the numbers. But I wanted it. I really did.

LJ put the car into park. "You're not going to tell me?"

"We don't have to tell each other everything." I teased.

"Fine, then I won't tell you what I was thinking for my mom's birthday present." He reached for his door, but I grabbed onto him and jerked him back. We'd always shopped for a gift together, but this year he'd said he wanted to get her something on his own. It was another hole poked in our fifteen-year friendship. Hopefully it wasn't another football jersey.

"What is it?"

He grinned, trying to pry my fingers off his arm. "Show me yours and I'll show you mine."

I shoved him away with a sound of disgust. "You're really the freaking worst, you know that?"

"So you say." He hopped out and jogged around the car to open my door.

Okay, maybe he wasn't the worst. I'd miss little things like this after we graduated. Right then it hit me. The fellowship. Five games left in his season. The end of the Monday Dinner Downer.

The whole thing was coming to an end. It should have been 100% happiness, but attending and avoiding these dinners had been a stable point in my FU college life. It would be weird to see it go.

He walked ahead of me and stopped on the bottom step, looking back at me.

"Sorry, just thinking." I racked my knuckles on the door.

"Thinking about what?

The door opened before he could ask any more questions, and for once I was happy at Ron showing up to give LJ a distraction, so he didn't focus his prying on me. But those feelings evaporated the second we made it over the threshold. Ron stood in front of us, face flushed with a dopey, embarrassed look on his face.

Someone else had been invited to dinner. A woman in her late thirties sat in the seat I usually sat in beside Ron. I shook my head, making sure I wasn't seeing double or hallucinating. There were two place settings on the side LJ usually sat on alone. I stalled, focusing on this woman with a brunette bob and nice mom eyes with crinkles on the edges smiling at me from the dining room.

LJ brushed against my side and stuck to me like my coat was made of crazy glue.

"Who is that?" The pit in my stomach I'd thought couldn't get any deeper turned out to have a surprise trap door in it.

And that's when the way he answered the door, so unlike any other time he'd answered, clicked into place. Flushed, slightly embarrassed, cagey. It was the kind of look someone might've had if they'd been caught making out.

"Marisa and LJ, I'd like you to meet Nora."

He kept walking, but I stayed rooted in place.

Nora slid her chair back and stood, smoothly, effortlessly. She had on a tasteful fall outfit—a cream sweater, black pants, black shoes, and a simple silver necklace. A perfectly nice and normal outfit. She walked around the table gingerly, like she didn't want to intrude.

Too late.

I glared at Ron. "Who is she?"

He waved us forward toward the table. "Come on. I'll introduce you."

LJ grabbed onto my sleeve and dragged me forward.

My feet hit the floor with Frankenstein steps. With each one a new trap door opened.

"We both haven't been the best about sharing, so I thought I'd share something with you." He smiled at Nora and stood behind his seat, holding onto the back of the chair like we were sitting down for a nice family dinner. Nothing out of the ordinary here.

"I'm so happy to finally meet you, Marisa. Ron has told me so much about you." She patted Ron's arm.

"Funny, he hasn't said a word about you." I cut my eyes to him.

LJ cleared his throat and extended his hand for a shake.

She took it, her smile wavered the tiniest bit.

My blood rushed from my head and I swayed, catching myself on the back of my chair.

Her smile was warm and so were her eyes. It wasn't until it faltered that I noticed the hand reached out toward me.

Not in the mood for pleasantries, I pulled my hat off and shoved it into my coat pocket. Was I being a child? Probably, but Ron had just sprung a girlfriend on me out of nowhere. No consideration, no asking, no warning.

I'd always figured football was his life. It was all he had time for and all he'd ever make time for. But here was a living, breathing example of how untrue that was. It tapped into a new well of anger I hadn't known existed.

He had a girlfriend, and he'd invited her to dinner.

A feeling built in the back of my throat, traveling up to my nose and burning in my nostrils. Pressure and moisture. I blinked, staring at the table. No grocery store lasagna tonight. Everything here looked homemade, down to the brownies sliced and stacked on a fall-themed plate.

LJ tugged my chair out. "Marisa, sit." He ducked his head and whispered into my ear. "Are you okay?"

Instead of answering, I plopped down without taking off or even unbuttoning my coat.

Stilted conversation flowed around me. Silverware, glasses, serving utensils and plates clinked and scraped against one another as everyone filled their plates. LJ plopped roast beef, mashed potatoes and green beans onto mine after several attempts to get me to pick up my plate.

"And the kids were so happy to pick out their costumes."

That sent a jolt straight through me. "Kids?"

Nora looked from Ron to me. "Yes, I have an eight-year-old girl and six-year-old twin boys. Ron was so great and took them out to find their Halloween costumes."

My head whipped from her to him.

He smiled at her. Not the forced, unsure kind he gave me, but a full-on smile. So comfortable. They weren't newly dating. It had been a while. He'd been playing dad to her kids for a while. He set down his silverware and wiped his mouth with a napkin. "It wasn't a big deal. I was happy to do it." His hand fell on top of hers.

I fisted my hands in my lap. "You took her kids shopping for Halloween?" The words wobbled and swayed. The burning moisture was back, slamming into the back of my nose and creeping toward the corners of my eyes. I cleared my throat.

"They're good kids."

"Right. Good kids." I gasped like I'd been flung into a vacuum. Gulping down a breath, I turned back to Nora. "How long have you two been dating?"

She shot Ron a concerned look. "A little over a year now."

They'd been dating for over a year. And he was pissed about me not telling him about the fire when he'd been dating Nora over here since last October. Had he taken her kids costume shopping last Halloween too? I'd been a ghost or a face-painted zombie for most Halloweens growing up. LJ's parents would've taken me shopping, but I hadn't wanted much, and God knew my mom couldn't spare a few dollars for a costume—not when there was grain alcohol in the tri-state area. "Wow, that's amazing. So wonderful you're bonding with them already."

Her smile was blown-glass brittle. "It took a while before we were ready, but they're getting along great. The kids adore Ron, and I was so happy I could come over to finally meet you."

"What made you think this was a good idea?" I glared at my father and wiped my sleeve across my nose.

He sighed. "I wanted to show you that I am not this horrible person you think I am."

This was worse. Because he obviously hadn't been to her kids. But he'd dropped off the face of the Earth and ignored his own. My neck heated, the blood drumming in my veins, and I twisted my fingers in my lap, trying to keep it all together.

"All you've managed to show me is that you've been more of a father to these kids you barely know than you ever were to me." My voice cracked.

LJ covered my hands with his.

If I looked at him, I'd shatter.

"You think you're the only one who's been through a lot." He shot a placating look of mild embarrassment to Nora. His look of 'I told you she was dramatic' or some other bullshit.

I shot up from my chair, anger waging war in my chest. "You know nothing about me or my life!"

"And whose fault is that, Marisa? We've been doing this for almost two years and you refuse to say anything more than a few words to me. I thought if Nora was here—"

"Because I don't want to be here. You had your chance to be my father, and you walked away without a second thought." Now the tears burned their way from my ducts. I'd sworn I wouldn't cry over him again. I'd thought I was numbed to whatever crap he could pull. Turns out I was wrong, and I hated not being able to control all these old feelings that made me feel like an abandoned little girl all over again.

He banged his fist on the table. "Is that what you think? You think I didn't give you a second thought after I left?"

"It sure as hell didn't feel like it when my mother rattled off the lists of all the reasons you'd split. When I waited up at night sitting on the front step on my birthdays hoping maybe, just maybe you'd come. When I'd tell Santa all I wanted was for Ron to come and rescue me. When my mom was so fucking drunk I had to drive us back from a restaurant at twelve years old." My hands shook. Old feelings of betrayal and anger roared through my head, making it hard to think. I was getting lightheaded. My chest tightened, and I sniffed, trying not to break down.

"I wanted to be there for you." He shot up from his seat.

"But you weren't." I brushed away the burning tears, the ones that showed up at the worst possible moment. These were the tears that came when I was trying to stay strong, and sadness and anger collided like a thunderstorm overhead. "And I was stuck with an alcoholic mother who was sure to tell me *every single day* how much I'd screwed up her life."

LJ rocked back in his chair, nearly tipping it over.

I looked to him, hating the shock and worry in his eyes.

"Marisa, why didn't—"

"I'm sick and tired of this. I didn't tell you, LJ, because you didn't even have the concept of what it was like to have a shitty parent. Your mom was late picking you up that first day we met because her car got a flat. She showed up apologizing a hundred times and took us both to get ice cream when you said I was waiting too."

I wiped at the tears blurring my vision. I ought to hold back. He didn't need to know this. It wasn't his fault, but right now lashing out was all I had. It was all I could do to keep myself standing.

"Do you know what the hell my mom was doing when I got home?"

Dead silence. The stupid clock in the living room ticked the seconds away.

"She wasn't even there. She came home at midnight after getting back from the casinos." A hysterical, watery laugh jumped from my throat.

My gaze swung back to Ron. "That's who you left me with. I was an eight-year-old little girl, just like Nora's, but you didn't take me Halloween shopping. You were on the road at games or scouting trips and then you just stopped coming home. You just stopped. I'm glad to know you can be a great guy." It was the knife I'd already thought had been twisted as far as it could go, but no. There was more. I wiped my nose with my sleeve, my face an absolute mess. "It's awesome you've got that fatherly instinct in there. Just sucks you didn't use it with your own kid."

There were no more words to say. My chest burned like someone was shoveling piles of coal into a furnace or chucked an entire keg into a bonfire and shrapnel cut through my body.

I flung open the door and fled his house. My feet slammed into the paved walkway and I cut across the lawn to speed up my escape. Blinded by tears, I raced past the houses along the street, gasping for air.

This time LJ didn't jump in front of me. He tackled me, wrapping both arms around me and holding me against his chest.

I shoved at his arms. "Stop it. Get off." Slipping out of his hold, I took off running.

"Marisa!" He could catch me—he was way faster than me—but he didn't.

He let me go.

With every step, a jolt shot through my body that wrenched ugly sobs from my throat.

With every step, the burn got hotter.

With every step, I hated the way LJ had looked at me when I'd blurted out the biggest secret I'd been keeping from him since we'd become friends.

Ron had a girlfriend with kids. An eight-year-old daughter. Twins. And he was so great with them.

I'd just spilled everything to LJ, the secret I'd kept from him since the beginning of our friendship. Stupid. So stupid to blurt things out like that.

My feet drummed against the ground until I skidded to a stop, grabbing onto the railing of the porch to The Brothel.

"Marisa!" LJ shouted. His car door slammed.

I flung myself up the stairs and jammed my key into the front door, closing it behind me and took off up the stairs to hide and pull a Keyton, never to be seen again.

But the latch didn't catch.

His footsteps behind me were as loud as my thundering heartbeats.

We burst through my door at nearly the same time.

He caught my arm and spun me around to face him. "Stop running." His gaze was fierce, bordering on pissed.

The burning pressure was back, pounding furiously in my nose.

His furrows softened and he held onto both my arms. "Stop running from me, Marisa. Please."

"Why shouldn't I run? Maybe I want to be the one running for once. First my dad, and then my mom every damn chance she got."

His face was filled with sadness and shock. "Why didn't you tell me?" The words bordered on desperate.

"Tell you what? That my mom, if she could even be called that, was an alcoholic? That I spent time at your house because I hated being home alone? Because I hated going to bed hungry? Because I hated her rolling in the middle of the night alone—or not?"

"All of it," his whisper was so intense it sent shivers shooting down my spine.

The ugly, wracking sobs were back like they were wrenched from the depths of my heart. It was an emotional detonation that only he could bring about.

He hugged me, holding me so tightly I could barely breathe. Or maybe my lungs had stopped knowing how to function.

Quieting, with the tears turning cold against my skin, I held onto him, clung to him. Still feeling seconds from coming out of my skin.

The house was quiet and we went upstairs to my room. My fingers and tip of my nose tingled at the change in temperature.

Tears flooded my eyes as my body thawed from the chill. All the things I'd kept from LJ were held back by a dam close to bursting. The downpour raised the water and it lapped at the edges of the wall I'd built up to separate that part of myself from who I was with him.

Throwing off my coat, I plopped down on the floor, wanting to get this over with.

From the look on his face, he wouldn't let it go.

He took off his coat and hung it on the back of my chair. "You could've told me."

"And become a charity case to your family?" I scooted back and crossed my legs.

He faced me, sat and crossed his. "Why would you think that? We'd have done anything for you. Still will."

"And become a mooch or someone you felt you had to keep around? No. That's not my deal."

"What the hell is wrong with you? Why do you keep talking about yourself like this?"

I shook my head, looking away. "You don't know what it's like to be…" I trailed off.

"No, don't stop. I've been your friend since the third grade. How could you think I wouldn't want to know?"

"There's more than a few things you don't want to know about me, LJ." Trying to share them in the past had only gotten me hurt. He wanted to be my knight in shining armor, but I wasn't his princess in the tower. I was his sidekick.

"Things like what?" He prodded and wouldn't let it drop.

"Things like the scar on my wrist was from the first time I tried to make soup by myself and my mom came in and spilled the whole thing and I reached for the pot like an idiot. Or the week I spent with you the summer before ninth grade, my mom wasn't visiting a friend in Chicago. I don't know where the hell she was. I still don't have any idea." I was pissed for the scared, lonely kid bumping around the house and feeling everything she was at the same time.

He held onto me and rocked me until the tears dissolved and my skin was itchy from the salt staining my cheeks.

"Why didn't you tell me it was that bad?"

"What could you have done?"

"Something? Anything?"

"Were you going to move me into your tree house? We were kids."

"Yes, but my parents would've helped. They'd have had you come live with us or tracked down your dad."

"You had a full house as it was. Adding me to the mix when everyone was dealing with so much already wasn't okay."

"Screw okay. My mom loves you like a daughter. I lo—I can't believe you kept all that from me for so long."

"What the hell does it matter? Why are you getting upset? You should be happy, I saved you from dealing with all my baggage. We played video games and ate crappy food in your room and the backyard, wandered the woods and hung out. We were kids."

"And you were a kid dealing with things you shouldn't have had to."

I shrugged. "I could say the same about you. You were handling all the stress of your dad being sick. You were helping your mom and Quinn. We all have to deal with heavy shit sometimes."

He scrubbed his hands down his face. "I wish you would've told me."

"Let me hop in my time machine and get right on it. There are some things you don't want to know." I stared at the floor, trying stop the flood. I barely had my head above water—dumping another bucket on top wasn't a smart idea.

"What else? Tell me. What things can't you tell me?"

About Venice and…

"And things like, I like you. I've always liked you and you don't feel the same way about me. So there. How about those new bits of information?"

His head dropped a fraction of an inch, eyes darting back and forth like he was running numbers in his head. He slammed his eyes shut.

Stupid. It was a stupid thing to confess.

I spun, facing my bedroom window and scrubbed my hands down my face.

"Marisa…"

"What?" I turned to face him.

A pained, bordering on tortured, expression cast a shadow across his face.

His arms wrapped around me, holding me tight against him, and his lips were liquid fire crashing down on mine.

CHAPTER 15
MARISA

Breathing heavily, blood pounding, my heart ramming into my ribs, I jerked back staring at him.

"What—?" My anger transformed into confusion.

His fingers gripped my face and slipped around the bottom of my ear, holding me to him while he delved deeper into the kiss. His tongue flicked against mine and I whimpered, drawing a groan from him, lost to the thumping beat of the blood coursing through my veins.

He let me go and stared into my eyes. There was no hesitation or confusion in them, only a hunger.

And my confusion reversed course and shifted straight into passion. The raging fire of anger was channeled into a need. The flood gates had opened, only this time it wasn't water—it was fire.

My swollen, aching lips transmitted a signal radiating throughout my body. The need crawling under my skin was hungry for more.

"I've wanted to do that for so long."

Panting, heated with a mental shout of 'finally,' I stared into his eyes, seeing the truth of his words. My heart was finally free to let all those feelings loose, and the tears almost made their return. This was pure, unadulterated bliss. "What the hell took you so long?"

His hands slid down my sleeves until they got to my hands and he intertwined his fingers with mine.

"When I'm standing here with you like this—" he lifted our hands and held them to his chest. "I have no freaking idea."

There were so many things to sort through, but now the need was winning out. "Then kiss me again."

He kicked my door closed and went in for another kiss. The first hadn't been a fluke, not by a long shot.

This wasn't a daydream. This wasn't a fake out. This was happening.

Before long, needy sounds filled the room. It took me far too long to realize they were coming from me.

I dropped my head to his shoulder. A nearly-silent prayer for him not to stop whispered across my lips.

His lips danced along the curve of my neck, intensifying the heat humming through my body.

My hands ran along his back, shoving at the sweater and t-shirt underneath.

He stilled and rocked back, cupping my cheek. "I want you, Marisa." An extra-long blink and his gaze was back on mine. "I need you."

A lightness in my chest unlike I'd ever felt before. He needed me. He wanted me. He'd have me.

"And I need you too." I stepped back, grabbing the hem of my shirt and swept it over my head in one smooth motion.

His gaze tracked straight to my chest.

The pulse between my thighs deepened, sending sparks of anticipation through my body. Then a small curveball. "Shit, do you have any condoms?"

Without a word he rushed out of the room and I heard one of the drawers in his room slam shut. He had a box stashed there. I'd found them when we'd been sharing a room and a little flare of jealousy had burned in my chest, but now I was glad he had them. I wouldn't let jealousy ruin this moment.

Bursting into my room, he glanced down at the small unopened box, he cursed under his breath.

No, no no. What if he was backing out? I reached for him. "What's wrong?" I trailed kisses along his neck and slid my hands toward the buttons on his pants.

"They're expired. Dammit." He groaned.

"You're joking." I grabbed the box. This was not happening. They gave handfuls of condoms away in the student center every week. Sure enough, the date stamped on the box was more than a year ago.

"Shit."

"I'll be right back." He bolted from the room so fast there should've been a plume of smoke behind him.

I sat on my bed. Why were his condoms expired? Now wasn't the time. And before I could let any doubts or fears creep back in, he was back with a strip of condoms.

"That's a lot of condoms."

He flung them on my bed behind me and ran his fingers along my chin. "I don't want to have to go back for more later."

The sparks turned to flares.

"Well aren't you a planner."

"I've been waiting for this for too long." His fingers skimmed along my back, slowly running under the heavy straps of my bra and camisole.

Tingling anticipation charged my skin.

I repeated his movements. A mirror of longing and hunger.

My breath hitched. "How long?"

His fingers trailed down the side of my neck.

Goosebumps trailed down my arms and the tempo of the throb between my thighs increased. "Too long."

Just how long exactly? Another thing to tuck away for later. It couldn't have been as long as I'd wanted this. I'd all but given up hope of one day feeling him like this, of being close to him as anything more than his friend.

His smell made me heady. It made me think of hiking on a sunny day in a forest. Fresh. Earthy. Real.

I tugged his shirt overhead, breaking the hold neither of us wanted to lose on one another.

He turned, tugging me forward by the loops on my jeans. His fingers grazed my waistband and slid under the camisole. Taking his time, his damn sweet time, he drew my camisole up.

The rough touch of his hands skimming along my sides and unhooking my bra sent dizzying desire radiating through me.

Both of us were naked from the waist up, standing in my bedroom, and my heart was beating so fast, I expected to look down and see the imprint.

"You're beautiful. And you're sure about this?" Did he always have to be so damn earnest and sweet?

But a beat hit. This would change everything. This wasn't a kiss. This wasn't an errant almost-hand-job. This was sex. A big first. It might be our last, the last of everything built over the past fifteen years of friendship. But I couldn't stop.

I wouldn't stop. I needed to know.

"Let me show you how sure I am." I shoved down my jeans and kicked them off before tugging the buttons of his and pushing them off his trim hips and down his muscled thighs.

They hit the floor like mine.

His eyes were closed like he'd slipped into a quick meditation, but his cock certainly wasn't relaxed. It stood up straight, thick, heavy. His lips moving, saying silent words.

My body hummed in anticipation. A flare of worry was quickly smothered by my hope and want.

A bout of hesitation hit me and then his eyes snapped open. "Just trying to calm myself down. I thought I was ready to see you like this, but holy shit, Marisa."

I chuckled, preening at the words. "If you like what you see, then come get me." I spread my arms wide.

He shot forward, spinning me around until I flopped onto the bed.

My hair fell into my face.

His warm, weighty body settled over mine.

I parted my thighs, letting him in. Letting him closer. The tension and worries I'd anticipated weren't there. There was nothing except the not-so-gentle hum of anticipation. My hummingbird heartbeat might as well have been one continuous beat making my skin flush and glow.

His corded muscles flexed, like it was taking all of his strength to hold back.

I didn't want him to hold back anymore.

He dropped his head and laved one of my nipples, rolling the other between his fingers, while rocking his hips against me. The slow, steady rub of his cock against my clit coaxed moans from deep in my throat.

I held onto his head.

The tongue-and-teeth combo was working wonders on my breasts. I hadn't ever thought they were all that sensitive. Apparently, they just hadn't met the right guy. LJ was that guy.

Heat and quivers coiled in my belly.

The charge running through my body heightened, and the sounds from where his hips ground against mine bordered on obscene. Even the tiniest particle of reservation evaporated. I wanted this. I wanted him.

I felt around on the bed and snagged the condoms. "LJ, here." I tore one off and held it up to him.

He stopped and looked up at me with rosy cheeks and a

flicker of confusion. "Right." He chuckled and lifted up, rolling the latex onto his shaft.

A happy sigh rushed past my lips when he dropped back down and nudged at my pussy.

His fingers brushed the hair back from my face, and he stared into my eyes.

If there was a time to not be a gentleman, it was now, but LJ being exactly who he was, it was why I loved him like I did. He ran his thick mushroom tip up and down my entrance.

"Come on, L." My heart tripped, stripping away all the layers between us.

He met my lips and drank from them in hearty gulps.

I clung to him.

My toes scrunched as he pushed inside. So much pressure. Full. So full. My mouth opened in a silent scream.

His head pushing inside. Stretching and spreading me.

I gasped, squeezing my eyes shut at the intensity, breathing through the pain.

He stared into my eyes, watching every breath. "Are you okay?"

"Mmhh." I nodded, not trusting my voice, and the sharpness of his invasion eased into a throb.

The feeling of fullness gave way to ripples of pleasure.

His thrusts built slowly, until they rocked into me harder and faster. Measured. Methodical. Maddening.

A tease after the wait. The pain was completely gone now. My breath hitched as the electric current increased.

"I thought the phrase was cock tease." I shifted my hips to get him to sink in deeper, faster, completely.

Each half stroke was torturous pleasure. And with one thrust, he buried himself in me.

I yelped and my back arched off the bed. Helpless lust crashed into me and stole my breath. But I needed more.

He glanced up from looking down between us. His pupils were massive and he shuddered, rocking me along with him.

Staring into my eyes, he raised up and I shifted my hips, opening my legs wider.

The breath was stolen from my lungs as his slow thrust invaded me, an invasion that sent sizzling pleasure rolling down my spine. The bliss blooming from deep within me turned to a euphoric moan as his slow, steady drive reached depths I relished and wanted to never stop.

"Are you okay?" His fingers brushed the hair from the side of my face.

Sweat beaded on his forehead. His control and caring, never wanting to push me further than I wanted to go, made it hard to keep my heart from swelling. He was watching me like I was the most precious thing in his life.

"I'd be even better if you stopped holding back." I shot him a lopsided grin and urged him on with a tilt of my hips.

He dropped his head back and hissed like he was in pain. An excruciating pleasure he couldn't get enough of and couldn't escape.

My bed rocked and banged against the wall like we were trying to demolish the place.

He wasn't holding back now.

How little he was holding back was written in the sweat coating both our bodies.

If anyone came home they'd think there was a drumline in my bedroom, but we weren't stopping.

I ran my fingers along the side of his face, reveling in the stubble and traveling up to tickle my fingers through his hair. "I'm all yours, L." It slipped out, I swiveled my hips to distract from the words. Stay in the moment.

This spurred him on. Rolling, grinding thrusts and the sounds of our bodies battling toward the peak now within view heightened every touch, taste and smell.

Rippling waves crested over me, dragging me to the

depths of bliss with each thrust stripping away my ability to do anything other than feel.

A brutal climax ripped through me and my moan was lost to a scream. I buried my face in the crook of his neck and held on as my walls clamped around him.

LJ hissed and kept going, his thrusts getting harder and sloppier. The silent mantra was back, only now I could hear it with my cheek rubbing against his chin, the short hairs tickling my skin.

"So fucking beautiful. Make it good for her. So fucking beautiful." On repeat.

A chuckle caught in my throat at the most LJ thing ever said during sex. I rode the waves, moving from peak to peak before he thickened inside me, triggering another oversensitive orgasm.

This time, I wrapped all my limbs around him, trying to stall the movement. It was too much. He was too much and even more might be the death of me.

He collapsed on top of me and I basked in the weight and heat of him. After so many times sharing a bed, I had to say this was my favorite position. Glowy, tingling, and blissed out, I held onto him, not wanting these feelings to wane and the rest of the world to barge in on our moment.

Instead of moving off me, he slid his arms under me and squeezed me hard against him. "That was…:"

I laughed and hugged him back. "It sure was."

He hopped off the bed and got rid of the condom before jumping back into the bed with me.

This time, his strong thighs were on the outside of mine and he molded his body to mine again, sliding his arms behind me.

His not-nearly-as-deflated-as-I'd-expected cock was nestled in the hair on top of my pussy.

I was blanketed by his body, his strength, his lo—

Now was not the time to put words out into the universe,

but I couldn't back up. And suddenly, the panic of someone downstairs having heard us sent an elbow straight to my stomach.

"Is anyone home?"

He drew his head back and rested his fingers against the side of my neck. "No one's here. They won't be back for a few hours." His fingers trailed down my shoulder, and the goosebumps pushed through my skin.

The cooling of my body was stopped and reversed by the growing appendage between us.

"Then we have time for another round." I grabbed his ass and squeezed a cheek.

"I'd say we have time for at least another couple, if you're game."

I grabbed the strip of condoms half-wedged under my lower back and waved them in front of his face. "How many do you think we can make it through before anyone comes back?"

His lips twitched. "I have no idea, but I'm ready to start this race in five." He took the strip from me.

"Four." I wiggled out from under him and got onto my knees.

"Three?" He got up onto his and tore open the package.

"Two." I pushed against his chest and he fell onto his back.

"One." He straightened his legs.

I threw mine over his and gripped him before lifting up and guiding him inside.

"Blast off."

CHAPTER 16
LJ

Marisa rode me, her hips dropping and rotating. Teeth-grinding pleasure was injected straight into my veins.

I cupped her breasts, toying with her nipples. She found her rhythm and I added my own thrusts timed to draw the moans, gasps and looks of surprise from her.

After so long holding back, I couldn't anymore. I didn't want to, not when she felt this good and made noises that tapped into a baser, primal side of me that didn't want to let her go. Not after we were finally together.

With the right tempo, it wasn't long before my focus shifted from making this good for her to holding back. It was too good. Watching her made it even harder to keep the reins on.

My silent chant resumed and I squeezed my eyes shut only to snap them open. I didn't want to miss a second of her parted lips and hooded gaze.

She stared down at me like I was a superhero who'd showed up with a basket of orgasms to hand out. Damn, I wanted to run out onto the roof to see if I could actually fly.

I gripped her hips, pulling her down harder and grinding up into her.

This set her off. Her head dropped back and she screamed my name before falling forward onto my chest.

Sweaty, sex-drunk, and satiated, I held her against my chest and brushed her hair to one side, massaging the dents in her shoulder from her bra.

Coming down from the sex high was happening faster than I wanted. All the reasons and roadblocks lined up in the back of my head, ready to unleash a downpour on our first time.

She kissed my cheek and let out a sigh of contentment.

I didn't want to move from this spot, but I had to get rid of the condom.

When I slid back into the bed, she had her thinking face on.

The door opened to the reservations, which lined up in a nice orderly fashion.

"Your condoms were expired."

"Yes." I'd hoped she'd have forgotten that. And I didn't have more than a few brain cells left after round two to come up with a good excuse.

"But they're good for like, five years."

I dragged the blankets down, my heart beating wildly for totally different reasons than a few minutes ago. She should know. Also, it was a solid cover, if I'd botched it for her.

"Yes."

"Was it a box you got from someone else?"

"No." I chuckled. "I bought them myself."

She moved under the blankets, the wheels turning and gears grinding even louder. "When?"

"Senior year of high school." I faced her with my head propped up on my arm, wishing I had another distraction cookie to shove in her mouth, but not wanting to hide this from her anymore.

"What?" Her eyebrows furrowed, and then she gasped and stared at me with her mouth slack.

I was tempted to nudge it closed with my finger.

My neck and chest burned with embarrassment. The red was probably a glowing beacon to planes flying overhead.

"You're a *virgin*?" When she said the word, it sounded like it was in a foreign language she'd never learned. She shot up, the blanket falling off her body. "Are you fucking serious?"

My face heated with embarrassment, like someone had shoved my mouth full of candles and lit the wicks. "Why not scream it from the rooftops? And not anymore." I sat up, keeping the blanket over my lap as if the soft sheets could hide my self-consciousness. How obvious had it been? Why'd hadn't I just come up with a good excuse?

"What about the girl you dated freshman year?" She shifted on my lap, straddling me, wrapped up in her own blanket with her arms draped over my shoulders.

My head rocked back, trying to figure out what alternate life she'd thought I was living. "I didn't date anyone freshman year."

Her lips pursed. "You don't have to lie. I saw the pictures online. She was a cute, super tall brunette with a pixie cut."

I wracked my brain trying to figure out who this mystery woman might have been, which wasn't easy with Marisa on my lap. At least there were two blankets between us, or I'd have trouble remembering my own name.

"She was tallish. Was in lots of pictures with you. Every game, even the away games, she was there."

"Tara?" I laughed before steeling my face at the glare from Marisa. She was being totally serious.

"Fine, Tara. Yes, what about *her*?"

"We were *not* having sex. She was the mascot."

"The mascot."

"Giant cartoon knight."

"Was a girl."

"Yeah. She traveled with the team to games and stuff. She graduated my freshman year."

Her grip on the sheet loosened and it slipped down her back. "Or the one girl sophomore year with the faux hawk?"

"Class project partner. She crashed here a couple nights because her roommate was insane. She kept stealing her underwear."

"What about—"

I cut off her list with my finger against her lips. The last thing I wanted was for her to go off on a wild tangent about me and my bedroom activities. Evading wasn't going to work. I need her to know.

"I haven't slept with anyone else—ever." My hands wrapped around her waist, thumbs brushing against the soft skin of her back.

Her face cycled through at least ten different emotions before settling on confusion.

"Why not?" She settled deeper onto my lap.

At least she believed me about that, but did I really want to tell her the whole truth? Would it seem pathetic and stupid? On the other hand, I'd already run the ball in this far, what was a few more yards?

I tilted my head and stared into her eyes, the same chocolatey brown ones that made me want to gorge myself on brownies. "They weren't you."

"LJ…" Her head tilted. The question blaring in her eyes. "No one?"

I stifled my smile. "I'm not saying I've never been kissed or anything. But it just never seemed right." The line between her not thinking of me as a manwhore or a nun was a hard one to toe. This was the worst possible place for her to be sitting for this conversation. There was nowhere to run. Nowhere to hide. I didn't want to go through a play-by-play of just how far I had gone, and I didn't need to think about how her experience eclipsed mine.

Or the guys she'd been with.

Her hands stilled their torturous swirls on my back. Her head ducked and she stared at the same spot in the center of my chest she always looked at whenever she couldn't look me in the eye.

Shit, had I screwed up? Was it terrible, and now she knew why? Embarrassment sent me from half-mast to floppy noodle in a split second. Was she going back and finding that it all made sense now? I should've just kept my mouth shut and pretended I didn't know why they were expired. Not that lying to her had ever been easy. Holding onto one big lie was pretty much my limit.

"Me too," she whispered.

It barely made it over the pounding of my heart trying to escape up my throat. "You too, what?"

She peeked at me before dropping her gaze again, licking those full lips that I needed to taste again. "I—I'm a virgin too. Well, I was…" Her lips twitched.

I rocked back nearly toppling her off my lap.

Her hands shot out, grabbing for my shoulder and I stared into her eyes, blown away by her confession and the years of jealousy I'd dealt with thinking about the guy who'd gotten to do more than just sleep beside her.

Her shoulder jumped and her fingers tickled the back of my neck, raising goosebumps all over my body. "It just never felt right."

"What? Why didn't you tell me?"

She jabbed her finger into my chest. "Why didn't you tell *me*?"

Holy shit, Marisa was a virgin. I'd devirginized her. Those words detonated in my skull. "I'd have made sure to go slower or…"

"If you'd gone any slower I'd have been fifty by the time we actually did it." A playful shove.

Relief that some things between us were still the same

brought a smile to my face.

"I was trying to be considerate. And take my time. And not come within three strokes." I wriggled my fingers into her side.

She squirmed and yelped, trying to get off my lap before sobering. "How was it?" The corner of her bottom lip disappeared into her mouth.

Lifting her chin with my finger, I stared into her eyes not wanting a shadow of doubt or worries to invade her head when she thought about what we'd just done. "I should be asking you the same thing. Isn't it usually guys who screw up the first time for the girl?"

Her fingers skimmed along my chest, tracing the patterns of my muscles.

My dick responded, ready to live up to my tease about making it through the whole strip of condoms.

"Maybe, but I don't have any complaints. It was amazing." Wonder filled her voice.

Breath trapped in my lungs escaped. My cheek twitched. "I know, I should've been doing it years ago."

Her gaze narrowed and she grabbed a pillow, whacking me with it. "Too late now. I've got the first place spot on your bedpost." She pumped her hands overhead and made fake crowd cheering noises.

"Have I told you you're the worst?" I relaxed against the wall, watching her gloating glow, still fully aware of our nakedness and unable to take my eyes off her. Things didn't feel one bit awkward. It felt like us, but better. I wanted more of this. A lot more. "Don't I get the same spot?"

Her lips curved in a sassy, smirk. "I guess I'll allow it." She slid off my lap and grabbed a t-shirt—my t-shirt—and pulled it on. Climbing on the bed, she sat beside me with her back resting against the wall. "What a pair we are—two 22-year-old virgins."

"Maybe there's more of us out there than we think." I

nudged her with my elbow, no longer feeling like I was alone or had been crazy for waiting for her. Not when we got to have this together.

"Maybe…" The lip nibble was back on.

"Are you having regrets?" My stomach knotted and soured. God, I hoped not. It was the best night of my life.

"No! Are you?"

"Not a single one." Then the mantle of reality and responsibility dropped onto my shoulders. After the blow-up Marisa had at her dad's house today, she wasn't in the best frame of mind. Emotions were heightened.

She might never have slept with me, if what had happened at his house hadn't happened.

I also didn't want her to use this as another thing to piss him off—for her sake, for the sake of what might be salvageable in their relationship, and for my sake. I hated the shitty, selfish feeling gnawing at my gut for even thinking of it. There were fewer than six weeks left in the season, and I needed to salvage what I could. "But maybe we don't tell anyone about this for now."

Her shoulders stiffened and her lip fell free from between her teeth. "We should keep this quiet."

I couldn't tell if it was a question or not, but I pushed forward for both our sakes. "Do you really want the guys— hell everyone who's ever said we have the hots for one another—to get the satisfaction? They'll never let us live it down, and they'll probably assume any time we're alone we're having sex. Then there's the other guys on the team. It could cause problems there, if we're out…"

She drew her knees up to her chest. "And then there would be all kinds of questions about our plans for the future. What we're doing after graduation. It's not like we're dating or anything." She shrugged. "Especially since I got the Guggenheim Fellowship. I'll leave for Venice two weeks after graduation."

The war between pride and happiness brought out the big guns, trying to push out hesitancy, heartache and hatred for a whole damn city.

"You did it." That piece of information had burrowed into my brain like a shard of glass over the past couple hours.

"I did." She sat up straighter, but pride and anxiety washed over her face. "I'm totally on board with the 'don't tell anyone' thing. It would bring up way too many questions." She put up her pinkie.

I hooked it and tugged her closer, letting our lips brush before running my tongue over the gap between her lips and demanding entrance.

She sighed and I deepened the kiss, wanting to spend the next seven months imprinting the memory of me on every part of her to tide her over while we were apart.

The front door opened. Heavy footfalls rattled the house.

I shot back and flew off the bed. "It's Berk." Picking up my clothes, I searched for my shoes. I jumped into my boxers.

"He might not even know you're in here."

"Hey, LJ, you here? I saw your car outside."

Shit! He'd be up here any second. "My shirt." I waved my fingers at her.

With one moment of hesitation, she put an opposite hand on either side of the shirt and whipped it up over her head before flinging it to me.

I tugged it on and grabbed my shoes.

The stairs creaked.

Diving onto the bed, I planted a kiss on her before rushing out of her room. Dropping my shoes beside my door, I got my jeans on and slid into my desk chair, shooting it five feet from the desk and banging into my bed.

Digging my heels in, I scurried to my desk and propped my head up on my hand and slipped open a notebook. My heart raced for a whole different reason right now and I swallowed, trying to look natural. Just a regular evening, here at home. Studying.

Berk popped his head in. "There you are. Why didn't you say anything when I came in?"

"I was studying. I probably zoned out or something. What's up?"

"Your notebook is upside down."

I glanced down at the lined paper in front of me and my stomach dropped. Scrambling, I turned it until it faced right side up.

"Sometimes when I'm quizzing myself in my head, I'll do that, so I can't read the answers."

"Okay, that's weird, but whatever. Can I talk to you about something? It's about Alexis." He dragged his fingers through his hair.

The relief was sharp and sweet. Berk didn't even seem phased by my excuse, too preoccupied with whatever was going on inside his head. Unfortunately, that thing was Alexis. His sister.

I groaned and slumped back in my seat. "Dude, after she tried to steal my wallet I know the answer will be the opposite of whatever she wants you to do. I'm not going back on the ban. She can be here, if you're here, but no leaving her here on her own."

"Come on, she's not that bad." He dropped his arms to his side.

She was the absolute worst. A former foster sister, he was overprotective of her even though she seemed to get into nothing but trouble. But I'd cut him some slack.

After the way my evening had gone, I didn't feel the need to go over every terrible thing she'd done in the three-and-a-half years I'd known him. I wanted to hold onto the fuzzy feelings nestled in my chest as long as possible.

"What's the issue?"

Berk rubbed his hand over the back of his neck. "Are you worried about the draft? About making it?"

Every day. "Sometimes, but all we can do is give it our all this season."

His fingers drummed along the side of his leg. "It's hard to think that in seven months we're either done with football forever and trying to find a regular job, or we're playing in stadiums with more cash than we know what to do with."

My gut clenched at the first possibility. "It's not going to happen. We're kicking ass this season. Other than the first game against STFU we've kept it together. Reece was a first round draft pick. He's set with his signing bonus."

"Yeah." The least convincing sentence ever. Why was he worrying about this now? He'd always seemed the most laid back of any of us when it came to his future. Secure in his place.

"How are things with your agent?"

"They're fine. He's a little slimy, but I figure most are." A sad flash flickered through his eyes. "It's a lot of pressure once this season finishes. A lot of opportunities for people to come looking for things from us. For people to start treating us differently."

"What exactly are you worried about?"

"Honestly? That after the draft I'll never know anyone who wants to know me for anything other than what I can give them."

"That's a cynical as shit way to look at things." A realization hit me that I'd never thought of for him, an only child who'd been in the system. "And another reason you're always swooping in to save Alexis. She's the closest thing you have to family." And he had the hots for Jules, but liked to pretend he didn't.

"Alexis is my sister. There's no other way about it. And it's not only about her."

"All we can do is try to surround ourselves with people who care about us."

"You're right." He squeezed the back of his neck. "Sorry to go all softie on you."

"It's what friends are for, right?"

He nodded. "True. It's great you've got Marisa, who'll always have your back. Friends like that don't come around too often. You guys are lucky."

"Damn lucky."

CHAPTER 17
MARISA

LJ's hands palmed my ass. The windows were fogged up, and I ground myself against his straining erection, teasing us both.

My lips were swollen and throbbed, but it wouldn't make me stop. "We're going to be late."

He didn't break lip contact. "I know, but it's okay. I'll tell them there was traffic." His fingers sunk into my hair. Even with the driver's seat pushed back as far as it could go, I was wedged between his chest and the steering wheel, which dug into my back. I couldn't stop smiling.

His fingers slid under my shirt, teasing and tickling.

A dead end, five blocks from his childhood home wouldn't have been my first choice for a make out spot, but holy crap had the last two weeks been infuriating. I'd had meetings with Venice late into the night, going over a lot of the plans for my fellowship and finding out what I'd need to enroll in the master's program.

I rocked on his lap, about to lose my mind with wanting him inside me again. The dreams had almost been cruel with the way the fourteen days had gone. There had never been long enough to give us the level of satisfaction we'd been craving.

LJ had practices and weight training sessions every day. He'd strained a hamstring after a strenuous work out and had been on the couch alternating ice packs and Ace bandages for a couple days. It came with the football territory. What he'd put his body through season after season was brutal, but he'd been lucky. He'd had no surgeries or serious injuries so far, unlike some guys who'd had their ACLs, shoulders, or worse operated on.

Not playing as much this season had gotten to him some, but it also saved him for the games coming up. Which would mean more travel. I tried not to let it get to me. It was what it was, but I wanted more alone time with him.

My bed was so freaking loud there was no way to fool around while anyone else was home. LJ's room was at the first door at the top of the steps and his bed wasn't much quieter. And we'd almost always had our doors open, so we could shout to one another about something. Suddenly switching to two closed doors wasn't the best way to keep what we were doing quiet.

Even the freaking floors were noisy. We'd learned that the hard way when Berk came upstairs asking if we were moving furniture.

There had also been two games since then with more travel time, which meant he'd been gone from Thursday to Tuesday both weeks. At least I hadn't had to worry about dinner with Ron, but talking to LJ and going through a play-by-play of what we were going to do to one another when we finally had a minute alone was driving me crazy.

Midterms had been rough. The chemistry classes would come in handy for the museum curation work, but man, did they suck.

Between his schedule and mine, other than right now, it

felt like it would be three months before we had a chance to have sex.

It was making me mildly cranky.

His phone buzzed in the cup holder.

We broke apart and I picked up his phone. Chest heaving, I pushed my hair back and checked the message.

My lips twitched, embarrassment radiating though me. "It's from your mom, she wants to know how much longer until we get there." Perfect timing. At least she wasn't knocking on the window asking what was taking us so long.

LJ banged his head against the headrest. "I told you we should've left a half hour earlier."

The responsible guy. My responsible guy. "I'm not the one who decided since we didn't have any toilet paper at the house, we should stop and buy some instead of just using napkins."

"You were shouting at me from the bathroom. What the hell was I supposed to do?"

"Oh yeah." I dismounted him and fell into my seat. "Roll down the windows, it looks like we were recreating that scene from Titanic in here."

He turned on the car and rolled them down.

A shiver shot through me and I flipped down the visor to check myself in the mirror. "What the hell did you do to my hair?"

I rummaged through my purse for a brush and hair tie.

"You weren't complaining when I was massaging your scalp."

"Well, I'm complaining now. I'll have to braid it. It looks like I was stuck in a category 5 hurricane."

"Let me do it. Turn sideways."

With a hint of side eye, I did as he asked and faced the passenger side door.

His fingers worked into my hair from the front of my head down to the nape of my neck, separating the stands. Working with quick hands, he braided one side while I braided the other.

I checked it in the mirror and tied off the ends with a hair tie. "You've gotten a lot better at this since the first time I saw Quinn after your handiwork."

"How many other fifteen-year-old guys would even attempt to braid an eleven-year-old's hair?"

Resting my head against the head rest, I looked to the one guy who'd been a fixture in my life since one of the worst years I'd ever lived through. He'd shown up in my life at the exact moment I'd needed him—when my dad left. "None."

The engine turned over and he pulled out of the dead end. "What did you say?" He glanced over.

"Nothing. Thanks for helping with my hair."

"Showing up at my parents' place with second base hair probably would've raised a few questions." The kind any concerned and loving parent would ask. The kind mine never had. Going to LJ's house was a knife that cut both ways. It was a window into a family I loved with my whole heart, and one I'd always felt I'd be on the outside of.

He pulled in behind Jill's burgundy sedan in the driveway. The two-story Cape Cod had white framed windows and gray siding. They'd had to repaint the garage after LJ and I had thought we were master sneaks after finding a can of red spray paint. Too bad we'd executed our plan by writing our names.

LJ looked up at the wreath hanging on the front door and the light above it flicked on. All the lights were on, and Halloween decorations were covering the lawn. Spider webs stretched along the bushes in front of the walkway to the front door.

He took my hand, squeezing it before hopping out.

He made it halfway in front of the car before I flung my door open and stuck out my tongue.

His hands flew into the air in defeat. "You're such a pain in the ass."

"Some things will never change."

Our fingers brushed as we walked side-by-side, sending tingles rushing through my body. The edges of my mouth twitched.

His pinkie finger hooked mine one paving stone from the front steps.

"Stop it."

"What?" His look of mock surprise and outrage turned my twitchy, twinkle of a smile into full-blown laughter.

I shoved him away and rushed for the door.

Jill pushed it open and shook her head with her gaze shooting upward. "You two. I swear, sometimes I'm tempted to check your birth certificates to double check that you're twenty-two and not ten."

"Happy birthday, Mom." He held out the blue and yellow gift wrapped box with curly ribbons stuck to the front and kissed her on the cheek.

She swatted his shoulder and he walked inside.

"Happy birthday, Jill."

Her arms wrapped around me and she squeezed me tight. "I'm so proud of you, sweetheart."

Her motherly kind of approval hit me like a thud in the center of my chest.

I squeezed her even tighter and inhaled her classic, floral perfume.

She led me inside. "LJ told us about Venice."

Two years would be time away from them. No more birthday dinners. They might not even be living in this house anymore if LJ got his way. He wanted to upgrade them to a brand-new house. Maybe a brand-new state. Possibly a brand-new life.

The living room and dining room were on either side of the small entrance hall big enough for a coat closet and a shoe rack. The kitchen was straight ahead behind the squeaky swinging door, and from the smells wafting out, Charlie had the birthday dinner special almost ready to come out of the oven.

Birthdays in the Lewis Household were the warm, family affairs that I'd always hoped I'd have for myself someday.

A cork popped. Jill yelped and grabbed onto my arm. "Charlie, I swear you're trying to give me a heart attack."

"I told you I was going to open the champagne as soon as they got here." He stood with a bottle wrapped in a towel, dripping the bubbly onto the hardwood floor.

Her hands flew into the air. "I thought you meant once we sat at the table or after LJ and Marisa had at least taken their coats off."

"Quinn's still in the shower, so we don't have to worry about her badgering us for a sip if we finish this off quickly."

LJ shrugged his coat off and dumped it over the back of the couch. He went into the dining room and picked up two of the flutes, holding them out so Charlie could fill them. And fill them he did, waiting for the bubbles to settle before filling them almost to the top.

"Jill." Charlie held out a glass to her and held out his empty hand to me. "I'll trade you. One coat for a glass."

"Unlike some people." A pointed stare in LJ's direction, I laughed. "I know where the coat closet is." I unbuttoned my coat and opened the closet behind me, putting it on a hanger and taking the glass from him.

"At least one of you does." Jill sipped from her glass.

Charlie stepped beside Jill and wrapped his arm around her. "A toast, to the most wonderful wife a guy could have. The kind who will tell me how stupid I look in a new pair of pants, but it doesn't stop her from squeezing my butt when I'm cooking her birthday meal."

LJ and I groaned.

The two of them looked at us in mock shock. "To Jill on her 49th birthday." He lifted his glass higher in the air.

"To Mom."

"To Jill."

We all clinked glasses and sipped our bubbly. Sometimes I felt like I was waiting for the studio audience applause when I experienced moments like this in their house. Even though I'd been invited and had witnessed them so many times over the years, I felt like an outsider looking in and trying to figure out how exactly this all worked. How could two people still be in love after all those years together?

Walking to the living room, I grabbed LJ's coat and hung it up beside mine. It was always easier to keep things tidy at LJ's. Everything had a place here, and I'd never wanted to be a burden. I was always ready to help out whenever I could.

"Way to show me up, Marisa." LJ called out from the dining room where he set out the plates and forks.

I finished my glass and set it down on the dining room table.

A thundering set of footsteps pounded on the stairs. "Marisa!" Quinn turned the corner and flung her arms around my neck, nearly knocking me over. She was almost as tall as LJ, which meant she had a solid inch-and-a-half on me even though she was four years younger.

"Quinn the Fin!"

It was a nickname she'd earned by spending most summers in the town pool. I'd take her when Jill and Charlie were at the hospital and LJ had football practice. I swear, one summer my nose hairs had been burned off from all the chlorine.

"Did I miss the toast?" Her shoulders sagged when she spotted the empty champagne glasses. "You guys took forever to get here, I was worried you were pulled off somewhere painting each other's nails or something."

A fork clattered onto a plate in the dining room. I cringed.

He was going to get us caught. Just what I needed, an awkward not-my-family dinner where we were grilled about what was going on between us.

She let go of me and grinned, her blue eyes twinkling with mischief.

LJ called out from the dining room. "Doesn't your big brother get a hug, Quinn the Fin?"

Peering around me, she narrowed her gaze. "I told you not to call me that."

A sound of mock betrayal cut through the room.

I covered my laugh with a cough.

"What the hell, I'm your brother."

"Only by birth." She folded her arms across her chest and rolled her eyes.

"I see you're ready for college, huh?" I hooked my arm through hers. "Come on, cut him some slack. He was so excited to come and see you."

"Could've fooled me. He hasn't been home in months." Under all the surly teenage sass was a hint of sadness. As much crap as she gave him, she loved him. They all did. They loved each other, which was why LJ worked so hard to make sure they didn't have to worry about money.

I got it. I absolutely got it.

"I've barely seen him, and I live with him. The season's been crazy. You know how it goes."

With a sullen nod, she dropped my arm and walked over to LJ and hugged him tight. "I missed you, doofus."

He smiled at me over her shoulder before initiating a bear hug. "I missed you too."

Squirming, she shoved him away. "You're the absolute worst."

"I tell him that all the time."

Leaving them behind, I went into the kitchen. The swinging door creaked.

Jill and Charlie jumped apart both facing the stove. It

looked like someone was getting the birthday smooches in early.

I didn't try to hide my smile. Apparently, LJ and I weren't the only ones to have our make out session interrupted. It was awesome that after twenty-five years of marriage they were still so into one another. It proved that not all relationships ended in a raging inferno. Most, but not all.

"Can I help?"

"No!" They shouted in stereo so loudly, my feet came three feet off the floor. I should've anticipated this reaction, even from LJ's parents.

Charlie untied the apron from around his waist. "How about…" He scrubbed his hand over his chin. "What about the…"

Jill added the lobster into the pot of mac and cheese. "She could scoop the cookie dough."

He leaned in and whispered into her ear.

A shudder ripped through her. "I'd blocked that from my memory. What about the…drinks? She could get out the wine."

My number one specialty. I'd never be like LJ's parents, hanging out in the kitchen making meals with someone. As much as I tried, it usually ended with an inedible monstrosity.

"Of course!" With a kiss planted on her cheek, he turned to me. "You know where the corkscrew is. The birthday girl will have white. I'll have red. Find out what LJ would like and serve up whichever you'd prefer for you. Also keep an eye on Quinn—she will swipe your glass."

In this house, people cared that you'd tried to take a sip of wine. She was a lucky kid to be surrounded by so much love. I grabbed the corkscrew and opened the two bottles.

They went back to their flirty low whispers.

I stepped out, feeling like I was intruding on their quiet, celebratory moment.

LJ wandered into the dining room and walked up behind me. We faced the doorway.

His breath tickled the hairs on the back of my neck. "We need to finish what we started in the car."

A shiver raced through my body. I dropped my chin to my shoulder. "Not for the next couple hours."

His finger traced down the curve of my elbow.

I jolted and splashed some white wine onto the table. "Shit."

Reaching for the stack of napkins at the center of the table, I yelped when LJ slid his hand into my back pocket and squeezed my ass.

"What are you doing?" I whisper shouted, gaze darting to the dining room archway. My heart triple beat. If anyone walked in here, there would be questions—lots of questions.

"Thinking about you." He said it so easy breezy, with a wolfish grin.

I stifled my smile, shoved him away, and wiped up the spill. "I swear, I'm sitting on the other side of the table."

He stepped back with a troublemaker tilt to his lips.

A rushing flush crept up the back of my neck, heating it inch by inch as I imagined his lips everywhere his eyes roamed.

Charlie came in with the giant platter of brisket.

Jill carried the mac & cheese, and Quinn had the greens and rolls.

I finished filling the glasses, including Quinn's with lemonade, which she went into a full pout over. Scooting my chair in, I took a sip from my glass, trying to calm my tension after almost getting caught.

And then the double cross. Quinn popped up from her seat. "I'll sit next to Mom, you sit next to LJ since you two will be bickering the whole time and I'll be caught in the crosshairs. LJ, switch with me."

My glare intensified at his triumphant smile.

"I guess I'll do it for you, Quinn. Don't forget this."

He slid into his chair and I promised a world of hurt if he tried anything while we were at the dinner table. Or maybe I'd have to make a preemptive strike.

Quinn launched into her college application breakdown. Five art schools spread out all over the country. There was an exchange of glances between LJ, Jill and Charlie while she showed me some of the new work she'd added to her portfolio. It wasn't just paintings; she had some breathtaking multimedia work. Her art aspirations were well placed and well deserved. The tuition for RISD was astronomical, and I knew it all hung on LJ's career prospects.

She'd make it, and so would he.

Other than a few failed footsie moments, dinner was uneventful. It was full of laughter, jokes, amazing food, and three of my favorite people in the world—scratch that. My favorite people.

We donned our construction paper crowns and sang Happy Birthday way too loudly and with tons of extra flair.

Jill blew out the candles on her cupcake and then we all dove in for the Lewis family traditional warm M&M chocolate chip cookies with vanilla ice cream. It was an absolute mess. The melting ice cream dripped down the side of my hand.

I licked it off and caught LJ's eye.

He looked back at me with an intensity so sharp I stopped breathing.

"Get the girl some napkins."

Jill's laughter-filled words snapped me out of the tingling tease tiptoeing down my spine.

We finished up our dessert and grabbed our coats. The three non-departing members of the Lewis family hugged me tight and LJ's dad hugged me last.

"Thank you for making it possible for me to be here today."

My throat closed up and the burn built in the back of my nose.

He rubbed my back and gave me an extra squeeze before letting go.

At the bottom of the concrete steps, I looked back at the house that held so many happy memories for me. So many times growing up, I'd wished and prayed I could have a family just like theirs someday.

LJ's hand brushed against mine, tugging me toward the car. He dropped it after a couple steps and walked around his car, opening my door for me.

Maybe keeping this all quiet was for the best. At least when it ended I might still be welcomed into this place that had become my second home—hell, my only true home.

CHAPTER 18
LJ

Marisa was quiet on the drive back, her arm propped up on the window. She handed me the money for the toll and stared out at the water as we passed over the bridge back into the city.

"What did my dad say to you?"

She jumped. "Nothing. Just thanking me for coming and dragging you along." Her eyes twinkled with subdued amusement.

I loved how easily she fit in with my family. How easily she'd always slotted in. Over the summer, when she wasn't here, her absence had been palpable. It had felt weird. But we'd have to get used to it. She'd be gone for two whole years. The thought lent a bittersweetness to her accomplishment.

I owed more to her than I could ever repay. It wasn't the only reason I loved her, but she'd been there for me as much as I'd been there for her. When my dad got sick junior year, I'd been all set to play in a summer league and had my scouting invites. Surgeries, chemo sessions, and trips to specialists had meant my mom and dad weren't home much, but Marisa gave up a scholarship to a summer Paris trip to help with Quinn.

She deserved her time in Venice more than anyone. What other sixteen-year-old would give up their summer dream to stay home and watch a twelve-year-old she wasn't even related to? Marisa. And she'd never stopped being there for me and my family.

"Anything else on your mind?"

"Just thinking of payback for the ass grab right before dinner." There was a wistful, plotting tone in her voice.

She'd flipped the coin toss and I was jogging to the line of scrimmage ready to continue the game we'd abandoned a couple hours ago.

Palming her ass right in my parents' living room after deciding we should keep things low key wasn't my best idea in the world, but watching her and knowing I could get close to her and touch her as more than a friend made it hard to resist.

Contending with the semi that had risen to attention had been the backfire on me.

"Wasn't licking the ice cream off your hand my payback?" Where I'd ended up with both elbows on the table and my napkin in my lap for maximum embarrassment protection.

"That was me not wanting to sacrifice a bit of the ice cream to a napkin. I'm greedy like that. And greedy for a repeat of last week." She rocked her head to the side with a blood-thumping, body-tightening look.

"As soon as I get you—" My head slammed back against the headrest. "Everyone's probably home and I have to be at the team bus by 6:15 tomorrow morning."

"And then you're gone until Monday. What about tonight?"

"Where—"

She glanced into my backseat. It was crammed for people

sitting, let alone what I'd want to do to her. "You and your stupid two-door car."

"My bed might as well be a fog horn. If we try anything with anyone home, they'll wonder if we're demolishing my walls."

"My bedroom is too close to the stairs, we'd have no time."

She rubbed her thumb against her bottom lip.

"Bathroom!" We shouted at the same time. Pins-and-needles anticipation ratcheted up with each block we got closer to the house.

Marisa ran her fingers along my thigh before squeezing it and making me jump. "Only if they're home. If not, we get naked like a quick-change artist covered in killer bees."

"How exactly does your brain work?"

"After all these years, you still don't know?"

I pulled up to the front of the house. Keyton and Berk's cars were parked right out front. The bathroom it was. The sink and counter were sturdy—or at least they'd get a killer test as soon as we made it upstairs. Hopefully, Keyton wasn't in his room, and maybe Berk was at Jules's house.

"Dammit."

When I opened the door, music pumped in from outside and a laugh or two cut through the low bass line. They were outside. The plans were still in play. We could make this work. My blood hummed in my veins.

"Is your bag packed?" Keyton called out from the doorway headed to the backyard. He had a foil covered tray in one hand and tongs in the other.

"Not yet."

"Berk and Jules are outside. Berk's starving even though we already had dinner earlier. I've got steaks, burgers and hot dogs to cook. You've got maybe twenty minutes before the food is ready, if you wanted to pack before you eat."

"Actually, I'm ful—" I cut my gaze to Marisa.

She creeped back toward the stairs.

"That's a great idea, man. I'll go get packed."

Her foot hit the bottom step. "And I am going to get changed."

That didn't sound suspicious at all…

Keyton clipped the tongs in our direction. "They'll be extra left over for you too, Marisa, so don't worry about food or anything while we're away."

"Thank you, Keyton! You're the best." Her hand slid up the banister and mouthed 'bathroom'.

He shook his head, chucking like it wasn't true, but right now he was my hero, keeping everyone outside. He ducked out the back door, disappearing down the stairs.

We both craned our necks to watch him walk out across the grass to the grill.

I casually walked up the stairs with Marisa trailing behind me before we got to the point our feet disappeared from view and rocketed up the last of the stairs.

Marisa ducked into the bathroom. "We've only got ten minutes, max, before someone comes back inside."

The door wasn't even fully closed before she grabbed onto my shoulder and pulled me close.

She reached around me and cranked on the shower. The spray drowning out the last of the music from the backyard and hopefully covering the noise we were about to make.

I jerked open the fly of my jeans and she shimmied out of hers.

My chest filled with the intoxicating hunger that reared its head whenever she stared at me like she wanted me just as much as I wanted her.

Grabbing my wallet from my back pocket and ripping it open, I fumbled it and almost dropped the condom.

Marisa's hands were all over my chest, under my shirt. In my hair.

I gritted my teeth and slid it on, the urgency and immediacy of getting inside her riding me almost as hard as I would her.

She jumped up on the counter beside the sink.

Testing and teasing her with my fingers, I found she was soaking. "Fucking hell, Marisa."

"I know, you should probably do something about it." She bit her bottom lip, one already pink and glistening.

Steadying myself with one hand, I sank into her. The warm, velvety walls clamped around me and she yelped.

I shuddered trying to hold back and my muscles tensed with how good she felt and the creeping suspicion someone would come racing up the stairs thinking Marisa was being attacked.

"This angle. Holy shit, L."

I rocked deeper into her, driving all the way home.

Her back pressed against the wall and the front of my thighs banged into the cabinet beneath it, but it was quiet. At least the counter was. Marisa not so much.

"Oh god. Do that again."

I laughed through my gritted my teeth.

Her legs locked around mine, restricting my movements. Grinding and thrusting, she moaned, and her hold on my shoulders bordered on painful.

There was a break in the music vibrating the floors and she screamed, body going rigid in my hold.

I raised my arm and covered her mouth with my hand. If anything, my hand gave her permission to get louder. The music kicked back on.

Pounding into her now, I chased my peak and she crested to another. The electric intensity wove deep into my body down to the cells of my DNA, making it impossible to hold back much longer.

The music from outside and the loud-as-hell steps meant I'd at least have some warning, but we were quickly approaching the time where there wouldn't be anything that could stop the explosion creeping to the base of my spine.

Exploding into her, I braced my hands on the edge of the counter on either side of her hips and rested my forehead against her shoulder.

"That was awesome." She laughed against the side of my neck.

"It was." I licked my lips and stepped back on unsteady legs.

Taking off the condom, I dropped it into the trash can and buttoned my jeans.

Marisa crouched down and fumbled around under the sink, coming back out with a pad. She unwrapped it and crunched it up and put it on top of the condom along with some toilet paper. "That's like throwing away plutonium. No one will look twice." She pulled on her pants and checked her hair in the mirror. "Check that out, the braids held. Maybe we'll have to make this the go-to style for a while." Her eyes glittered with amusement in the mirror.

A content settled in my chest like I'd been covered with a weighted blanket.

"But then I can't run my fingers through it." I tickled the escaped curls at the base of her neck.

She jerked away and spun around, facing me. "Maybe I'll sneak into your bed tonight." Her fingers trailed down the center of my chest.

A shout from downstairs broke through the re-heating licking at my skin. "Guys, some of the food is ready if you're hungry."

"We should get down there." She stared at the center of my chest.

"What's up?" I tipped her chin up.

"Nothing." Her smile was wide, but it didn't match her eyes. Distracting me with a quick kiss, she opened the door and looked both ways down the hall before stepping out.

"Hurry up and pack your bag, then come down after me."

I hooked her arm and barely held back my smile. "I'll go down first. I'm already packed."

I pecked her on her open lips and rushed downstairs.

"Devious," she whispered after me.

Bounding into the kitchen, I grabbed sodas for me and Marisa before heading outside.

"Hey, Berk. Hey, Jules."

Jules waved her cup in my direction and covered her mouth with her hand. "Hey, LJ. Where's Marisa?"

"What do you mean? Why do you assume I know where she is?" Had they heard her? Shit, our cover was blown.

Everyone looked at me with a head tilt to go along with it. Okay, maybe the denial was a little too hard.

"Because Keyton said you two came back together."

A stuttering laugh of relief broke through the questioning silence. "Oh yeah, I haven't seen her since I went up to my room."

Berk took the last bite out of his burger I swore had been whole a minute ago and didn't cover his mouth one bit. "So, a whole thirteen minutes apart. That must be a record for you two."

Berk nudged the tray of barbecued meats toward me.

A plate with buns sat beside it.

"I'm still stuffed from my mom's dinner, so no meat for me."

"Dude, if I'd known that, I wouldn't have piled so much onto the grill."

"Don't worry about it. Marisa will need food for the next four days, so it won't go to waste."

Jules set her cup down on the grass beside her. "She doesn't cook?"

"No!" We all shouted at once.

She jolted and her hot dog flipped off her plate and onto the ground.

Berk scooped it up and hook-shotted it into the trash by the back door and grabbed her another one. "We try to keep Marisa's time in the kitchen to a minimum for the safety of all living things in the vicinity."

Keyton closed the grill. "She's the worst cook in the world and I can only assume she has a cast iron stomach or is part synthetic life form."

I lifted my drink to my mouth. "It's not *that* bad."

"What's not that bad?" Marisa breezed into the circle of chairs.

I wanted to pull her onto my lap, hold her hand, and kiss her like Berk could with Jules.

Handing her the cup, I met the eyes of everyone else in the circle. "Nothing. Getting up early in the morning."

"All packed?" She sat in the plastic lawn chair beside me. So close our fingers brushed. I kept myself from hooking my pinkie around hers.

Keyton lifted his cup in my direction. "Berk said he'd drive us to the bus in the morning and pick up some breakfast along the way, unless you wanted to drive yourself."

Marisa froze with her soda halfway to her mouth.

The whole house to ourselves.

"I might hit the snooze a few times. I'll drive myself."

Her lips twitched and she flicked the rim of her cup. A sideways glance told me the morning plan was a go—now we just needed to get through the next eight hours until everyone else left.

———

FRESH, CRISP AIR. CRUNCHY, CRINKLY LEAVES. THE BEST FUCKING way to start off a travel day.

The spot on my chest where she'd nipped me before screaming my name pulsed. I rubbed my hand over the mark, happy to have a reminder of our morning.

After Keyton and Berk had shouted from the bottom of the stairs that they were leaving, we'd waited a total of three minutes before running into each other in the hallway and falling back into her bedroom.

Three team buses idled in the parking lot dotted with players' cars. I slung my bag under one of them and climbed the stairs. The FU Trojan with his sword pointed toward our next win was painted on the side.

Inside the muted interior of the bus, some guys had their hats pulled down over their eyes. Other had headphones on and phones out. The normal rowdiness was non-existent this early in the morning. A luxury charter bus wasn't the worst way to get around, but long hours on the road made even this thing unbearable. At least it was only a twenty-minute drive to the airport.

I grabbed a seat behind Keyton and Berk.

"Look who finally decided to join us." Keyton peered back at me, an eyebrow raised in suspicion.

"The snooze is addictive." I tried to play it off, but Shakespeare in the Summer wasn't exactly in my wheelhouse.

Berk spoke through the gap in the seats. "How are you feeling about your chances of getting on the field with this one?"

And just like that, my untouchably great mood soured.

The defensive line coach walked down the aisle, checking off names on his clipboard. Coach stood at the front of the bus. His gaze swept over each row and hit mine with extra heat. "I'd say, not good."

CHAPTER 19
MARISA

"How long are you holding out on me that you and LJ are sleeping together?"

I choked on my water. It burned my lungs and dribbled out of my mouth. I flailed and knocked my notebook off the dining room table in Ford's apartment where Liv and I were studying for tonight.

"You asswipe. I've been here for twenty minutes. You waited for me to take a drink to ask that question." I used my sleeves to clean my chin.

"You're right, and you took forever to open your bottle of water."

I picked up my notebook and whacked her with it. "And that's crazy. Why would you say that?

"Please, I'm the queen of don't-even-think-about-dating-that-guy relationships, remember?" Liv and Ford had been a big fucking deal to her older brother, Ford being his best friend and all. Although not anymore. Apparently, they hadn't spoken much at all since Ford and Liv decided they didn't care what he thought and they wanted to be together. If only it had been that easy for me and LJ.

"Plus, you've checked the time at least twenty times in the

twenty minutes you've been here. I was like that all the time when Ford was traveling to games."

Deflecting and evading these questions had become second nature, a holdover from all the times I hadn't wanted everyone to know I was pining after my best friend that had continued until LJ had said we should keep what we were doing just between us. "Still not convincing enough. He's my best friend. Of course, I'd want to know when he got in."

"I thought I was your best friend."

I glared. And LJ said I was a pain in the ass?

"Plus, you have a used condom stuck to the back of your jeans."

I shot up from my seat. "Sonabitch. I threw that away." Spinning in circles, I tried to find the gross latex.

Liv perched on the edge of the couch, lips twitching like she was a second from cracking.

Grabbing an overstuffed pillow off the couch, I lobbed it at her. "You're the worst." My screech could probably be heard in New Jersey.

"Oh, my bad. It was just some tape." She burst into laughter and pulled the piece of tape off the back of my jeans, waving it in front of me. "Not sleeping together, huh?"

I flung myself onto the plush ottoman beside me, staring up at the exposed-beam ceiling. Well, so much for maintaining my cover. I'd make a terrible cop. But now it wasn't so scary to let someone in. Liv had always suspected something was going on between us, even when I'd thought it wasn't possible.

I glanced around, checking over my shoulder like anyone else was inside other than the two of us. "We've been sleeping together for almost three weeks now. Technically, only a couple times because of his stupid football schedule, but we've definitely crossed over the line from friends to more than friends. There, are you happy?" It all came out in a rush. I felt a flood of relief that someone finally knew.

"Supremely," she beamed. "I swore one day you'd just trip and end up on his dick with all the flirting you two did all the time."

"We didn't flirt."

"Right?" She nodded, looking at me like I was a delusional doofus. "You two have been foreplaying for at least a decade."

"Gross. We were twelve."

"You didn't have the hots for him when you were a preteen?"

"No, that was squarely high school territory. The first summer after football camp where he took off his shirt and the bird chest was gone." Right before diving into the pool. I swear, I choked on my gum when he emerged from the water, glistening with rippling muscles.

"Do the guys know? Have you two been driving them from the house with your hours-long sex sessions?"

"Ew, what the hell?" And if there had been a doubt in my mind about whether we should shout about sleeping together from the rooftops here they'd been evaporated. "Is that what you and Ford were doing when you got together under the cover of night and, oh, posted to the internet."

"Only for a few hours." She flinched and glared.

Whoops, probably crossed a line there bringing up the voyeur sex clip of Ford and Liv celebrating her 21st birthday in May.

"No, we haven't told anyone. And you can't tell anyone either." I jabbed a finger in her direction.

Liv was an excellent secret keeper. It was part of the reason things had gone south with her brother. It turns out brothers tended to not like you hiding that you're dating their best friend behind their back. So if anyone was a vault and knew how important it was to keep this quiet, it was Liv.

"Your secret is safe with me. Does this mean you two are

dating?" She made a swoony face I was seconds away from clobbering with another pillow.

"Things are fluid. There aren't any real plans beyond just enjoying the time we have together. He'll be headed to the draft in April and I'm going to Venice for two years." I shrugged. "There's no point in making long term plans right now."

"Come on!" She slammed her hands down on the pillow on her lap. "You two have been dancing around this for so long and now that you're finally banging you're like 'oh, we're just keeping it casual.'"

"What else am I supposed to do? I can't give up Italy and he's not going to give up football. Our lives will be crazy, why throw relationship expectations on top of that?" I'd run through it all hundreds of times in my head. Asking either of us to give up our dreams would lead to anger and resentment. It was better to hold onto what we had and let it go when the time came rather than clinging to it and destroying each other.

"Because you two care about each other."

"We've been friends for a long time, but I've been burned before when it comes to expecting too much from the people in my life. You can't be disappointed if you don't have expectations." We'd avoided any serious talks, and I planned on keeping it that way. Then at least I could pretend I wasn't falling in love with him and didn't know how I'd make it being apart from him for two years.

"So the plan is you go to Italy, he goes pro and then what? You never see each other again?"

I shrugged, not wanting to answer the questions that had been rolling through my head since I landed in August.

"Be serious. Do you honestly think he's going to get drafted and then never speak to you again?"

"It's a crazy life. He'll be traveling all the time. Tons of attention. And I won't be there. How can I expect him not to get caught up in the pro football world?"

"I know Ford plays hockey and not football, but we've made it through the ups and downs of him traveling just fine."

"That's different."

"How are we different? We've known each other since I was a kid. I was crazy about him from afar for forever. We had a kiss and then he broke my heart. Short of a mallet to the head, he was the most stubborn guy ever when it came to us hooking up."

"But you've been inseparable since you moved in together. Plus, Ford's older and a total quiet-type cutie. LJ soaks up all the attention. He loves it, but pretends he doesn't. Once he's playing more in the pros, they'll be kids running around in his jerseys. And as much as I've needled him about it, he's smoking hot. There will be women swarming him."

"It happens. But you trust him."

Those daily lectures from my mom and how wonderful her college romance with Ron had been echoed in my ears. After he'd been drafted it had been more time on the road for him, and more fan attention, until he was injured and switched to scouting and eventually coaching.

Long road trips. Long stretches away from home. And a long line of broken promises in his wake.

"Things will change. Once he's playing more this season the spotlight will be brighter."

"Why isn't he playing much right now?"

"He hurt his hamstring and he said he'd been slacking." A poke in the back of my brain told me it was a lie—one I hadn't dug deeper into. Football had been a verboten topic since I came to FU. When we talked football, the conversation might veer into Ron territory. Not to say I didn't watch LJ's games or want him to kill it out there, but I wasn't showing up to practices or bugging him in the gym like I used to growing up.

"He needs to get his act together."

"He does." We finished up our work. Liv's entire outlook was less doom and gloom than it had been last semester, but not talking to her brother still hung over her the whole time I was there. It must've been nice to have a big brother to look out for her growing up, but that didn't mean it was sunshine and rainbows all the time.

I knew that more than anyone. Sometimes when I'd bring up my mom or Ron, she'd look at me and I could tell she wanted to tell me to be thankful I had any parents at all—hers had died when she was younger. But mine had showed me time and time again that being alive didn't mean they were parents.

"When's Ford back in town?"

"A week." She collapsed back into the couch. "These long stretches suck. He's on the road for twelve days this time."

"It must be hard."

"At least it keeps me focused on graduating. Changing my major as a second-semester junior hasn't given me tons of time to cram everything in before we graduate."

Things like as much time as I could manage with LJ. The internal battle waged between wanting to spend every waking moment with him and not wanting to get too used to it. The clock ticked down to May. Italy had felt like a solid escape plan, leaving on my own terms, doing a job I'd dreamed of finding, and starting my career.

But there was a piece of me that wanted to be the ultimate football girlfriend. It wanted to let him handle everything and stop fighting so damn hard to put distance between us and asserting my independence. To just give in. And it made me hate myself for even entertaining the idea. It felt like the code was written into my DNA by my mom; one slip and I'd transform into her, bitter and angry when it all fell apart.

Nonetheless, I left Liv's the second the alert came in notifying me their flight had landed. It was still quiet when I got back to The Brothel. It was better to be with him than to be apart thinking about all the things being with him meant.

I wasn't sitting at my desk waiting for the precise moment the door opened. Nope, definitely hadn't re-read the same five sentences running through the timeline for disembarking, baggage claim, loading onto the bus, and driving time to the house.

Berk flew up the stairs first and dumped his things in the bedroom across from LJ's. He peeked his head into my room. "Hey, Marisa. Glad to see the house is still in one piece. I'm heading over to see Jules. See you, bye." He was gone before I could get a word out.

Keyton came up next, ducking in. "Hey, Marisa. Everything good?"

"There aren't any scorch marks on the ceiling. It's all good here."

A stifled smile ghosted across his lips. "Glad to hear it."

His eyes darted toward the stairs. "LJ will be up in a bit. He's still a little keyed up after the trip." From the dip in his voice, it didn't sound like he meant obnoxiously singing FU game cheers and doing cartwheels in the living room.

With a rap on my door jam, he opened his mouth and closed it before walking into his bedroom across from mine.

The last set of footsteps were quieter, more weary and worn. I hadn't gotten to watch the game today, only reading the highlights. Had he screwed up a play they didn't mention?

I waited for him to pop his head in my door. I kept waiting.

He didn't stop off at my room. On the other side of the wall separating our rooms, there were muted sounds of unpacking, but not a word or move toward the hallway.

Leashing the nagging worries swirling in my head, I went

to him, leaning against the doorway. If I had the talent, I'd break out a slab of marble and sculpt him. Instead, I'd resigned myself to appreciating art in all its forms. Even the grumpy football player doing an impersonation of a bear unpacking.

His folded clothes sat in piles on his bed. It always felt good to know there was one thing in the domestic arts he sucked at where I could help.

He jerked clothes out of his duffle and shoved them into his empty hamper like he had a personal vendetta against them.

"Don't you know you're only supposed to be this angry when you lose?" I picked up a sock that had landed by my feet in the furious unpacking.

Crouched, he shook his head. "I need a couple minutes."

Instead, I checked the hallway. Keyton's door was closed. Wasn't I the one talking about putting distance between us less than an hour ago? I closed his door and sat on the floor beside his desk.

"Want to talk about it?"

"No."

"Want me to pry it out of you?"

"No."

"Want me to tickle it out of you?"

His steely gaze was my only response. He picked up the bag and shoved it into his closet.

I stood, grabbed his coat from the back of his door and held it out to him. "Let's go."

Turning, he crossed his arms and planted himself like a tree.

"Oh come on. How long have we known each other? Do you think you can wait me out?"

———

"You're always so grumpy when you're hangry." I licked marshmallow off my finger.

"I wasn't hangry."

"Says the man on his fifth s'more."

The freezing November air numbed my nose, which was probably running by now. There weren't many people here on a Monday night, but I'd chosen to sit outside instead. Fire & Ice wasn't far from campus, but far enough for LJ to work out whatever was going on with him on our quiet walk over.

On the table between us, we had a platter complete with chocolate bars, graham crackers, marshmallows, skewers and a small fire at the center.

Our knees bumped into one another's under the table, not in a playing footsie kind of way, but in a 'we're sitting at a children's table' kind of way. I couldn't say I hated it with the heat from the fire providing warmth the metal chairs weren't.

I stuck a peanut butter cup on my graham cracker and pulled my marshmallow from the fire, sandwiching it between another graham. Holding out the treat across the table, I tilted my head, trying to catch LJ's eye. "Come on, L. You know it's your favorite."

Tension had eased out of him on the walk, but there was still an uneasiness to him. He had a cagey, ruffled air. He reached for the s'more and I pulled it away a little getting him to come closer.

He came with it and grabbed for the chocolate and peanut butter treat, coming out of his seat.

When he did, I popped up and kissed him. Nothing more than a peck really. It caught me off guard how easily I'd done it and how much it made sense now. Before I'd have laid into him or cracked a joke, but the kiss felt natural.

And I wanted more.

His lips were firm, but soft against mine. Warm, tasty and I wanted to feel them on mine even longer. But not here. Not now.

I checked over my shoulder. The place and street were deserted like before, but LJ's eyes went wide before he laughed. The last bits of tension were wrung from his body.

"What was that?" He peered around like I had and snagged the s'more from my hand.

"It was a way to get your head out of your ass."

"Looks like I'll have to find more reasons to shove it up there." His gaze heated as he bit into the graham crackers, making a mess of his hands in the process. "Damn, this is good."

"Only one more. We don't want you puking in the backyard like you did in sixth grade."

"It was worth it."

"Now will you tell me what's up?"

"I didn't play much during the game and my agent is freaking out, which is causing me to freak out."

"Why isn't Ron playing you?" After talking to Liv, the nudge in the back of my head was more of a shove. I'd told him to tell me if there was a problem. I'd made him promise me that going to dinners wouldn't be an issue and I'd told him that he didn't have to come at all, but he insisted. I needed to believe that he'd tell me the truth—eventually.

"Do you ever think it's weird you call your dad, Ron?"

"No changing the subject. Why isn't he playing you?"

He smooshed his s'more together. "I don't know."

"Maybe you should've brought it up at Monday dinner. Who else on the team gets a solid hour of undivided attention with Coach Saunders?" I hadn't been back since the Nora dinner and I didn't regret it one bit. I'd need to go back eventually, just so I wasn't screwed with next semester's tuition, but I was biding my time and dragging my feet in subjecting myself to another round of fatherly dinner theater.

"His attention is pretty divided. And usually focused on you."

"Let's not ruin this dessert by talking about him." It was

bad enough I had to see him on the sidelines of all of LJ's games, I didn't need him ruining my dessert.

"You brought him up." His verbal ducking and dodging wasn't nearly as fast as he was on the field.

"And now I'm un-bringing him up." I made video rewind noises with my mouth. "You had a great play. Those blocks were brutal. How about the three quarters leading up to that?"

He licked some of the chocolate off his fingers.

"They were cutting it close. It was down to the wire."

He made a noise of disapproval. "There are only three games left before playoffs." That was more to himself than me.

"Then you'll have to get out there during practices and make sure the defensive coach doesn't have a reason to hold you back. Maybe he's trying to give the underclassmen a chance with so many seniors leaving. You remember how bad it was freshman year for you guys."

"Yeah, you're probably right." He looked away and stuck another marshmallow on the fire. "I'm glad you made me come out tonight, Risa."

Did I say it was freezing out here? The way he looked at me reached deep inside my chest and started a mini bonfire right on my heart.

CHAPTER 20
LJ

"Bye Weeks are the best weeks of the season." Keyton lit a folded piece of newspaper on fire and stuck it into the coals on the grill in our back yard. During the spring and summer, back yards were packed with other students on the weekends soaking up the sun.

The November snap had hit, so we were all winter grillers in this house.

"Three more games left until the playoffs." Only three more chances if our streak died and we didn't make it to play-offs this year. My stomach knotted in a fist-tight clench.

"You're going to ride out this season without playing? Just give up like it's no big deal."

"I know it's a big deal. And appreciate you bringing it up when I'm trying to relax for five seconds." It came out more biting than I meant it to.

But he shrugged it off and rolled right over the way I snapped at him. "Marisa hasn't talked to her dad about it?"

"I haven't told her."

Keyton stopped mid-step. "Why the hell not?"

"There are more important things."

"Ah, okay, so you don't actually care about getting drafted

and those fat paychecks mean nothing to you. I didn't realize we had another Nix situation on our hands."

"Nix's dad played pro for almost a decade. He's never had to worry about money a day in his life. That's not my life. Do you think I've got a fat inheritance tucked away somewhere and I'm working my ass off for fun?"

"Then why aren't you doing everything you can to give yourself a shot? You need to have Marisa talk to him."

"I can figure it out on my own." I pushed past him and took the lead up the steps back into the house.

"Yes, because you've been doing such a bang up job of that already." He grumbled, walking up the stairs in my wake.

"We can store the booze out on the deck to keep it cold."

"We've got a game in two days. This is not the time to get blitzed."

I turned at the top of the steps and spread my arms wide. "Not like I'll be in for more than a play. What does it matter?"

"If you don't ask Marisa to talk to her dad, you're never going to get enough time on the field."

"I'm not going to put that on her. She's been at my side through some rough times. I can sit through some weekly dinners, so she can pay for college."

"At the expense of your future?"

"What's at the expense of your future?" Marisa walked out of the kitchen with a pitcher of brightly-colored booze.

Keyton shook his head looking around the room.

My muscles tensed. My gaze sharpened. My stomach clenched.

A muscle in his jaw ticked. *Don't do it.*

"Is no one else going to say it? Really? Fine. LJ's been side-lined by your dad for ninety percent of our games... because of you." Keyton threw out the words like he'd finally reached the end of his rope—a rope no one had asked him to carry.

"I told you to shut the hell up." I lunged at Keyton. Berk

grabbed me, his arm coming up around my neck as I went for Keyton's.

"Because of me." Marisa's voice broke through my over-whelming urge to shut Keyton up.

I stopped struggling against Berk and spun around.

The look in her eyes told me the damage had been done. "It's not because of you. It's because he's being an unreason-able asshole."

"Because of me." She stared at him with hurt brimming in her eyes. "Because I'm making you come to his dinners."

I stepped forward reaching for her arm. A pit twisted and turned in my stomach. All my lies were coming back to haunt me. "It's not a big deal."

"It's a big deal if it's keeping you from playing." She jerked back, crossing her arms over her chest, pissed. It radi-ated off her in waves.

"And you've done way more than that for me." I let my arm drop, but moved closer.

"This is your future we're talking about. This is all you've ever talked about. What you've wanted since we were ten years old." Flinging her arms out to her side, she shook her head like none of this made sense. I'd learned that a hell of a long time ago.

"And it'll happen." I had to believe it would happen. That I made the most of my time on the field to make it possible.

"Not if you're not playing most of the games. You said it was because you'd slacked off in the pre-season, but he's stopping you from starting this season because I've dragged you to his house every week."

"So what? The time I'm on the field, I make it count. It's my turn to be there for you. After everything you've done for me and for my family, of course I'd do that for you."

"How many times have I told you, you don't owe me anything? There's nothing left for you to repay. There's no ledger with your debts tallied up."

"I don't give a shit. My dad wouldn't be alive if it weren't for you. I'll freaking follow you wherever you want me to go."

"I'm not... I don't want you following me around doing whatever I want because you feel indebted to me. We're supposed to be friends—I don't want you feeling like I'm lording something over you that I'd have done no matter what to help Charlie."

She shoved the pitcher at Berk, the contents sloshing over the side and spilling down his chest.

Her footsteps shook the house as she charged upstairs and slammed her door.

"What the fuck?" I stared at the empty steps. "What did I say wrong?"

Berk wiped at his chest and dropped a hand onto my shoulder. "Maybe she's afraid that's the only reason you're still hanging around. Or like she's an insurance policy in case your dad gets sick again."

Jules piped up from the living room where she was sitting with Alexis. Just great. Even more people in the house to witness this. "Girls don't like feeling like you're not with them for them."

I launched into some backpedaling and diversions about never being more than friends with Marisa. The last thing we needed in the middle of this was even more people with opinions about our relationship—or whether it even was a relationship.

I stared up at the ceiling, feeling more like she'd poured the pitcher over my head. Cold fingers of dread and distress trickled down my spine. I'd never wanted her to feel like anything I felt for her had to do with her saving my dad's life.

Taking the stairs two at a time, I stood outside her bedroom door and knocked. She'd go to see her dad. One hundred percent her next course of action would be ripping her dad a new asshole, but that wouldn't be the best thing for either of us.

After the double hit of her discovering my lies and finding out her feelings about the bone marrow transplant, I needed to make sure *we* were okay.

Hostile silence reverberated from the other side of the wood separating us. "Can we talk?"

Nothing.

"It's not like I don't know you're in there." I barged in.

"Get out." She jerked her hair into a sloppy ponytail.

"We need to talk."

"Now you want to talk? I've asked you why you weren't playing much this season and you lied to my face multiple times."

The blame settled squarely on my shoulders. "What was I supposed to say?"

"How about 'Marisa, your dad is a colossal dick and he's benching me because we're friends and I've been going to Monday dinners, even after I promised I'd stop if it affected my spot on the team.'"

"And then you'd never give him a chance."

"What's your obsession with me giving him an ounce of my time? You offered to come to dinner, so I didn't have to go alone, so I'd actually show up and didn't have to talk. I don't want to know him. And now you've made it to the point where there are only two more games left in the regular season. Have you lost your mind?"

"If you didn't go to dinner, he wouldn't sign off on your tuition and maybe you'd have to transfer again or not finish school." It had been a floundering Hail Mary pass to keep her in school, to make sure I didn't have to suffer through another year like I had freshman year. I'd just wanted three more years to spend together before we were officially adults.

"This is your life. Stop treating me like I'm holding this thing I did over your head forever."

"I was trying to protect you."

"I don't need your protection, and I never asked for it."

"Like you didn't need it with Chris."

It was a low blow. But it needed to be said. Sometimes she did need help and protection and I wanted to be the one she turned to.

She staggered back. "That was an asshole move." The words shot out of her mouth like a confetti cannon of contempt.

"This is real life. Not what's happening out on the field." I raked my hands through my head. "Let me try to figure this out."

She threw her hands into the air. "You've been doing an excellent job so far. Two games. There are two games left before playoffs. You're lucky you guys have had a great season and hopefully there will be a few more chances."

"I can—"

"And if you can't, like you haven't been able to do for the past two seasons? What then? What about your dad's medical bills? Your parents' house? Quinn's college? All these big plans. You're willing to put them on the line to give some asshole who might as well have been a sperm donor a chance?"

She charged toward the door, but I got in her way.

"We're not finished."

"We sure as hell are." She shoved against my chest and barged out of the room. Her steps thundered down the stairs.

I dropped to the edge of her bed, staring at the empty doorway. The words echoed in my head. Did she mean it?

CHAPTER 21
MARISA

blazed down the street to his house with sweat clinging to my skin under my coat. Heat traveled up through the zippered top of my coat and heated my chin while the air chapped my cheeks.

A house away from his, a kid sped toward me on a bike bundled up with knee and elbow pads and a helmet on.

"Levi, come back." An older girl, equally padded up, called after him.

He turned and rode toward her.

Behind the girl, running alongside an identical-looking little boy with a towel wrapped around his waist to steady him, was Ron.

His words of encouragement sliced through the air. "You've got it, Landon. You're doing it."

The coals of the fire burned even hotter. Incendiary rage detonated in my head like emotional napalm.

My skin tingled like I'd stumbled onto a pack of lions ready to tear me limb from limb. Only these weren't physical threats, but mental ones gouging deep into old wounds I pretended were healed. I wanted to flee, but I couldn't.

Landon's feet were moving a mile a minute and it wasn't

until they were ten feet from me that Ron looked up. He stopped, catching Landon around the waist with the towel. The bike toppled over, but the little boy stayed anchored around the waist. He didn't let him fall.

He started. His forehead creased in concern, and it made me hate him even more. "Marisa, what are you doing here? What's wrong?" He steadied Landon on his feet and walked toward me.

"You're what's wrong." The words barely escaped through my gritted teeth.

He looked from Landon to me and crouched down, facing the boy toward him. "Head over to play with your brother and sister, Landon. I need to talk to Marisa." So doting, gentle, and kind.

My blood simmered in my veins. Not that he was being nice to some kid I'd never met before, but that he could be that to some kid who wasn't even his own.

The little boy looked from me to Ron and nodded.

"Do you want to come inside?" He reached for me. Comforting, gentle bullshit.

I jerked my arm away and stepped back.

Weariness radiated off him, but once again—too fucking bad. "What did I do now?"

"There's a laundry list. Let's start with you not playing LJ because of me." The burn was back, building brighter in the back of my nose. "What the hell do you think you're doing? His future is on the line. His career and providing for his family are on the line."

He lifted the Fulton U cap like he needed to air out the top of his head. "I wondered how long it would take him to cave."

"Was this a test? Some screwed up mental game?" The kids behind him all turned to watch us. Maybe it was best they saw exactly what kind of guy he was and who he'd been pretending to be.

His gaze cut away and back to mine with arms folded over his Fulton U Coaching Staff polo. "Life is all about choices. The things we value and the things we don't."

The front door to the house swung open. "Lunch is ready." Nora stood in the doorway, smiling and waving for the kids to come in. She froze when she spotted me, a worried look crossing over her face.

A perfect little family. He got to play house while trying to destroy the closest thing I'd ever had to a home.

I clenched my fists at my sides and glared, trying and failing to keep my breathing under control. Trying not to let myself spiral into the splotchy-vision breakdown barreling down hard onto me.

"He came with me to those dinners because he's my friend. I needed support and he was there for me. Whenever I've needed support he's been there for me and you used that friendship against him." My voice cracked. I hated how tears burned in the corners of my eyes. I hated how much I wanted to feel nothing whenever I looked at him. And I hated how he'd used me against LJ.

"All I was trying—"

"You were trying to take away the only person who's ever truly loved me because you're *jealous*. I thought I hated you before, but you've sunk to a whole new level."

His jaw clenched and the vein in the side of his neck bulged. "This wasn't about jealousy. It was about making sure you two didn't repeat the same mistakes your mom and I did. Football cannot be more important than the people you care about."

"It was for you!" I took a step toward him and shoved a finger in his face. "You left. You left me with her and you never came back. Hell, football is still the most important thing in your life." The tears burned my cheeks in the winter wind. "The deal was weekly dinners with you, except on game nights or when you're scouting or when you're at a combine or whenever else it fucking suits you. Or it's time to hang out with Nora and her kids. It seems you've got plenty of time for them."

"It's every other weekend. When Nora has the kids." His lips pinched and his head dipped.

I hoped the weight of shame buried him.

"Yes, football is also important. I have a job and a lot of people who depend on me."

"So does he." I screamed so loudly it echoed on the empty street. My throat throbbed, raw and blazing. "Why the hell do you think he's been working so hard? And you're worried about him being selfish?"

"He needs to know—"

"No! He doesn't need to know anything. He needs to get a fair shot at the draft. You will play him in every game for the rest of the season, so his draft prospects aren't damaged any more than they have been already."

Tight, clipped words escaped his mouth. "You're not going to tell me who I can and can't play, Marisa."

"If you ever want to see me after today, you will put the best inside linebacker on the team in the last two games before the playoffs. And we both know that's LJ. It's what he's worked for and what he deserves."

"And if I don't?"

"I'm done." I threw up my hands, ready to follow through on what I'd said. It wasn't a threat, it was the truth. "I'm done with you. I'm done with you and your pretending you care about me. I'm done with you forever. You can play house with your new girlfriend and her kids and forget you ever knew me. Forget I ever existed because you're a selfish bastard who doesn't care about anyone other than himself, and Nora and those kids will be better off the second they know that."

The front door to his house was still partially open. "Did you hear that, Nora? Run the other fucking way." I raked my blistering gaze over him, not able to believe I'd let LJ think for even a second I could ever think of him as my dad.

"What about your last semester? I still haven't signed the forms yet." How long had he been sitting on his ace in the hole?

My laugh dripped disdain and disbelief. "I'll pay for it. I'll use the money I saved for my fellowship. I don't care; I'm done doing things on your terms. If you ever want the chance at having any kind of relationship with your own daughter—your actual daughter, you'll do what's right." I spun to leave.

"Does he know you're here right now, putting your future on the line for his?"

"No." Whirling around, I marched back up to him. Angry sadness chewed through my chest at the thought that he couldn't believe I'd sacrifice what I had for someone I cared about. "And he'd stop me if he knew. He didn't want to tell me why he wasn't playing because for some insane reason," I smacked my hands against my forehead, "he didn't want me to hate *you*. He wanted me to make up my own mind without his interference. He was trying to give you a chance and you threw it away with some macho 'now I decide I'm your father' bullshit."

"I *am* your father."

"Since when? Since you left when I was eight? I didn't see you. I didn't hear from you. I didn't get a single present, letter, note, signal flashed in the sky—nothing. You left me with her. You left me to fend for myself and I will never let you hurt someone I love."

I wiped my nose with the sleeve of my coat.

"He's my friend. My best friend. The best friend anyone could ever have."

From the look on his face it wasn't the least bit convincing. Fine, if he couldn't do it for me, then maybe he'd do it for the one thing I knew he loved.

"You know it's what the team needs, and what you know is right. Maybe once you can act like a decent person."

I choked back a sob and wiped away the tears chaffing my cheeks. "You can choose to be a real father to me just this once." I held one finger up in the air, but not the one I wanted. "And do the right thing. Or you can start that new family over with Nora and pretend I never existed, because I'll only ever think of you as dead."

Spinning, I fled, running until I reached the end of the block. Around the corner and out of eyesight, I collapsed against the tall wooden fence and dissolved into a flood of tears.

Every step closer to me closed the door to the future LJ had been dreaming of his whole life. He'd talked all the time about how great it would feel to buy his parents a new house, to pay for Quinn's college, to know that the next time his dad, mom or Quinn needed anything, that he could take care of it without a second thought.

And he'd almost lost it all because he was too stubborn for his own good.

With The Brothel in view, my steps slowed. With each one, it felt like a lead weight had been added to my ankles, like my energy had been siphoned off with a garden hose and a gas can.

Sitting at the top of the stairs leading to the porch was LJ.

I held onto the railing to steady myself. My face felt like a splotchy, wind-burned mess.

"You went and talked to him." The corners of his mouth pinched.

"I did." Rushing past him, I opened the front door. Inside, I figured I'd hear grilling, drinking and laughing going on, but it seemed the party was over. Another thing ruined because of me.

His steps followed behind me. "I told you not to do it."

"And I told you not to be an idiot."

"What did you say to him?" He dashed past me and stood on the stairs, blocking my path.

I gripped the banister and ground my teeth. Helping him was out of the question, but he could sacrifice everything for me? "I told him the truth, and I told him if he ever wanted to speak to me again, he'd do what he knew was right."

"Risa." A long suffering sigh of disappointment and misery descended around him like a cloud. "He's your dad." He sat again, planting himself in my way.

"When will you understand that this isn't a missed football game or forgetting to pick me up from school? This is never being there for me. My parents have never been there for me. My mom isn't capable of taking care of herself, let alone me, and Ron cut out when I was just old enough to miss him. My parents aren't your parents, and not every parent deserves a second chance—or even a first chance. Sometimes drawing that line is the best thing you can do to protect yourself." Just when I'd thought there were no more tears to cry, they were back.

But this time I wasn't sitting on the frozen sidewalk. I collapsed on the step in front of him.

LJ's arms enveloped me and held me tight against his chest.

I clung to him like I'd stop breathing if I let go.

He buried his face in my hair and ran his fingers along the back of my head until the sobs turned to hiccups of embarrassment. "You know you're the strongest person I know."

"I'm not. I'm really not. If I were, I wouldn't have come running to Fulton U to get Ron to pay for college." I looked up at him. "And because I hated being away from you in New York."

"It only took you three years to finally admit you find me absolutely irresistible." A gentle smile played on his lips.

A watery laugh spilled from mine. "Yet somehow you still manage to be the worst."

He brought me into his room and kicked off his shoes.

I toed mine off and followed him to his bed.

With strong steady fingers, he unbuttoned my coat.

I stilled his fingers and stared into his eyes. "You shouldn't have lied to me. You shouldn't have kept this from me."

His nod was grim. He peeled my coat off my shoulders. "I know. I didn't want you to hate him and I didn't want you to not be able to pay tuition. I didn't want you to have to leave again." Staring into his eyes, the tears returned for a totally different reason. With one look, he made me feel a kind of wanted I'd never felt before and didn't know if I'd feel it again. It was scary to see the depths of his care and know it might not last forever.

We climbed into bed together, our arms and legs tangled and our heads on the same pillow.

He ran his fingers through my hair, pulling at the strands stuck to my face by tears.

"I love you, Marisa."

This wasn't the first time he'd said it, but this time it felt different. It felt heart-stoppingly, soul-scorchingly different.

CHAPTER 22
LJ

Keyton leaned, bracing his arm on the locker beside mine. "Listen, man. I'm sorry. I know you said not to say anything, but sometimes you're just too damn stubborn for your own good."

The tightness in my muscles had nothing to do with powerhouse practice or skipping stretching. I dropped my pads onto my shoulder in the locker room and dragged my jersey over my head.

"Nothing to do about it now." The stadium rumbled above us. Stands filled with frozen fans.

"How's Marisa?"

"I'm more pissed at you for getting her angry than Coach." My cheek twitched.

Marisa and I had spent the last couple days in our own world, disappearing into quiet spots on campus. I knew I should've gotten my own place senior year.

He held out his hand. "Are we good?"

Tilting my head, I met his eyes. How many times had I done something like that for Marisa's own good? Sometimes we had to push the people we cared about. It's what friends did. I grabbed his hand and jerked him closer, patting my fist against his back. "We're good."

With a nod and half-smile, he let out a breath. "Thanks. I was worried you'd boot me out of the house or something."

"No way. If I did, Berk might try to move Alexis into the spare room."

"She's up to something, isn't she?"

"When isn't she? But Berk will have to figure that out on his own."

Coach Saunders pushed into the locker room and all the chatter quieted down.

I snapped straight, staring at him and trying to keep the daggers sheathed. Marisa had told me all about the cozy family scene she'd stumbled into when she confronted him. To think I'd thought he deserved another chance.

Pulling out the clipboard, he stared down at it. "Change up to the starting line-up today. Lewis is swapped in for the start. Everything else stays the same." He didn't spare me a glance. "We're out there in ten."

Air forced its way out of my lungs and I couldn't draw any back in. I was starting. Starting for the first time in twenty-four games.

The coaching staff followed him into the PT and recovery room off the main locker room.

A hit nearly knocked me off my feet, but I didn't slam into the floor. Instead, I was smashed into a set of jersey covered pads. "You're starting." Berk bellowed, nearly taking out my ear drum.

"I won't be if I'm deaf and can't hear the plays." But my grin flashed like a winning scoreboard.

Berk dropped his head and glanced over his shoulder. "I'm glad Coach finally got his head out of his ass."

"That makes two of us."

We rushed down the tunnel, the chill from the late November air biting even harder as we came out of the overheated locker room in full pads. The second string guys jogged up and down the sidelines to keep warm. The rest of us knew we'd be hot soon enough.

The fog of our breath drifted into the air and commingled into a Fulton U fog. Heat cannons were cranked on, but out of their narrow field of reach, the cold snapped against my skin.

Our QB ran out to the center of the field for the coin toss. The thundering boom of the crowd reverberated through to my bones.

The ref made the call, and the defense was up first.

Rushing out onto the field, I closed my eyes, knowing my spot without needing to see it. We wouldn't need to come from behind this game. We wouldn't cut the final score close to the end of the last quarter. We'd win and I'd show everyone by just how much with me here to stop every play coming my way.

Pacing behind the linemen, I found my target and ran through the hours of tapes we'd watched to dissect the opposing team. My goal was simple. Don't let anyone past me.

Impede. Interrupt. Intercept.

The ball snapped and everything moved in slow motion. Gaps developed and I exploited them ruthlessly, knowing every minute I was out here was one more minute closer to winning the game. Every blocked inch put the offense in a better position. Every breath was one closer to going pro.

———

HOME GAMES MEANT HOME PARTIES. THIS ONE WAS A BONE-rattling, ear-ringing, adrenaline-revving party where we were seconds from being lifted off our feet and carried around the house.

At least we hadn't had to supply the booze. Kegs were rolled in without anyone even asking, and the music from speakers we didn't own rumbled the floorboards beneath our feet.

Some of the underclassmen were in the house, and I'd tap them tomorrow to clean this up after inviting themselves over.

For right now, though, I basked in the near-shut-out post-game vibes. This was a post-game party where I'd been on the field for every defensive play. This time, Marisa laughed in the kitchen talking with Jules until Berk joined them.

But now they'd both disappeared, probably making out somewhere. He'd been cagey lately, since the Dough Ho situation with Jules. *Someone* had found the dirty notes he and Jules had been anonymously sharing. Well, Jules had been anonymous. Berk had been going crazy trying to figure out who was sending them, and, lo and behold, it was our sweet as pie, curvy, quiet neighbor across the street. *Someone* had discovered these notes and somehow linked them to Jules. *Someone* had posted them online during Jules's online baking show, which led to an unfair shitstorm of assholes tearing her apart online. So *someone* was a total asshole who Marisa had said needed her ass kicked.

Berk refused to see reason when it came to Alexis. Who was I to lecture him on anything like that?

Marisa had been right in front of my face for forever, but I'd fought against my feelings. Right now, I wanted to rush over to her, throw her over my shoulder, and find a nice quiet spot to make some noise. She'd probably punch me in the solar plexus and glare if I did.

It had been my idea to keep things quiet for my own selfish reasons, but now I wanted to shout about her from the rooftops, and I couldn't.

Marisa didn't want to bring down the accusations and behind-our-back whispers about why I was playing now. People might link her and her dad as the reason, and over-shadow my hard work. I'd been the one who suggested we keep things quiet, so that was my big idea biting me in the ass.

With twenty high-fives and ten recreations of my game-winning interception, I inched forward through the party. Finally getting the recognition for all my hard work felt good. Not only was I seeing it on the scoreboard, but people were grabbing onto me and freaking out, giving me a play-by-play of moves I'd literally done. Their excitement was infectious. I'd missed it after riding the bench for so long. Hopefully, I'd get even more of it next year.

Every few feet, I'd raise my head and catch Marisa's eye.

Even though I couldn't hear her laugh from where I was, I saw it, and it had been ingrained in my brain. She'd give me shit all night about soaking up all the fan attention.

Fifteen minutes later, I finally made it to her side.

Her eyes lit up and she served up an ice-cream-sundae smile for me. "Been enjoying all your adoring fans?"

"They're okay." I shrugged.

"You're so full of it. You love every second of it." She preened and put on a queen wave, pivoting at the waist with her elbow bent and only her hand moving.

"I do not."

A guy slammed into my back, knocking me into Marisa and bringing our lips inches apart.

Her eyes widened.

I couldn't tell if it was with worry or desire. The tempta-tion rode me hard to close the gap and finally show everyone how close we truly were. Before I could make a decision, it was made for me. My arm was jerked back and I was turned around.

I reached out for her waist to steady her, but she jumped back.

"The floor is slippery." She dropped her gaze, looking around at the empty, dry floor.

A beer was shoved into my hand, amber liquid sloshing

over the edge of the rim. "The interception was insane. I had to get you a drink. One more game and we're going to the playoffs again."

"Thanks." I drank my beer and watched her out of the corner of my eye.

I got a look here and there, but never too long. It was like she didn't even want people to know we were friends, let alone more than that. We hadn't even put a label on what the 'more than that' was.

"Beer pong. We're up!" Marisa tapped the back of her hand against my chest. "Let's show them how it's done." She downed her drink and marched out to the back yard without a coat on, even though there were still small sad, gravel colored patches of snow on the ground from our freak pre-Halloween storm.

"Do you want your coat?"

"I want to kick some beer pong ass. Let's go." She smiled, no longer seeming cagey. It was the quieter, more intimate moments in front of others she shied away from, but when it came to the big loudness in front of other people, she seemed the same. At least that was one part of whatever we were now that was no longer confusing.

Now I just needed to unlock the rest.

CHAPTER 23
MARISA

I flexed my fingers on the keyboard and my tongue was heavy in my mouth, my throat and chest tight. It was giving up, but there wasn't any other way.

"Don't do this, Marisa. Just wait a little while longer. I can come up with something."

LJ perched on the edge of my desk, hovering.

"The final payments to Venice are due in May. They need to secure my housing and the only way they can do it is if I pay. There's no way I can come up with the money before then, even if I tutor seven days a week."

"But I'll have the money by late April. Early May at the latest."

"Your money. The money for you and your family." I wasn't going to fall into the trap of becoming someone LJ felt he had to take care of. I'd been taking care of myself for a long time now.

"Stop being so damn stubborn. Or at least hold off on paying the tuition bill."

"If I don't pay it now, I can't register for classes and there's only one section of Managing Museums offered in the spring and I need it to graduate. If I wait, I'll get locked out."

"Maybe…dammit. Come on. Just wait."

"What's the point in waiting?"

"Fuck, I'm going to get some cookies to soften the blow. I'll warm them up and we can have them with milk, okay?"

"I'm not going to say no." I offered up a half smile.

His face was a cross between deflated and dejected.

"Stop acting like you're the one who won't be going to Italy at the end of this summer." Saying it out loud hurt. My lips went numb and I sucked in a choppy breath. I could maybe get a position at the museum or a local gallery. My hands were clammy and shaky.

At least I'd be able to see LJ, but what if he ended up on a team thousands of miles away? My stomach clenched like I'd done a keg stand after a tuna-and-Cocoa Puffs sandwich.

"I know how much you wanted this." He leaned in and ran his lips along the line of my neck. His nose tickled me and I scrunched up my shoulders, pushing him again.

"Go get me my cookies, so I can drown my sorrows in sugar, vanilla and chocolate."

He took my hand and rubbed his fingers across my knuckles. "It won't be all bad. I know you wanted to go, but I'll make this summer worth it. We can take a trip, go somewhere amazing. Penthouse suite. First class all the way."

The temptation was strong. So strong, I wanted to lean right into it and forget all my problems, but I needed to course correct. "Stop spending money you don't have."

"You saw the game. Three interceptions, and we won by the biggest margin all season."

"Someone's getting a big head."

He glanced over his shoulder before dropping my hand onto his crotch. And no, it wasn't his phone or a remote in his pocket. "I mean, something's big." The deep, syrupy way the words dripped from his lips did a number on my heart, sending it speeding. A playful noise of disgust shot from my throat. "Go get my damn cookies."

He laughed and hopped up from the desk, darting into the hallway.

The cursor blinked in the search bar of my browser. I typed in the student accounts website and logged in. My big dreams of going to Italy dried up with each keystroke.

I hadn't heard a word from Ron since I'd screamed in his face for a solid fifteen minutes.

But I wasn't going back to Monday dinners, which meant I was on my own.

I wiped my hands on my jeans and clicked through the student accounts portal. Rummaging through my drawer I found the unused book of checks, which I'd need for the account and routing numbers for the archaic website. It looked like the first website ever created.

The big number in bold at the bottom had sent bile flooding to the back of my throat that last time I logged on.

Typing it in, I was glad LJ wasn't here, so he couldn't see my fingers shaking.

I filled in all the information and clicked submit. A big red notice popped up at the top of the page.

Error: Overpayment not accepted.

The number I'd memorized while trying to think up a way out of this situation wasn't there anymore. Instead, at the bottom of my account balance was a big, bold $0.

Checking through the transactions on my account, I saw that the last entry was a staff tuition waiver applied yesterday.

He'd done it. Ron had turned it in.

I slumped back in my chair and stared at the screen. Surprise and shock detonated in my head. This had to be a mistake. I refreshed the screen twice.

LJ's steps thumped on the stairs.

Scrambling to log out, I closed the laptop screen.

"Maybe after graduation, we could do a road trip first."

He walked into the room with two glasses of milk and a plate heaped high with cookies.

"A what?"

Setting the plate and glasses down, he spun my chair around, whirling me in a circle. "A road trip. We could drive down to Florida or up to Niagara Falls. We could drive to California."

"What is going on with you?" My gaze darted to the laptop and my lips parted to tell him. The disbelief still clouded out almost everything else.

He beamed, excitement glinting in his eyes. "If you're not going to Italy, I want to make this a summer you won't forget. I'll have plenty of free time and more money than I'll know what to do with, if things go as planned."

"Let's not count our eggs before they hatch." There was no point in telling him now. I needed to find out if the balance was real. If it was, I could still go to Italy. I could turn in the money like I'd talked about with the Venice committee and fly to Europe for the next two years.

"This also means you can come to my games. Maybe be there for some of the pre-season." His excitement increased with every new step in this plan he was creating. A plan where I didn't go to Italy. A plan where we'd be together. But what happened if all that changed and I wasn't by his side every step of the way? What if I left for two years and he was here being a pro football player and forgetting all about me?

———

"Marisa!" LJ's voice carried up the stairs.

"In my room. Those ten-year-old tour groups are brutal." I'd kicked my shoes off and was sitting on the edge of my bed, massaging my feet. My go-to tour guide outfit of my only skirt and a white button-down shirt was wrinkled and needed to be washed. Wednesdays were my turn to do school tours, and I'd need to buy new shoes before I lost a toe. Now I could, since my bank account hadn't been drained paying for my last semester's tuition. I'd checked in with the student accounts team about the payment, and they'd assured me it couldn't be reversed.

He thundered up the stairs. "How did the tours go?"

I kneaded my thumb into the arch of my foot. "How do you think they went?"

"I thought you were going to buy new shoes." He knelt and took my foot into his hands. Powerful thumbs dug into the cramped muscles.

Painful pleasure coursed through my body and I fell back onto the bed, gripping the sheets. "Don't you dare stop."

"Why do you keep wearing these?"

His fingers were torturous magic.

I groaned and hissed with each deepening massage pass. "All those PT sessions have paid off."

He switched to the other foot. "No one's home." The dance of his fingers moved from my foot to my ankle to my calf.

"I mean, I'm home." Propped up on my elbows, I dropped my head back trying to pull together the strength to lift it.

The magic of his fingers bordered on obscene.

"Risa, pay attention." He stopped moving and I growled, actually bared my teeth and growled.

The massaging stopped, but not the movement of his fingers. They crept up my legs, over my knees and to the insides of my thighs. "No one else is here. Berk is with Jules and Keyton has class."

"Oh."

He pressed on the insides of my thighs, spreading them, rubbing the sensitive skin. "Which means we have some time to ourselves."

"It's been a while." My breath hitched. The nervous,

twitchy side of me fought against the hunger blooming in my body and centering on the throb between my legs.

His fingers inched higher, and, being the helpful friend that I was, I lifted my hips, letting him pull my panties from under my ass. "It's been too long."

Almost two weeks. Between my museum shifts, tutoring, and LJ's practice and game schedule, our paths felt like they were crossing less and less. Most people would think finding time to have sex with your roommate would be easy, not so much when you were trying to be secretive about it and our beds were noisier than a construction zone.

Other than some under-the-blanket action on Movie Thursdays and him tracking me down in the Art History department for a mini makeout in the alcove of Renaissance art replicas, the drought had been long and hard.

He bunched up my skirt.

I'd never been happier for that clearance rack purchase than when he dragged his hands over my legs.

His thumbs brushed along the crease where my thighs framed the prize his eye was most definitely on.

"I need to do this more often." His breath whispered against my pussy.

My muscles tightened in anticipation. The throb deepening and ripples fluttering through my stomach.

The first brush of his tongue sent liquid pleasure rushing through my veins. The added fingers ratcheted my back off the bed. The combination with the addition of extra attention to my clit flooded my body with a sexual tsunami. All sounds were drowned out by my moans and the blood hammering in my ears.

My fingers clutched at his hair and his ears were nestled—well, more like clamped between my thighs.

Panting and flushed, with dots dancing in front of my eyes, I fell back onto the bed. The collapse was complete.

LJ chuckled still on his knees, his belt jingling.

"Hey, guys—" Keyton's voice broke through the sex daze with the silver lining of a round two. "Have you seen my...wallet."

A bucket of ice water drenched on my body would've been less jarring.

We all stared at each other.

Keyton's mouth hung open, keys still on the keyring on his finger.

LJ was on his knees between my thighs.

I lay on my back with my skirt hiked up to my waist, sex-flushed.

Those football reflexes kicked in first. Keyton slapped his hands over his eyes like a six-year-old during a kissing scene.

LJ jumped up and flung the blankets over me, while standing in front of me and faced the door.

"Sorry!" Keyton turned his back to us. "I was looking for my wallet. I didn't see anything."

He saw everything. As much as I wanted to be horrified, the fact that we'd been tiptoeing around this for nearly two months and still hadn't learned to close the door was pretty hilarious.

Giddy panic laughter bubbled up.

Drawers opened then slammed shut in Keyton's room.

LJ retrieved my panties and handed them over.

I shimmied into them still under the blankets with my heart ping-ponging in my esophagus. Kill me now. Send lightning bolts straight through my bedroom window. Maybe I could slam my head in my closet door, or just walk in there and never come out. He'd seen everything. I would have laughed if the panic hadn't strangled the air out of my lungs. All these months of being careful and I did an OBGYN spread right in front of my open door.

Damn LJ and his talented fingers and tongue, distracting me from the front door opening and the creaky-as-hell stairs.

LJ peeked his head out of my room.

I dragged myself off the bed and gripped his arm, partially hiding, partially using it to keep me upright.

Keyton froze coming out his door, sliding his wallet into his back pocket. The scarlet crawl of embarrassment crept up his neck under his collar and up to the bottom of his jaw.

It matched mine.

LJ skirted along the wall, walking toward him like a horse he didn't want to spook. "I was…"

"Checking a bite. A sting. I had a bee sting." Wow, I was next-level brilliant. The entire time I'd been putting on my underwear and that was the best excuse I could come up with? A bee sting. In November. A week before Thanksgiving.

Keyton's nervous laugh filled the hallway. "If you say so."

Joining LJ in the hallway, I faced Keyton. "Could you not say anything to anyone?" A panicky edge crept into my voice. "Please?"

This wasn't how I needed anyone to find out about me and LJ. Plus, there was the whole draft, graduation and Italy thing looming in the distance. The more people who knew about us, the more people who'd have an opinion on what we should do, and I didn't even know what I wanted to do—or what he wanted to do.

"Don't worry about it. I won't say a word. But you might want to close the door next time." He jumped down the stairs and back out the front door.

Watching him retreat like he'd walked in on a bear foraging in the hallway, I laughed. The kind of laugh of relief you do three minutes after your non-bang buddy roommate had seen you naked from the waist down.

"Why didn't you want to tell him?" A trace of disappointment ran through the question.

I dragged my fingers through my hair. "Tell him you were going down on me?"

"No, tell him about us."

"*You're* the one who said you wanted to keep it quiet."

"Months ago." He rubbed his hand over the back of his neck. "But we've been…"

"We've been LJ and Marisa with sex. Things have been busier than ever this semester. It's only going to get worse. Do you want Berk to know? Reece and Nix? The gloating alone would be annoying. Then questions about how long and what next—we don't need to deal with all that pressure."

He sighed. "You're right." Not sounding a hundred percent convinced, he stepped closer. Maybe he didn't think it made sense now, but in five months, after we'd graduated, it would. Once the real world intruded and we began to drift apart.

I ran my fingers over his arms. The hair tickling my fingertips. "We're alone again, right?" Peeking out my doorway, I checked the front door.

"We are."

I pulled him out of the doorway and fully into my room, closing the door behind him. "Then let's finish what we started." The cool metal of his jeans button and zipper pressed against my skin.

We didn't have much time left. Better satisfy every hunger pang while I could.

CHAPTER 24
LJ

The final game of the season. Thanksgiving. Christmas. Playoffs. Another championship.

Some months felt like they dragged on while others felt like we'd been shot into the future by cannon. Through it all, there had been one constant to anchor me to the present. Marisa.

Poor Keyton had been subjected to some of our 'couldn't hold back anymore and attack one another' sessions, since he was the only one who knew about us. Berk was at Jules's more and more.

He'd also finally gotten it through his thick skull about Alexis, and he and Jules were happier than ever, although none of us had the full story. Not to say things weren't the same for me and Marisa.

No one even knew we were now more than friends. After the season ended, it seemed natural to tell everyone, but Marisa kept stalling. There was always a reason to keep things quiet and suddenly my act of self-preservation back in October felt like an albatross around my neck.

I'd leave for the last combine before the draft tomorrow.

I'd gotten the invitation. My agent had nearly blasted out my ear drum when I called him to let him know.

Coach Saunders would be there, along with Keyton, Berk and a few other guys from our team.

And there were my classes on top of everything else.

"Jules is the best neighbor ever." Marisa kicked the front door closed and walked in with a clear container and a cup of sauce balanced on top. She was in her museum tour guide clothes, which was part of the reason my plan would work without raising suspicion.

"What did she make us this time?"

"Churros and a chocolate sauce. I didn't think I could love her more, but I do. I so, so do."

She loved Jules, but had yet to say it back to me since I'd said it to her in November.

I couldn't say it didn't hurt. It felt like a sliver of glass buried in my skin, but determination pumped through my veins to get her to see it. To get her to say it.

It was time for me to tell her this wasn't junior high and high school love. This was a crazy, can't-imagine-my-life-without-her kind of love.

"I've got a surprise for you."

"You do?" She glanced up at me with half a churro in her mouth. Setting them down, she held one out to me, dangling it from the ends of her fingers.

I wrapped mine around her wrist to steady her hand and took a bite. "We're going out."

"We are?" She licked the cinnamon sugar from her fingers.

My nostrils flared and I tightened the reins so I didn't scrap all the plans I'd put in place and make Keyton break out the headphones. "Yeah, let's go."

"I'm still in my tour clothes. I don't need to change?"

"Nope." I grabbed our coats and tugged her toward the front door.

"Where are we going?" She buckled up and I pulled away from the curb.

"Somewhere special."

The traffic fell in between rush hour and the nightlife crowd, so we moved through the city quickly.

"What's the occasion?"

"We're together." I dropped my hand onto her knee, brushing my fingers over the fabric.

She laughed. "That was a next-level answer. Your wooing skills are at peak capacity right now."

"I try my best."

The deflection with humor. It was easy to fall into our normal, silly, antagonistic pattern, but tonight I wanted it to be more. We pulled into a city lot and I opened her door.

"You coming?"

"What are you up to?" Her eyebrows furrowed and lips pinched.

"You could come with me to find out."

She slid her hand into mine.

I checked the address one more time, and we walked down an alley before popping out on the other side of the Northern Liberties strip of businesses and shops.

"Here we are." I stopped and looked to her.

"Seriously?" She jumped onto me with her arms wrapped around my neck.

I smiled into her hair and hugged her back. The plan was working. Part of me was afraid we'd get here and she'd tell me this was the one particular artist she couldn't stand. "I saw the flyers in the Art History department."

"So you brought me to the opening?" She held her hands to her chest and looked at me like I'd showed up with a diamond bracelet.

"Something tells me art is your thing."

Inside the gallery waiters walked around with wine and champagne on trays. There were fancy hors d'oeuvres.

We handed our coats over to the coat check and wandered through the wild world of modern art. "How'd you get tickets to this? Professor Morgan could only get two, and by the time I saw the email they'd already been taken."

Leaning in, I whispered in her ear, wanting so badly to run my lips along the curve of her neck, and to find a dark corner and show her how much I'd missed her. Not traveling since the championship had made it easy to forget how much being away from her sucked.

But we wouldn't have to do that again. We'd have the summer. Maybe we'd even go to Italy. It wouldn't be the two years like she planned, but I'd make it up to her. We could spend the whole off-season in Venice if she wanted.

Gondola rides, good food, and great nights together, wrapped up in one another.

The temptation to rush back home and say screw the art increased when I rested my hand on the small of her back. "Nix's restaurant is doing the catering. He put in a word with the organizers."

Tonight was for her. I couldn't come up with a way for her to still go to Italy, but I could wander around this place and pretend I knew what any of it was—for her.

The food, drinks and company made this the best night in a long time.

"L, this is amazing." She stood in front of artwork spot-lighted in the center of the room.

None of it made any sense to me, but I loved watching her take it all in. "I've been wanting to come here forever."

"Why haven't you?"

She shrugged. "The museum. Tutoring. Classes. And the bus schedule to get here would've taken forever."

"You could've borrowed my car."

She whirled around, stalking toward me. "Who are you and what have you done with LJ?"

My laugh was shotgun loud. "When have I ever not let you borrow anything of mine?"

"Ninth grade biology."

"I didn't want you swabbing my jock strap for bacterium cultures. Sorry for having a little dignity."

"It was for science!" She laughed and grinned. The future fog cleared when she looked at me. All the hazy uncertainty crystalized, and it felt like there wasn't anything to worry about. One smile. One laugh. One look.

"That's exactly what I wanted our entire bio class to know. 'There's a strange never-before-seen growth in this petri dish.'"

"It knocked you out of your no showering phase, didn't it?" Every guy went through a funky phase, but right now I could certainly use a shower—with her.

We wandered around the gallery.

Her excitement as contagious as the first time she'd wandered through the Philadelphia Museum of Art making us both late to the field trip bus.

I slipped my arm around her shoulder on the way back to the car.

She didn't pull away, but held on to the front of my coat and hugged herself to my side. "Thank you for tonight. It was perfect."

"Anytime." All the time. I'd take her to every art exhibit I could get my hands on, once I signed on the dotted line.

Back at the house, it was silent. Not 'everyone's upstairs' silent. 'Long gone' silent.

The lights were on at Jules's place, so Berk would be there for the night.

Keyton's door was open with all the lights off.

She stopped in the hallway with her hands out at her side like it helped her hear better. "No one's home."

I stepped behind her, letting my chest press against her back. "I know."

She shuddered. Not from cold. The heat was cranked in the house. Her chin dropped to her shoulder. "Seems like we should probably do something about it."

We fell into my bedroom.

The raspy, rich tone of her voice sent bolts of pleasure down my spine and straight to my cock, which was determined not to be ignored any longer. Her ass nestled on my lap and the rubbing against the grain of my jeans tortured me.

With both my hands, I ran my fingers through her hair, pressing against her scalp and parting her thick, soft locks.

She moaned and dropped her head back, letting me massage her. "Scratch what I said earlier. This is perfect."

Ducking my head, I ran my lips along her collarbone and up her neck.

Her fingers tightened on my shoulders, kneading and stroking them.

I followed the curve of her neck to her cheek, I didn't stop until I'd reached my prize—her lips.

Every taste was always too short and left me starving for more. She stole my restraint and my breath away. It was like she smashed a window, snuck in, and snatched it from my lungs.

But I needed more. And so did she.

She parted her lips and our tongues met, hungrily restrained. Craving, yearning, burning.

My heart pounded in my chest like an animal waiting to be released for the full meal laid out in front of me, but the restraints were still on.

One hand dropped to the back of her head, sliding down to her neck, my fingers dancing along the delicate skin.

She broke our kiss, her lips red and swollen. "More, L. Haven't I been patient enough?" Sliding off my lap, she tugged her shirt up over her head and dropped it to the floor. She reached behind herself and unfastened her bra.

I ran my fingers over the curve of her breasts and teased the stiff peaks of her nipples.

Goosebumps broke out over her skin and she shuddered, her eyes hooded and churning with the urgency I tried to keep at bay. I wanted this to last. I wanted this to never end. I wanted to brand myself on her memories, filling them with the same greedy feelings I couldn't beat back.

Her pupils dilated, swallowing up the chocolate brown almost entirely.

My fingers skimmed down the backs of her shoulders to the band across her back.

Her cleavage was at eye level. The soft mounds of her breasts swelled over the cups of the bra.

With one flick, the fabric went lax, falling down and exposing her to me. Her nipples pebbled and she sucked in a breath as I lowered my mouth to one and then the other.

She dropped her arms and her bra was completely off, falling into the pile of clothes growing at our feet.

I cupped her breasts and rolled her nipples between my fingers, teasing them with my tongue and teeth.

Her gasps and moans guided me.

The excitement built fast and hard, and my erection strained, pressed against the zipper of my pants. Touching her at this point was a liability. The faintest brush of my dick against her soft skin and I might embarrass myself. After all these months, sometimes it felt like the first time.

I backed her up to the bed, laying her down, spread out in front of me.

She was finally mine.

Her hands were all over my neck, back and shoulders. Her fingers raked through my hair, holding me against her chest. Shudders rippled through her as I slid lower.

My nose brushed against her thatch of hair and her hands stilled as I parted her folds and ran my tongue through her sweetness. Circling her clit, her body shook and shuddered as

I took my time, savoring every taste, smell and feel of her body pressed against mine.

"How?" She propped herself up before her head rolled back. "How the *fuck* are you so good at this?" A moan escaped her lips.

I chuckled, but didn't let her words deter me from my prize. Making this every bit as good for her as it could be for me was my number one goal. I'd take my time even as my dick throbbed and I got lightheaded, almost unable to contain myself.

Running my hands along the smooth insides of her thighs, I kept up the constant pressure and attention to every part of her pussy. Tasting, sampling, devouring.

Her fingers tightened in my hair as I slid one finger inside her and added another.

The trembling of her thighs told me how close she was. The panting, gasps got sharper, higher and even more musical to my ears. With one more broad stroke of my tongue against her clit, she came undone, screaming my name with her thighs locked tight around my head, deafening me to her cries.

That was the most satisfying sound in the world. Pride welled in my chest that I'd drawn them out of her.

Her leg lock loosened, and I crawled back up her body, gritting my teeth as my dick rubbed against the bed and nudged at her heated core.

I braced my hands on either side of her as she looked up at me with a wide smile.

"That was an unexpected end to our evening." She laughed like someone had told a joke for her ears only.

The pounding demand from my erection waned the tiniest bit. "Most classy art gallery visits don't end with hot, crazy sex once you get back home?"

Her eyes widened and she hitched her legs around my waist, digging her heels into my ass. "They might not, but they sure as hell should. It was fan-fucking-tastic. It was sophomore-year-championship-trick-play good."

She rubbed her hands over my shoulders, urging me closer.

To drop down onto her and give us both what we'd been denying ourselves and finally gorging on one another like there was no tomorrow.

She was beautiful. Perfection. Everything I'd always wanted.

I ripped off my jeans. Fumbling around on the bed, I found the smooth, metallic package. Ripping it open with my teeth, I lifted up, separating our bodies just enough to slide the latex on and settled myself between her thighs. The head of my cock rested at her entrance, heavy, throbbing and ready for her.

She urged me closer, harder, faster and I gratefully accepted the invitation.

I'd never been with anyone else. I didn't have even a whisper of an idea that it could be better with another woman, and I didn't want to find out.

Sweaty and tangled in my sheets, we collapsed on one another. Her smooth arms and legs rubbed against the hair on mine. Content to never move again, I felt the words building in my throat.

"I love you, Marisa."

She kissed my chest and her smile widened. "I love you too." She said it like any other time the words had passed her lips.

I could let it pass. I could let it pass by like saying hi or bye to a friend, but I needed her to know. Tucking the hair behind her ear, I rubbed my thumb along the underside of her chin and held her gaze.

"Love you, love you. I love you, Marisa."

She stiffened, staring back at me like this wasn't inevitable. Like it wasn't impossible not to.

"And I have all kinds of plans for us once I get back from Chicago and once I'm drafted. Plans that include you."

Her lips parted, but no words came out. Instead, she burrowed deeper against my side and hugged herself tight to me.

All the ideas about what happened after graduation had been mine. She'd been focused on right now. But I needed her to know we weren't over after graduation. What if her plans with me ended when we walked across that stage?

CHAPTER 25
MARISA

L J had been weird all day before he left. He'd professed his love for me, not we've-known-each-other love, but the kind that reached deep down into me and touched a scary place where future plans were made and expectations were set.

This was the no-man's land I'd tried to stay away from all my life. The land mines set there had a way of blowing up huge. I'd wanted to tell him how much I loved him too, how I couldn't wait for us to go through with all the crazy plans he kept throwing out there, but the words stalled in my throat.

We still needed to go slowly, and his life would be changing in ways he couldn't imagine in the next three months. It was better to leave some things left unsaid, some protections still in place. It was better to have an escape hatch.

The whole day before he left, he was quiet. He'd talked to his mom early in the morning and had gone out for a walk. He didn't even make fun of the sandwiches I'd made us for lunch. And he'd gone to bed early, which made sense.

His flight for Chicago had left at 5am, along with Berk, Keyton, Ron, and other guys from the team. But there hadn't been any stolen kisses, touches, or even looks all day.

Worry wound deeper in my stomach. This whole time I'd been preparing myself for the end, but I wasn't ready yet. I didn't think I'd ever be ready. And it scared me. Shook me to my core how hard it would be to leave him or worse, watch him walk away.

The mid-day phone call while I'd been studying for finals hadn't helped soothe my anxiety. A drive across the bridge sent my body into shoulder-tight, hands-clenched, lock-jaw stress mode. I parked in the hospital lot, breathing deeply before psyching myself up to go inside.

The pungent smell of antiseptic was miles away from the curation room in the museum. This wasn't just clean. It was 'pour a bucket of bleach on top of everything and scrub it down' clean.

A stocky nurse who looked like she hadn't left the hospital in days worked efficiently, looking up the information for my mom. "Your mom has been transferred to one of the clinic rooms. They should be finished with her brace. It was a clean break, so no surgery is needed. Room five down that hall." She pointed behind her.

"Thank you." It had taken two calls from the hospital to get me here. Part of me had been expecting the worst when I picked up. The worst part was, I didn't know if I was relieved or not when they said she'd fallen and broken her leg.

Outside her room, I psyched myself up to go inside. I took deep breaths, but not so deep that the cleaning products burned my nose. Armor up. After almost two months without hearing from her, I had to remember and anticipate exactly how she'd needle her way under my skin.

It was already thinner than normal.

"My daughter will be here soon. Could you be a dear and see if the doctor might prescribe me some more meds before she gets here."

"Ma'am—"

"Mom, I'm here."

This gave the nurse enough time to escape to the door. "The doctor will be here with your discharge orders in a few minutes."

She sat on the hospital bed looking like she'd been on her way to a night on the town. Or maybe she'd been coming home. "It's about time you got here. I've been waiting forever."

"What happened?"

"Stupid Eddie had to go home and see his wife, so I was home all by myself. I tried to get my hands on the spices in the cabinet by the stove."

Spices—aka, the booze stash.

"I slipped and here I am." Her hands shot out in a voila to her leg in the brace.

For a long time, I'd waited for a phone call to say she'd had an accident, hooked up with the wrong guy and ended up hurt, or done something else to end her run of luck when it came to booze and guys. Getting out of the hospital with nothing more than a bum leg was a minor miracle.

"Let's get you home. Do you have food?"

"Of course, I have food."

"Edible food?"

"You were always such a picky eater."

Water off a duck's back.

An orderly showed up with a wheel chair.

Despite all her grumbling and complaining, we got her into the chair. Her twenty-pound purse sat on her lap.

I picked up the rest of her things in the room and shoved them into her bag. "Ready to go?"

"Why are you rushing me? You have somewhere better to be?"

Anywhere. Literally anywhere.

I shouldn't have come. When the hospital said I'd been listed as my mom's emergency contact, I should've told them they had the wrong number.

Instead, whatever remnants of daughterly obligations existed in me were tapped into by the censure in the hospital worker's voice when I'd asked about other ways she could get home.

My goal was simple. In and out.

"I've got to study. Midterms are coming up. LJ's in Chicago for the combine today and I need to get home by three to watch it."

"You barely stop by for Christmas, don't even give me a call for New Year's and now you're rushing me out of the hospital."

I'd avoided her almost all of winter break and hadn't gotten even the hint that she wanted me to show up beyond a slurred call at 11pm on New Year's Eve. I guess that boyfriend of hers with the kids wasn't around anymore. Good for him.

I stopped by the nurse's station for instructions on what to do next.

"The discharge papers are almost ready. You can wheel her out to the front of the hospital, pick up her prescriptions and then get your car and pick her up."

"Does she need them?" Mixing alcohol and pills was never a good idea. "Some of her other medication..."

The nurse flipped through her chart. "She didn't mention anything, but the prescription is for extra strength ibuprofen. The risk of interactions would be minimal, but I can double check, if you give me the names."

"No, that's fine. We'll be okay." Relief that she hadn't been proscribed something stronger pushed some of the worries away. If she stepped up her addiction to real pills, the next call I got might not be so innocuous.

The discharge nurse walked me through the rest of the forms I needed to fill out.

An orderly pushed my mom's wheelchair. Her foot rested

on the foot rest in a brace. Arrows and signs pointed toward the pharmacy.

"I can get her pain meds and meet you out front." The man nodded and pushed her in the opposite direction.

One person stood in line at the window. At least this wouldn't take too long.

My muscles were wound tight, there was a faint throb at the front of my head, and my stomach was clenched like I was preparing for a blow. Never again.

Italy looked even better with each day. I still hadn't talked to LJ about it. Like an escape pod I'd tucked away in case things went bad, but also because I couldn't give it up just yet. I'd dreamt about wandering the city and the country since I was little, like a princess locked in a tower, only mine had been built of glass bottles. One summer hadn't been enough to scratch the surface, but leaving...what happened if I left?

The last time LJ had told me he loved me, it had scared me. Those were the kind of words you couldn't walk away from. They were the kind that meant promises, and I'd been let down and left behind so many times before it made it hard to believe they could be true.

And that they would remain true. What the hell did forever even mean? I could barely think past graduation.

"Marisa?" A familiar voice broke through my insecurity spiral.

"Jill." Like a ray of sunshine breaking through clouds hanging over me, she walked up and hugged me.

"What are you doing here? Is everything okay?" Her smile was warm, but eyes creased with concern.

"It's my mom." Who I don't want anywhere near you. The meetings between LJ's family and my mom had always been cringe city with me finding any way possible to make a quick exit for us both. "She hurt her leg."

Charlie walked up behind Jill. "Hey, Marisa." His hug was

strong and comfortable, fatherly. The closest to one I'd ever had. The closest to one I'd ever have. Letting him go, a jab of sadness knocked into my stomach.

Jill's eyes widened, looking past me. "Terri, what happened?"

I turned, and sure enough, the orderly was pushing my mom toward us. No. No. No. I needed to go.

Misery was written all over the orderly's face. Who knows what she'd done to badger him into finding out what was taking me so long after the five whole minutes she'd had to wait while I filled her prescription.

My muscles, which had thawed a few degrees, were right back to ice solid.

"Tripped while rescuing orphans from a burning build-ing." My mom's sarcastic tone dripped with an attitude she always had around anyone she assessed to be even remotely nicer, happier, friendlier than her, so everyone.

Jill let out a startled laugh. This time I did see a different smile from her. It was thin and reedy, polite and appropriate, but nothing like the one she'd given me. "Sorry to hear about your leg."

My mom opened her mouth, but I cut her off, not wanting her to set her sights on landing a dig in no matter what.

"Is everything okay?" I looked between them. The anxiety knot in my chest doubled turning into dread.

Jill tugged at her earlobe. "We're here for another round of tests after Charlie's six-month check-up. There were some issues with the last one. Some were inconclusive, so they wanted to do a few more to double check." Uncertainty flick-ered in her eyes.

My vision tunneled. "More tests?"

The last time had been so hard on Charlie and Jill. They'd both been so strong, trying to keep their family's heads above water while dealing with so much. He'd been so frail and pale, pain etched in every gaunt line while he tried to keep a brave face. The dread pit deepened, sending sharp spurs into my stomach.

"Does LJ know?" All moisture was sucked out of my mouth.

He'd freak out. The first time his dad was sick, he'd found me on the bleachers between third and fourth period in tenth grade, laid his head in my lap and broke down. The tears didn't stop for a long time, but I'd been there for him. I braced myself for needing to be the strong one again.

"I let him know yesterday. With him flying to Chicago, I didn't want to, but he'd made me promise to always let him know when we were going in for a visit."

My head was woozy and light-headed. His quiet detachment before getting on the plane. I'd chalked it up to nerves about performing in front of every pro scout in the country up against all the top players from every other team. But now…

"I hope everything will be okay."

Her gaze brightened and she straightened her shoulders. "I'm sure it will. Don't worry about it. I'll leave you two, so you can get your mom home."

His distance. The worry, but he hadn't said a word. He hadn't told me. Why wouldn't he have said something? I'd always been there for him before, and he'd kept it to himself. The spiral sped faster. The rails were coming off.

"Let me know if you need anything, Jill."

She patted my shoulder and nodded.

All those plans he'd made had probably entailed the Marisa Magic lasting. If something happened to Charlie, would he even want me around? Would I be cast out? How would he even be able to look at me again? I mustered up a numb-lipped smile and cleared my throat.

The fact that I was even feeling sorry for myself shifted my worries to disgust with myself.

I wanted to stay. I wanted to be there with them and make

them laugh and joke while they waited. I wanted to not have to spend another minute with my mother.

I walked alongside my mom while the orderly pushed her to the curb.

"Wow, you're really getting in there deep, aren't you? Offering up help without a grumble or someone even needing to ask. How many times did they have to call to get you to come?"

My jaw ached. "Stop it."

"What?" She feigned innocence, complete with big wide eyes and fingertips splayed on her chest.

I left her at the front of the hospital and went to the short-term parking lot to pick up LJ's car. Part of me wanted to keep going straight onto the highway, instead of pulling around to the front of the hospital.

At the entrance, there were moms cradling new babies, people on crutches, and my mom sitting in a wheelchair in her cast, radiating bitter drunkenness.

Waiting to pull into an empty spot, I tapped out a message to LJ.

Me: Good luck today. Thinking about you. I'll be watching at 3!

The text bubble popped up, indicating he was typing, and just as quickly disappeared.

My throat tightened, legs wobbled and my heart squeezed like someone had gripped it tight, twisting to test the integrity. Failure was imminent.

After helping her into the car, I stopped off at the grocery store and bought her enough lunch meat and bread to last a week. It took longer than I'd hoped, and the count-down to three got even closer. I'd planned on watching it at home alone where no one else would be bothered by my shouting. I definitely hadn't planned to watch with my mom.

Every mile on the road in LJ's car, my head was a maelstrom of anxiety. I compulsively checked my phone at every red light, but the phantom buzz came up empty every time.

Walking into my mom's house—I couldn't call it mine anymore—felt as weird as it had when I'd stopped by on Christmas Eve. It looked and smelled the same, but it wasn't home. I had no home.

I unpacked the groceries, flinging boxes and packages on the counters to put them away quickly. My ears buzzed, panic-inducing thoughts swirling in my head.

"This is what you get for me?" On crutches, she hobbled into the kitchen.

I shoved the food into her barren fridge. Half-empty bottle of olives and room service ketchup bottles rolled around on the shelves. "Sorry, let me move this prime rib and Caesar salad aside to make room for the groceries I paid for with my own money."

"I'm not in elementary school. What's with all the lunch meat?"

"It's better than what you left me with growing up." I snapped, inching closer to the edge.

A dismissive snort was her only reply. "You were fine. All you had to do was run to LJ's house and everything would be taken care of."

The muscles in my neck tensed, anger seeping into my veins and ears ringing. I slammed the fridge shut, contents rattling inside. "Maybe I wanted my mother to take care of me."

"You were more than capable." Another blow-off.

"I was a child."

"Your father went off and lived his life, doing whatever the hell he wanted. Why shouldn't I have been able to do the same thing?"

Bringing up these old feelings was picking at the oozing stitches I'd pretended were fully healed. "Sorry I was such an inconvenience."

"No need to be dramatic."

My cheeks heated. What was the point of trying to change anything about her? "Do you need anything else before I go?"

Her voice softened. "You're leaving already? We've barely had a chance to talk."

I bit my tongue so the 'why the hell would I want to stay?' and a reminder of how much convincing it had taken to get me here didn't fly out of my mouth.

Laundry loaded, a bed made up on the living room couch, and an elementary school sandwich later, she'd exhausted every possible way to keep me in the house.

Checking the time, I wouldn't make it back to the house before the combine. *Shit.*

Leaving my mom in the kitchen, I walked to the living room and flicked on the TV and sat on the coffee table.

Commentary was layered over the distant sounds of the nearly empty stadium where players lined up for drills, sprints and showing off all their skills and power to the teams watching.

"Up next, we have the linebackers. There's a lot of talent, and of course the competition is always fierce."

Eight other guys went through the motions, their names and times flashing on the bottom of the screen.

My mom rattled around the house, clinking bottles and grumbling. If she fell trying to get a drink, I'd be tempted to leave her.

LJ's name flashed up on the screen. Even with the dark cloud hanging over my head right now, pride flared in my chest seeing that and hearing the announcers go over all he'd done in the past four seasons. Normally, I'd be jumping up and down and cheering at the screen. I wanted this so badly for him, more than I'd ever wanted anything for me. Because I loved him.

I gripped the edge of the table and held my breath.

The drills began like they had for the other players. His

times flashed onto the screen, compared to the other guys. He wasn't first in any, but he was consistently in the top three, while other guys bounced around in the rankings.

A final shrill whistle and he finished. He jogged to the sidelines with sweat pouring down his face. Winded and intense, he stepped up next to the sideline reporter like all the other players before him.

Although I could see him on the screen, I still checked my phone like he'd message me at this exact moment.

"Those were outstanding times out there. How are you feeling about the draft?"

LJ's face and cheeks were splotchy red as he dragged a towel over his neck. "Feeling as good as any of the guys out here. There's a lot of tough competition, and I just hope I proved myself out on the field."

"You killed it, L." I shouted at the screen. Pride glowed in my chest, shiny and bright.

He'd worked so hard. He hadn't played up the sideline silliness like he normally did. No grinning or winking. He was stone faced, serious.

I folded in on myself with my arms around my waist, staring at him, larger than life on the screen. An ominous cloud of desolation hung in the air.

"There's a lot on the line and school is wrapping up for you. Are you looking forward to graduation?"

He dragged a towel down his face, schooling his face even as he sucked in air by the lungful. The light pads he wore rose and fell with every breath.

"Yes and no. There's a lot to leave behind, but I'm ready to start a fresh new chapter."

"I'm sure there are a lot of teams out there who'd be interested in helping you with that."

"I hope so. I'm ready to work hard and do my part on whatever team I'm on."

"We've got the draft coming up in April. Who'll be

coming with you on draft night? A girlfriend happy to see you go pro?"

"No, no girlfriend for me." There wasn't a chuckle or a cracked smile. Nothing. Shaking his head, droplets of sweat rained down around him. "My parents will be there. I'm going to make them proud."

I stopped, stalling, and watched him move on to the next question. Choking on air, my lungs burned and the room tilted, my vision blurring and dimming. I didn't know what I'd expected him to say, but it wasn't that.

"Looks like you let that one get away." Mom crutched over from the living room entryway to the couch. "Too bad. He'll be swimming in football groupies by the end of the semester. Hell, there are probably a few there ready to bag themselves a pro player before he signs his check."

"He's not like that," I snapped.

"Neither was your father, but all that time on the road, he forgot who was waiting for him at home. Time it. By the time he gets back here, he'll be knee-deep in coeds who will do whatever the hell he wants."

I stared at the screen long after they'd switched to the next position drills.

My skin felt burnt and blistered.

"And his dad's probably sick again. You should've gotten in there while you could. Your welcome mat will be rolled up as soon as the chemo starts up again. Unless maybe they want to take that handy bone marrow again. Charge them this time. He'll have the money." She waved her arm in the direction of the screen LJ was no longer on.

Without another word, I left the house, got in the car that smelled like LJ, and drove the well-worn path back to The Brothel. Tears burned at the edges of my eyelids, but I blinked them back. My chest hurt with a deep and heavy hurt, like I was losing a part of myself.

On the drive back, my head throbbed, shoved full of all

the insecurities and fears about crossing the line with LJ. Across the bridge, the throbbing against my skull turned to pounding and hammering. I kept my hands ten and two, making it an uneventful drive, except for the pit stop five minutes from the doorstep where I pulled off to the side of the road. I fell out of the car to my hands and knees and puked what remained of the sandwich I'd scarfed down before I left for the hospital.

Sitting against the side of the car, I wiped my mouth and gathered myself with long shaky breaths. I dragged the air into my lungs, climbed back into the car, and made it back to the house.

Inside, I fought against every instinct to bolt. With trembling fingers, I paced my bedroom, phone pressed to my ear, and ran my fingers through my hair waiting for the other line to answer. It went straight to voicemail, and, like no one else I knew under 50, I left one.

I sat, staring at the phone willing it to ring. All my mom's words screamed through my head, ripping through my skull.

Instead of a return call, a text came through.

LJ: Not a great time. I'll be back in town tomorrow. We can talk then.

That was it.

With one text, he'd wrecked all the things I'd given him. My friendship. My trust. My love.

I dropped to my bed, fingers curled around my phone and trying to catch my breath.

My vision blurred, adrenaline screamed through my veins, and my sob was locked in my throat.

This was the moment. The moment he left.

Even if he came back on Friday, something had changed, and I should've been preparing instead of pretending.

CHAPTER 26
LJ

Checking my messages after I left the field had been a mistake. There was one from Marisa and another from my mom. The test results would be back in a few days.

Sitting in a hotel room in Chicago, I was ready to rip the paintings off the walls. He had to be okay. I'd pushed myself harder than I'd thought possible on the field today. My dad's life might hang in the balance of however many zeroes were on the end of my contract.

I wanted—no, needed to take away all the financial worries that might hit them. I needed to take care of Quinn and make sure Marisa still got her European tour. I needed to take care of them and this was the only way I could do it.

Talking to anyone would only make it worse. Talking to Marisa would make me want to be there right now. It would make me want to max out a credit card to get on a plane tonight, not tomorrow morning at seven am with the rest of the guys and her dad.

He stood right on the sidelines beside the interviewer with the rest of the guys ready to go out onto the field.

I'd gritted my teeth not to let a word slip out about Marisa.

He'd won his championship and taken away Marisa's chance of a lifetime. She'd been right. He didn't deserve a second chance. He didn't deserve a second of her care or attention.

I'd wanted to believe she was wrong, but she wasn't. Fuck him.

She'd called when I was in the locker room, but I'd been expecting a call from my mom, and her dad had been there with us, going over all the final numbers for the day.

Stewing, I struggled to settle down back in the dry, heated air of the hotel room. At least I hadn't had to share one. But there would be a worn path in the floor by tomorrow morning.

A pound at the door dragged me from the bench-clearing flood overwhelming my head.

I jerked it open. Keyton stood in the hallway.

"We're going to get something to eat. Let's go."

"I'm not really—"

"It wasn't a request. Get your shoes and wallet and let's go. Berk will meet us down there. He's talking to Jules."

A silent elevator ride down to the hotel restaurant later, Keyton sat cross from me in a chair while he'd made me take the booth like they were afraid I'd take off and go right back to my room. It wasn't the stupidest conclusion. I'd thought of trying it the whole time he'd been going over his menus.

The sports bar restaurant had jerseys framed and hung on the walls. Smells of fried food and beer on tap flooded the whole place. TVs on the walls replayed the Sports Center combine results from today.

I sunk down deeper into my chair.

Keyton set down his menu. "Do I need to call Marisa?"

"This has nothing to do with Marisa."

"You're only ever a pain in the ass like this when there's something up with Marisa." He averted his gaze. We'd kept all talk of me and Marisa and how he'd caught us to a minimum. There were a few times our loud-as-hell beds had probably given us away, but other than that, we'd kept a low profile. Too low.

"It has nothing to do with Marisa."

Other than me wanting her here. I wanted her with me to tell me everything would be okay and to not freak out until all the tests came back. It was so much worse when I couldn't see her or touch her.

"Are you worried about how today went?"

Another row clicked into place on the Rubik's cube of looming catastrophe. Not only was I dealing with fear of my dad being sick again, but now I could add in a dash of my numbers not adding up to the pro scouts. My stomach, which had been not interested before, now outright rejected the idea of putting anything in my mouth.

"You've got it handled. We all saw how you did out there."

"Who? LJ?" Berk slid into the seat beside Keyton. "You're a lock, man. First or second round. No nefarious past. No performance issues. It's not like you showed up late and missed the first half of one of the biggest games of the season or anything." He shook his head and laughed, gulping down the water in front of him.

At least I wasn't the only one who'd had a fucked up season. Berk had almost been kicked off the team for fighting an opposing player during the season, but it had all faded away like a mirage, and he'd kept tight lipped about it.

"What's your assessment of me?" Keyton turned in his chair.

"It's harder with a tight end." Berk waited, but neither of us took the 'that's what she said' bait. Read the room, Berk.

"You're probably looking at second or third."

Keyton's shoulders dipped a little. Not with sadness, but

relief. "I'd be happy with fourth. I don't even care. I just want to play."

Berk spun the laminated half page menu on the table, flicking it with his finger. "Not go on tour with your secret rock band?"

"What?"

"The guitar. It's not an easy instrument to sneak in and out of the house."

"I don't play."

"What's the story then?"

The server came over and took our orders. I went with a burger and fries, but there was no way I was going to be able to choke down more than a few bites.

Berk drank some of his soda. "We're not dropping this, Keyton. Graduation is a little over two months away and you still haven't spilled the beans. We don't hear you playing late at night. Is it electric? Or do you only play when no one's home?"

Keyton's gaze flicked to mine. "I don't play. I'm holding onto it for someone."

"You're schlepping a guitar around in college for someone."

"Yeah. No story there."

Berk leaned across the table. "I highly doubt that."

But he let it drop. I wasn't much company for the annoying needling game.

Food arrived and I pushed it around my plate.

"If you're not going to eat it. I will. All the snacks Jules made for me are gone." Berk slid my plate toward him without waiting for a reply.

Keyton let out a low, rumbling laugh. "You mean the two gallon-sized Ziploc bags of cookies are gone?"

He shrugged. "I was stress eating."

"My friends and I were wondering if you're the guys up there." A college-aged blonde and two friends stood between

Berk and Keyton's chairs and pointed at the TVs replaying the combine highlights.

"We are."

"That's so cool. We're in town for a national sorority meeting, but our football team sucks, so we've never seen any of our players on Sports Center."

"Well, there was the one time they put up the worst plays of the season and our team made it twice."

Polite chuckles and half smiles were all they got.

"Can we get a picture with you guys? Maybe it'll be worth something once you go pro." They smiled and bounced on the toes of their feet.

Keyton read the table. "Now's not really—"

Two of them slid into the booth beside me and pulled Berk and Keyton in, cramming the six of us into a seat meant for three.

The quicker we did this, the quicker they'd leave.

After more selfies than I'd taken in my entire life, they left with hints dropped about a club not far from here. Evasive maneuvers and fascination with the nicked and worn table tops were enough to end the interaction which had gone from annoying to painful.

"I guess that's something we'll have to get used to, right?" Berk's uncomfortable chuckle did nothing to raise the stale mood. "I'm going to call Jules." He threw down some bills and jumped up from the table, rushing off like he was afraid she'd find out he took some pictures with a few overzealous fans.

On our floor, Keyton stopped outside my door. "I hope whatever's going on with you works out okay. You don't have to talk about it. I know sometimes it doesn't help one bit, but we've got your back no matter what it is, and Marisa's the number one lined up for you. It's hard to find people who'll go to the mat for you like that." He rocked back on his heels, turning and walking toward his hotel room.

I sat on the edge of the bed trying not to let all the worst case scenarios eat at me. Things were so close to falling in place. So close to finally being perfect, I couldn't deal with being blindsided right now.

———

BACK AT THE HOUSE, I RAN UP THE STAIRS TAKING THEM TWO AT a time. I burst into Marisa's room.

She pretended she didn't check when I landed, but I knew she did. Only she wasn't here now.

Her computer, my old one from last year, wasn't on her desk. She didn't normally lug it around to classes. It was a brick and a half. And her backpack wasn't here either, although she didn't have classes.

Maybe she was studying in the library. But she hated studying there, especially when she had the house to herself.

Me: Marisa, I'm back. Where are you?

A text bubble popped up and disappeared. No message came through.

I called my mom and paced in my room before heading downstairs to sit by the window.

My head dropped and shot back up. I rubbed my eyes, barely keeping them open and checked my phone again.

No response to my message. It was almost midnight.

She never stayed out this late.

Now the scenarios were spinning in my head.

I sent another message.

Me: Where are you? Are you okay? It's late.

The text bubble popped up again. Some of the tightness clenched in my gut eased.

Marisa: I'm fine.

Me: When are you coming home?

Marisa: I'm not coming back tonight

Me: When are you coming back?

Marisa: Go to bed. I'm sure you're tired.

Me: Where are you?

Marisa: Out. I'm not responding anymore. I'm fine. Goodnight.

Standing in the center of the living room, I chucked my phone at the couch. Frustration filled every cell in my body. I needed her here. I wanted her here. The only thing that had kept me from losing it with the news of my dad was knowing Marisa would be waiting for me at home.

I'd been ready to drag her to bed. Screw anyone else knowing about us.

"You're up late." Keyton sat on the middle of the staircase, staring at me from between the bars.

"Marisa's not coming home tonight."

He scooted down a couple more steps. "That's unusual." There was a measured tone and cadence to his voice, like he was waiting to see exactly how I felt about that.

Shitty. Angry. Anxious. That's how I felt about it.

"Did something happen?"

"No." I scrubbed my hands down my face suddenly feeling all the weight bearing down on my shoulders. "I don't know."

"Is this relationship stuff or something else?" He stood at the bottom of the steps.

"Are we even in a relationship?" I dropped onto the couch and braced my forearms on my legs, squeezing my hands together.

"Not that I haven't tried to purge the image from my head, but you two certainly seem like you're more than friends."

"I want us to be. I've wanted us to be, but she's throwing up road blocks every step of the way."

"Maybe she's scared." He lifted one shoulder. "When people are scared they do some crazy things. Terrible things they wouldn't normally do." A haunted look crossed his face.

"What is she scared of?" I looked to him, wanting someone to have answers to the questions roaring in my head.

"That'll be up to you to find out." He patted my shoulder and headed back upstairs.

I interlocked my fingers at the back of my head and stared out the window at the quiet street outside. Tracking her down was the first thing on my list, but fear gripped my heart. The stakes had been raised. The results still weren't back from my dad and now Marisa was gone. I couldn't lose two people I loved, and there was only one I could do something about. I wasn't going to give up without all the answers I needed.

CHAPTER 27
MARISA

"Marisa?"

I shot up from the comfy leather couch in the Art History department, shoving the blanket behind me. "Professor Morgan. What are you doing here?"

She stared back at me, taking in the limited sprawl of my things with her keys gripped in her hand.

"What are *you* doing here? Are you sleeping here?" There was no censure in her tone, only concern.

"No, of course not." It didn't even sound convincing to me. Not with the overstuffed backpack, bedtime ponytail and blanket bulging behind my back.

She tilted her head.

My shoulders sank and I slumped back.

"How long have you been sleeping here?"

"Only one night. I came in after the cleaners left on Friday. I figured I'd have the weekend to figure something out."

"You don't have anywhere to go?"

"Not really."

She picked up my backpack. "Come with me."

"I swear, I'll leave right now." The last thing I needed was a write-up for crashing in university offices or something.

"You're not in trouble." She slung the backpack onto her shoulder. "I have a guest house you're welcome to stay in. You've had the worst luck with living arrangements, haven't you?"

"Something like that." Only this time, it was a self-imposed exile.

"It was a fire last year, wasn't it?"

"Yeah." I gathered up my blanket and tried not to feel like a mooch for bumming a place to sleep off my professor. "You don't have to offer up your house. I can find somewhere else to stay."

"Don't worry about it. If you use it, I'll feel less terrible about actually having a guest house."

"When you put it that way…" I followed Professor Morgan out to her car. She kept the conversation light, sticking mostly to discussions of art.

Inside the guest house, she helped me make the bed and set out towels. "I don't want to pry, but you can talk to me if you need to. I'm an art historian, not a therapist, so my advice might suck big time, but it's worth a shot."

The one-bedroom guest house with a full kitchen and bathroom was nicer than most hotels. Professor Morgan had done well for herself, although her worn leather briefcase, broken-in slide on flats, and the way she could never stay away from the cookie spread at any of the Art Department events had never screamed 'rich person'.

I picked my bag up from the floor and put it in the armchair beside the bed. "A lot is going on right now, and I'm probably not handling it in the most mature way possible." Not in the slightest, really, and I hated myself for it. I'd sent Jill a text to see how Charlie was doing. I hadn't been able to eat without worry. He wasn't someone who deserved this, and even though it was crazy, it felt like I'd failed him—them. That I'd messed up somehow, and he'd have years stolen from his life because my bone marrow wasn't strong enough or good enough.

"We all have our moments." Her dry chuckle did nothing to put my mind at ease. "Is this school, family or guy related?"

I sat on the edge of the bed and peered up at her. My mind was a churning cauldron of chaos. I hadn't been able to think straight since the last text from LJ. I'd been scared to go back to the house, especially after seeing the pictures he'd been tagged in on social media, where he'd been cozying up with some football fans at a bar. Why didn't he just take me out back and shoot me to put me out of my misery?

Charlie was possibly fighting for his life and LJ was out playing superstar. I didn't know what was scarier, talking to LJ or not talking to LJ. I'd been tempted more than once to call Jill and find out what was happening with Charlie, but that would be too much loss for one day. Hell, for one lifetime.

"All of the above."

She sat beside me. "A triple whammy. It's hard to know which way is up with those."

"It sure is."

"If you want to talk. I'm here. Well, actually, over there." She pointed to the white-trimmed, brick, two-story house that had to be way outside a professor's salary range.

"I appreciate it. And I'll be out of here as soon as I figure out my next steps."

"No need to rush." She popped up. "Here's a key. And here's my phone number, if you need anything." She scribbled the digits on a notepad by the front door.

"You really don't have to do this."

"We all need a little help sometimes. Don't worry about it and you can pay it forward the next chance you get."

I mumbled a thank you.

She closed the door behind her.

Walking to the bedroom, I stared at the phone I'd turned off a couple days ago. My fingers brushed against the dead, black screen. I needed to prepare myself, to fortify my mind and my heart against what was coming.

I'd also sent an email to the Venice team apologizing for how late I'd been in giving them the information they needed to enroll me in the master's program.

Curling up in bed, I hugged one of the freshly laundered pillows and buried my face in the soft down. I missed him.

The tears spilled down my cheeks, catching me off guard. It took nothing more than a thought before I was a mess all over again. Bleary-eyed and sniffling, I drifted off to sleep trying not to think about everything I was about to lose—if I hadn't lost it already.

———

THE SMELLS OF THE MUSEUM USED TO BE COMFORTING, AN ESCAPE from the real world where everything was labelled, cataloged, protected. Today, all they did was remind me of where I'd be going in three months after graduation.

Staying at Professor Morgan's place for the past two days hadn't been so bad, other than the crushing loneliness and fear of facing my real life outside the one-bedroom Pottery Barn guest house.

I left all my classes through alternate exits, or skipped them, if I could. Not that LJ was looking for me. I wasn't sure which would be worse: that he might be waiting for me outside of each class or that he was avoiding *me*.

Had there been any news from Charlie's doctors? The knots in my stomach had been grating and grinding, making it hard to choke down anything. The fear of hearing the disappointment or anger in their voices if the cancer had come back had kept my phone turned off, no matter how much I'd wanted to know.

Today, I was at the museum, in my museum tour clothes, with my museum tour group—twenty-nine seventh graders who looked as happy to be here as I did.

At least this gave me something to fill my time with other than obsessing over the betrayal of LJ brushing off my call and going out for drinks with random women, or the panic that I'd failed one of the people who meant the most to me.

I walked through the ground floor of the museum, droning on through the lines I'd long since committed to memory. My heart wasn't in it one bit.

"This is the Arms & Armor exhibit. Wander around and see if you can answer the questions on the crossword puzzle and we'll meet back here in ten minutes." Some of the boys perked up and rushed off, heading straight for the wall of swords and maces.

The twenty-eight seventh-graders took off in ten different directions with their buddies. Their teachers were on herding duty.

"Marisa."

My heart stuttered and I turned to face the familiar voice I'd hoped to avoid for as long as possible. "What are you doing here?" I gripped my anger tight. It was a much safer, less scary emotion than all the others rushing through my head.

His face twisted with disbelief. "What do you think I'm doing? I'm not here to take in the art."

"I'm working." I seethed, keeping my voice low. He'd announced to everyone that he was single and ready to mingle, and he'd hooked up with some chicks just hours after texting me to say now wasn't a good time. "You need to leave."

"I wouldn't have had to show up here, if you'd answered my texts." His eyebrows dipped, and worry eclipsed anger, which brought out the little red flushes on his jaw.

"Time apart seemed like the best idea." My heart thudded in my chest, blood hammering in my ears.

"After a five-hour flight, I get to the house and you're gone."

"Why do you think that might be, LJ?" The anger that had been partially extinguished roared back. I replayed his words over in my head. "You said the only people going to the draft were your parents."

"I did. What was I supposed to say? Any time I've mentioned maybe telling people we're together, you recoil like I asked you to shove your head into a fire."

"You didn't have to say my name, but you could've said there was someone. Not that you had a giant glowing available sign over your head. Women were posting pictures of you cozied up to them after you sent me a text saying you're too busy to talk. Your messages came in loud and clear."

Confusion flashed across his face. "They were fans who wanted a picture. One picture and me, Berk and Keyton all left for our rooms."

My lips parted.

"Alone!"

A couple people stared at us as they passed by.

I flashed a smile before turning back to LJ. My cheeks felt like splintering glass.

He clenched his hands at his sides. "I wanted let everyone know. After the fight with your dad I was all for telling whoever you wanted."

I stepped in closer and jabbed my finger at the center of his chest. "You're the one who suggested it in the beginning." And once the word had gotten out on campus that he and I were dating, everyone would have been laser-focused on how he'd suddenly gotten more game time, or maybe Ron would've changed his mind and benched him completely. "You set the rules."

"Because any other time we've ever gotten that close, you've backed off like our kiss senior year."

I shook my head trying to follow his time jump and find out how that was somehow *my* fault. "You kissed me and then said thanks for saving Charlie's life, like it was my reward for donating bone marrow. I didn't want you to like me because I'd helped your dad—and what if it hadn't worked? You'd have never wanted to speak to me again."

"Is that what you think?"

I folded my arms over my chest and glanced to the side. The kids were wandering closer with their papers. A herd of them headed toward us. We needed to finish this now. I wanted to claw back the words and say I was sorry, but the fear and shame rode me hard, making it impossible to see anything but his eventual exit and my disintegration. "It's what I know."

His jaw clenched and he leaned in, growling, with eyes darting to the people strolling through the exhibit admiring the artifacts. "I thought we should keep it quiet because I didn't want you to blurt it out at dinner with your dad to piss him off and ruin any chances you two had to maybe get on speaking terms." He stepped closer, but I held my ground.

I gritted my teeth and checked over my shoulder for the marauding middle schoolers. "Aren't you the fucking saint? You didn't want him to know because you were trying to protect your chances in the draft."

"Yes, also that." His shoulders sagged before his eyes blazed again. "Can you blame me?"

"No, I can't. Of course you should've put your future first and I have to do the same for myself. It's good this happened." I rocked back, trying to put some space between us. "It's good I know where we stand because…" I licked my lips and sucked in a breath. "I'm going to Italy."

His mouth opened and snapped shut. Head shooting up and eyes bulging. "But you don't have the money."

My mouth was sawdust dry. "My dad signed the tuition waiver at the end of last semester. When I went to pay, the balance was already at zero." I shrugged like it was no big deal. Like my heart didn't feel like it was being clawed out of my chest. This was the beginning of the end. Why draw it out?

He stepped back. "You've known this since November."

"I hadn't decided." I truly hadn't, but thanked my lucky stars I'd had the Plan B to fall back on.

"You've been keeping this from me since November."

"It's not like I was hiding it. I just didn't mention it." The heat dropped off at the end of the sentence. The vehemence had been replaced by guilt.

"I tiptoed around Italy because I didn't want to bring up any bad feelings you might have about not being able to go. All the plans you let me think about what we could do this summer and how we'd spend it before training camp…" He shook his head and stared at me like I was a stranger.

Nausea roiled in my stomach.

"How could you keep this from me?"

The words stalled in my throat and bile rushed to overtake them. There was no going back now.

CHAPTER 28
LJ

flashed back to all the conversations. All initiated by me, made more and more elaborate by me. "The whole time I was making plans for us, you were planning on making your big escape." The gut punch was unlike any I'd felt on the field. It was a cleats-meet-soft-belly punt without warning.

"This isn't about me." She shook her head, eyes glistening, and I wanted to shake her.

I threw up my hands and let them collapse at my sides, frustration throbbing in my head. "Of course this is about you, Marisa."

All of this was collapsing slowly on top of me, and I couldn't stop it. It was hard to breathe. "I'm scared, Marisa. The draft. My dad." I let out a shuddering breath, trying to hold it together. "I need you to be there for me."

Her nostrils flared and her chin quivered. The sheen on her eyes glistened brighter. "Your family is strong. You guys made it through it before. You've got the guys. They'll have your back." She dipped her head and stared at the center of my chest.

Who was this woman in front of me? She wasn't the one I

loved. This was the scared shell she'd put on to protect herself, and nothing I'd say could get through that. It was hardened and secure.

"My dad could be sick again."

She brushed a finger under her eye and met mine. Dampness stained her cheek. "Looks like the Marisa Magic has finally worn off." She cleared her throat.

"This was never about what you did for us—for him. It was about me loving you."

"Do you honestly think you'd still love me if he was sick again?" Her voice cracked. "If he's sick again and my bone marrow didn't work this time? How could I look any of you in the eye again?"

"So your plan is to just never look at any of us ever again? Move to Italy and forget you ever knew us?"

Her lips trembled, but she kept them locked together.

I let out a humorless laugh and shook my head, staring at the armor and weapons behind the glass and mounted on the walls behind her.

If someone had come up and pounded me in the chest with a broad sword, it couldn't hurt worse than what I felt right now.

"You're right, Marisa."

Her lips parted.

"We were never going to work. You've been running away from the beginning. Bags packed, and foot halfway out the door, ready to bolt at the slightest hint of a future."

I stepped back, needing to put space between us. "You've always said you can't understand how he did what he did, and that you're nothing like your dad. Turns out you are wrong. You're exactly like him, pushing away and running from the people who love you."

A sound escaped her throat, halfway between a gasp and a sob. Her face fell, dropped just like my heart had and still was, sinking to the bottom of an abyss deep under the sea, being crushed by the pressure.

"Bye, Marisa."

I turned and shoved my hands into my pockets, walking outside into the still blisteringly cold early April afternoon. My legs felt waterlogged, like concrete should have been breaking under every step.

Numbness radiated through me, muffling and clouding everything.

Sitting inside my car, I stared out the windshield and gripped the steering wheel. My breaths were choppy and strained, and my blood screamed through my veins.

Unable to hold back, I released a scream and slammed my hands against the wheel, jerking it so hard I thought it might rip free from the column. Exhausted, I collapsed back into my seat and watched people walking by in their coats and hats, smiling, laughing, and holding hands. Kids ran to catch up with their parents.

This was a lot like the first time I'd left the hospital after visiting my dad. The rest of the world carried on as though mine hadn't imploded, like it hadn't been broken and shattered.

I'd been sliced to the bone, and the surgeon hadn't even had the decency to pump me full of anesthesia first. Defeated and deflated, I fell over the steering wheel and looked up at the white stone building where Marisa was. I hadn't thought there would ever be a day in my life when she wasn't by my side, whether physically or not. But now, I was riding out into what came next all alone.

———

IT WAS DARK BY THE TIME I GOT BACK HOME. I DON'T EVEN remember where I went. Everything was a blur. The fog of my feelings was so thick, it was hard to breathe.

"LJ?" Keyton called out from his room.

I gripped the top of the railing. "Yeah, it's me."

"Is Marisa here too?"

Steadying myself, I closed my eyes. "No, she's not here." I walked to his doorway.

He sat on his bed with a sketch pad and pencil balanced on his lap. "Where is—" Following my gaze, he dropped the pencil and flipped over the pad, clearing his throat. "Where is she?"

Leaning out his door, I looked down the hallway.

"Berk's not here. He's at Jules's place."

"Right. Listen, what you saw before with me and Marisa…"

His gaze dropped to the floor between us, a tomato red creep crawling up his neck.

"Just forget about it, okay? There's nothing to worry about anymore." I slammed my eyes shut. My heart feeling like it was being torn apart muscle fiber by muscle fiber.

"Who was worried?" He jumped up from his bed. "She's not staying with Liv, is she?"

"Honestly, I have no idea."

"You two broke up?"

"Can you break up with someone you were never even really in a relationship with?"

He sat on the edge of his desk right beside his window. "Maybe, maybe not, but that doesn't mean it won't still hurt like a motherfucker."

"Tell me about it."

"What happened?" He stared back at me, not with suspicion or skepticism, but open like he really couldn't figure out what would've gone wrong.

I slumped against his wall. "Honestly? I have no fucking clue. Things were great. At first, I wanted to keep things quiet because of her dad. And she went along with it, but later I didn't want to sneak around with her."

"She didn't feel the same?"

"She flipped it around on me. Then, I was the one who wanted to be open about it, and she wanted to keep it quiet. Like she was hedging against us ending—planning for it."

I slid down the wall and stared out the window beside Keyton.

"She wasn't ready." It wasn't a question.

"When we were together it was better than I ever thought it could be. I love her." I felt burned out, like the husk of who I'd been only a couple days ago.

"It's scary shit, having someone love you that much. It's scary feeling like you don't deserve it, and if it goes away, then what does that mean about you?" He dropped down to the floor with his back against the desk. "And when you're the one loving someone when they can't see it for themselves, you're bound to get burned. They almost can't stop themselves from trying to prove to you that your love's not real. They try to force your hand until they prove it to you."

I lifted my chin in the direction of his bed. "Is that who she is to you? The one you loved who burned you?"

He leaned over and grabbed the notepad off the bed and stared at it for a long time. "No, I'm the one who did the burning. And she was right to run." He slid the notepad across the floor.

Staring back up at me was a pretty girl, a little younger than us, with a hidden smile and clear eyes. "You drew this?" I handed it back to him.

"It's all I can seem to draw."

"When did you last see her?"

"Almost four years ago. At high school graduation."

"You haven't seen her since."

"I don't think she'd want to see me. We were...complicated. More complicated than we should've been, and we didn't have the history you and Marisa have."

"The history didn't do much good."

"I wouldn't say that."

"Do you think she'll ever forgive you for whatever you did?"

A faraway look shadowed over his face. "Some things you can't come back from. Some things haunt you even when you try to move on." He stared down at the paper and ran his finger along the sheet.

"I hope you get to see her again. Maybe show her you've changed." After knowing Keyton for three years, I couldn't imagine him ever hurting anyone. Maybe that was how it happened. The ones you least suspected could reach right into your chest and pull out your heart. I pushed up off the wall and walked to the door.

"I hope you're right. You—" He stood and set the notebook down on the desk. "You should at least hear her out when she comes back."

"I don't even know if she will." I shook my head, still not believing she'd be leaving after telling me she wasn't.

"She will. She loves you, and that's some scary shit. Once you realize it, there's no going back."

"I don't know. She hated how her dad ran out on her family, but he was trying to reconnect with her. Her mom isn't the greatest, so having him there would've been great."

Keyton tilted his head staring at me for a long time before letting out a breath. "I know it's hard for you to understand." He rocked back on his heels and glanced up at the ceiling like the words he was looking for were up there. "Sometimes parents fucking suck. I'm not talking about getting grounded for bad grades or having to take out the trash. They're the people who're supposed to love us most, but it gives them an in. They can also be the people with the first crack at hurting us most."

Bile churned in my stomach. This didn't sound like he was talking in abstracts.

"Your parents are great. They love you. They're proud of

you. They'll be there for you. Some of us aren't so lucky. We've never had any stability or feeling that if our life goes to shit there's a safe harbor for us. Sometimes you're on your own and sometimes it's better that way. Just because two people made a kid doesn't mean they're true parents and it doesn't mean they deserve all the chances in the world."

He crossed the room and dropped his hand onto my shoulder. "If her dad is the stand-up guy who can be a dad to her, then that's for her and him to figure out. You can't force it. It's got to be her choice on whether she wants to let her father be a dad. But it can't go at the speed you think it should."

With a squeeze, he let me go.

Shoving my hands into my pockets, I nodded. "Night."

I closed my door, changed, and crawled into bed. My clothes spilled out over the top of my laundry basket in my closet.

Keyton had been right about so many things. Fixing was what I wanted to do. My fingers itched to dive in and get to work, smoothing everything out.

There was no walking this back, only the long hard road of pushing ahead.

She had to figure this out after I'd put all my cards on the table. She'd decide what to do with her dad. There was no room for my interference anymore.

I couldn't make us work if she didn't believe in us—in me. I couldn't make her stop running. I couldn't make her love me like I loved her.

CHAPTER 29
MARISA

The door opened behind me. All the laughter, kids' TV shows, and music was amplified when it wasn't muffled by the door.

"Marisa?"

I looked up from the cold spot on the top of the concrete steps in front of Ron's house.

Surprise was scrawled all over his face. "Are you okay? What happened?" He leapt down the two steps and crouched in front of me. His hand hovered over my arms wrapped around my knees, like he was afraid to touch me.

I didn't blame him. I was pretty toxic. I was surprised LJ hadn't figured that out years ago. He was right. I'd been waiting for this shoe to drop from the moment he'd first smiled at me looking up from his multiplication worksheets.

"Sorry." It came out like a froggy croak. I cleared my throat. Coming here had been a mistake. I didn't know why I'd done it. Why, out of all the places in the world I could've gone, had I shown up here?

I dropped my arms and scooted to the edge of the step.

His hand came down on my arm, stopping me.

"Don't be sorry. Please, tell me what's going on. You're scaring me." The concern in his voice broke me.

I burst into tears. Deep, racking sobs dredged from the depths of my soul. The kind that left me gasping for air and fighting against the invading lightheadedness.

Ron moved beside me and wrapped his arm around me. He held me close, and I buried my face in his chest, holding onto his sweater like I might blow away at any second.

His noises of comfort only made it worse. The low murmur that it would be alright was something I'd only ever gotten from LJ's parents the one time I'd broken down after a bad fight with my mom.

The sobbing gave way to tears, which gave way to embarrassment.

I pulled back. Ron let me sit straight up, but didn't take his arm from around my shoulder.

"Come inside." I looked behind us. Someone had closed the door, probably not wanting to hear the hysterical breakdown of that random girl on the doorstep.

"No, it's okay. I shouldn't have come. I'm sorry I did."

"Please don't say that." The pain in his voice sliced me deep.

I wanted to be angry. I wanted to fall straight into that emotion around him. But more than that, I wanted answers.

I needed to finally ask the questions that had taken up residence in the dark, cobwebbed corner of my brain that I pretended didn't exist and that I didn't care about.

"Did—" Sucking in a shuddering breath, I shivered not from the cold, but from the fear overtaking every cell in my body. "Did you ever—" My voice cracked and I wiped my nose with my sleeve. "Did you ever miss me?" The tears I'd thought were finished filled my eyes. I blinked to keep them from cresting over the edges of my eyelids. "Did you ever wish you hadn't left, or that you'd come back for me?"

The words came out in a rush, like my mouth didn't trust

the rest of my body not to take off running down the street before they all came tumbling out.

He stared back at me, ruddy faced, with tears dripping off his chin onto his sweater. "Every day."

"You didn't even come after me when I left."

His jaw clenched. "I wanted to. I wanted to run right after you when LJ did, but Nora suggested I give you some space. She thought I should wait for you to come to me, if I hadn't fucked things up beyond repair already. Whatever relationship we had—we have—needed to be on your terms. Not mine."

I stared into his eyes, which swam with uncertainty and the smallest shred of hope.

Clearing his throat, he covered his mouth with his hand and stared up at the sky. "I've made a lot of mistakes—more than you ever need to know about—but they all pale in comparison to not being the dad you deserved. And that's a regret I'll carry for the rest of my life. But I hope it won't be one you have to. Wait one second." He jumped up and rushed back inside.

I sat on the steps and fished some tissues out of my pockets, using ten and shoving them back into my pockets before he came back.

The door opened again and he sat beside me with a piece of paper held between his two hands. It was long and thin, with numbers and letters written on it. "I wasn't ever sure if I'd give this to you."

He looked over at me. Sweat beaded on his forehead even though it was in the 40s. His hands shook, and he held out the paper to me. "The top one is the email provider. The middle is the username and the bottom one is the password. I owe you so much more than is there, but I hope maybe it'll help answer some of the questions you have."

I stood, and he did too, his eyes darting to the paper between my fingers.

"I have always and will always love you, Marisa."

I nodded, but didn't hug him back, still trying to figure out what was going on and what waited for me when I logged into the inbox.

Professor Morgan's house wasn't far from Ron's. I ran most of the way. I was still in my coat, sweaty and clammy, as I dove for my computer.

With trembling fingers, I had to type in the password twice along with the username ForMarisaSaunders before it would log me in.

The inbox loaded and I slammed my laptop closed. My chest was tight like a fist was squeezing it, not letting my heart fully pump. I unbuttoned and slid off my coat. With shaky fingers, I took my laptop from the desk in the living room to the coffee table.

I sat on the floor and took a long, unsteady breath before opening the laptop lid again. All the emails had loaded.

There were over 1500 of them. I reverse sorted them by date to see the very first one. I gasped and covered my mouth with both hands. It was dated the day after my dad left. Daily emails stretched out over the first three years he'd been gone. Weekly for five years or so and monthly until they picked back up to weekly once I'd started at Fulton U. I went back to the first email and clicked the unread message.

———

TO: FORMARISASAUNDERS@GMAIL.COM
    FROM: ronald.saunders@gmail.com
    SUBJECT:
Dear Marisa,

I hope you'll never have to see this. I hope tomorrow I'll be able to come home and you'll run up to me and give me a big hug like you always did when I came home from the road. But now I'm not sure of much, least of all when I'll be able to see you again.

No matter what happens, I want you to know I have always and will always love you. And I hope this message never makes it to you. I hope I can delete this account or forget about it, but a part of me is scared to death it won't be the case.

Love you always,
Dad

———

I CHOSE ANOTHER EMAIL A YEAR LATER.

———

TO: FORMARISASAUNDERS@GMAIL.COM
FROM: ronald.saunders@gmail.com
SUBJECT: Happy Belated Birthday
Marisa,

I'm struggling today. I really am, and I wonder how much to even tell you in these emails. Your birthday has come and gone. Did you get the presents I sent? Your mom said she'd give them to you, but at this point I don't even know. She's missed more court dates than she's made, and each one seems to mean I'm further away from finally being able to see you again.

I refuse to bad mouth your mother to you, and I hope she's doing the same. I truly love you and miss you so much. It hurts knowing I won't be able to watch you open your Christmas presents again this year.

I've turned down two jobs on the west coast because I don't want to be too far away, in case you need me, but every day it seems like my chances of getting to hug you on your birthday are worse and worse.

Love you always,
Dad

———

I SKIPPED TO THE EMAIL FROM RIGHT AFTER I CONTACTED HIM about coming to Fulton U. As much as I'd hated to reach out to him, once I found out about the tuition waiver and knowing LJ had been there, I'd been willing to send the email. New York had been everything I'd hoped for, but I'd missed LJ. It hurt how much I missed him. So I'd leapt at the chance to go to Fulton U where I had the perfect cover for following him there. They had a great museum studies program, stellar museums and the one person I didn't want to live without.

But sending the email hadn't been easy. And two months of psyching myself up to meet with Ron after he'd said yes.

———

TO: FORMARISASAUNDERS@GMAIL.COM
     FROM: ronald.saunders@gmail.com
     SUBJECT:
You're so grown up now, Marisa. It makes me so proud and hurts me so deeply that I've missed all your milestones. It's been so long since I've seen you, it's hard to reconcile the strong, determined young lady who showed up in my Coach's office with the little girl missing two front teeth who I carried around on my shoulders.

Coming back to Philly was the best choice for me because it meant I was closer to you, and the risk paid off, but from our first talk I don't know if I'll ever be able to make any of this up to you. Actually, I know I won't. For some reason, saying those words to you is so much harder than writing these letters. I still don't know if you'll ever see them. You'll probably think I was crazy for talking to myself all these years.

I hope we can bridge the gap between us and get to know one another. It's my fault I missed so much. I should've fought harder, no matter what the lawyers or judges said. I should've, but I gave up because it hurt too much to get my hopes up only to have them killed over and over again. It's no excuse. What kind of father doesn't fight for his little girl? I was a coward, afraid I couldn't do right by you, and now I don't know if I'll ever even get to know you.

You're a beautiful, driven woman, and I wish I'd been the father you deserved.

Love you always,

Dad

———

TO: ForMarisaSaunders@gmail.com
   FROM: ronald.saunders@gmail.com
   SUBJECT:
Marisa,

You were right about so many things today. It hurts to know how true it all was. So much of my frustration and anger was taken out on someone you love, who loves you too. I see the way you two communicate with a look, never saying a word, and I wish I knew you that well.

I don't and he does. In a lot of ways, I see myself in LJ, but he's proven he's better than I was. He's willing to make the big sacrifice plays to protect the people he cares about. Maybe my testing him was trying to see how far he'd go, but I already know it was farther than me.

He's exceptional on the field. Even without playing, his star will rise, and I'm afraid of what that'll do to you two. I don't want to be the reason another person in your life lets you down. I do hope he's a better man than me like I suspect he is, but I'm still afraid that once his star rises, it'll end with you hurt again.

I'll do what's right because I don't want to lose you. I never wanted to lose you, but I think I might have. Forever. I hope that's not the case. I feel like I use hope so often in these letters to you, but here's one thing I know. I love you and I'll always love you.

Dad

———

I READ THE LAST EMAIL WHEN THE SUN ROSE OVER THE HORIZON. My eyes felt like they'd been buffed by sandpaper. A mountain of tissues sat in a pile beside me on the bed. I'd gotten snapshots of my dad's life over the past fourteen years: the way he'd jumped at the chance to take the position at Fulton U, how hard it had been for him to not say a word against my mother. Even if the emails didn't go into details, I could fill in the blanks—hell, I'd lived them.

The presents he'd sent. The visits he'd tried to make. The court dates that came and went without the chance to see me.

My brain understood it all. I could piece together how difficult it had been, but in my heart, that little girl still wanted her dad to be the guy who rode in on the horse to save the day. Only, this wasn't a fairytale. It was the real world, and in the real world, there were court orders and job opportunities, and none of it worked out how we wanted it to.

This didn't solve anything, not by a long shot. The gaping wound in my chest that I'd tried to cover over when it came to Ron wasn't deepening, though. It might even be healing a little.

And it showed me how alike he and I were. Just like LJ had said.

I fell back in the bed and stared at the shadow pattern on

the ceiling from the slitted blinds. The first people I was supposed to depend on had failed me. There was no other way to slice it, even knowing more about my dad's side of things—so how could I have expected LJ to weather the storms coming our way?

Only, I should've.

He'd been the one person I could turn to no matter what. The one person who'd never let me down. The one person who'd lied to protect me when all it did was hurt him. He'd proven himself time and time again, but at even a hint of trouble, I'd run. No, I'd pushed him away.

He'd been right about me, but I wasn't going to be that person anymore.

All I could hope was it wasn't too late to show him how much I loved him and salvage our relationship.

CHAPTER 30

LJ

C lasses dragged. Spring workouts dragged. Even fielding questions from fans about what was coming next dragged. It all slowed to an excruciating pace, grinding out day after day.

Even hearing that my dad's results had all come back negative and he could now switch to annual visits instead of every six months hadn't lifted my spirits like it should have.

There was a Marisa-sized hole in my life, and I hated it.

The look on her face when I'd told her she was like her dad had felt like someone had reached inside my chest and squeezed my heart to the point of failure. But I couldn't take it back. I couldn't be with her if she didn't believe we could make it—if she wasn't one hundred percent as heart-poundingly, body-tinglingly, soul-scorchingly in love with me as I was with her.

"Hey, you want to head out? The taxi's here." Berk poked his head into my bedroom. "You okay?" He stepped inside the darkened room.

"I'm good." It was a bitter pill to swallow that I couldn't even talk to him about Marisa. Telling him everything now felt like it would only invite more questions, and they would be questions I either didn't have the answers to or didn't want to answer. Looked like my plan had worked out.

A hysterical, not remotely humorous laugh came out like a wicked witch's cackle.

Berk froze and tilted his head. "Are you sure you're okay?"

No. Not even a little bit. I stood from my chair and grabbed my coat. "Hell, yes, let's get fucked up."

Without waiting for Berk, I rushed down the stairs.

Jules and Keyton stood by the front door.

They both flinched when they saw me.

Was it my five days of stubble? My probably-smelly pits? Or was it my Joker smile? "Who's ready to go out?" I clapped my hands and rubbed them together. "Let's go out."

Berk padded down the stairs. "Are you sure you're good?"

I wheeled around. "Totally. Never better."

He looked from Jules to Keyton. "Maybe we should wait for Marisa. Is she still keeping Liv company while Ford's traveling?"

I was running out of excuses. Not exactly wanting to face the fact she might not come back. I channeled my sadness into the need to get blind-fucking drunk.

Keyton barged in before I could drop into full hyena laughter. "She said she had a study group tonight."

"Yup, she's long gone. Let's go." I jerked the door open and headed outside. Inside was too close. The walls pressed in with every minute I sat there thinking about what happened next.

It would be a lot better to get blitzed. I didn't have to be responsible anymore. The season was over. The combine was over. There was nothing left to do but wait for my future to be decided by some big wigs in stadium sky boxes, and hope my agent turned up with a draft invitation.

That would mean I'd go in the first, second, or possibly

third round. But right now, all I could think about was the woman I'd loved not being able to love me back, which called for booze. A lot of booze.

"LJ!" A collective shout from behind me.

I spun around.

Berk, Jules, and Keyton stood beside the open door to the taxi waiting in the middle of the street.

Berk cupped his hands around his mouth. "The taxi, remember?"

Marching back toward them, I kept my gaze diverted and walked around to the front passenger seat of the car.

The three of them silently got into the back seats. Their doors closed with a muffled thud. In the mirrors, I could see them whispering and exchanging glances.

The bar was already bursting with people when we arrived.

Inside, Berk herded us to a booth, which was already occupied. Reece and Nix sat in the middle beside Seph and Elle. Exactly what I didn't need right now: the whole gang back together.

Jules grabbed Elle in a former-roommate reunion. All the guys exchanged bro hugs and sat, but my knee bounced under the table as everyone filled the group in about what was going on with them.

Reece's update on his first pro season was the most interesting. Everyone wanted to know about our agents, draft rumors and what else we had going on.

I wanted to get up from the table and get a drink. My chair scraped against the floor and I nearly took out a server with a tray of drinks. "I'm going to order at the bar. I'll get something for everyone."

A server stood beside our table with a notepad out.

"Second round. So we don't have to wait to order." I disappeared into the crowd of people and went straight up to the bar, finding the only free spot beside the high-backed barstools that only trendy places had.

I waved for the bartender's attention. She came over after taking a couple other orders.

"Can I get four Sam Adams and three vodka cranberries? And two double shots of vodka right now?"

She took my card and started a tab, returning with the double shots of vodka while she made the rest of the rail drinks and opened the beers.

"Is one of those for me?" A brunette on the stool beside me leaned in with a light and airy smile.

I glanced down at the shots and back up at her. Lifting one, I handed it over to her.

If I squinted and turned my head to the side, she could look like Marisa. No dent on the bridge of her nose though.

She raised the glass and clinked it against mine. "To a wonderful night."

Keeping my gaze on her, I knocked my shot back, letting it burn all the way down. To a wonderful night.

———

THE POUNDING AT THE FRONT DOOR DIDN'T STOP. HALFWAY down the stairs, the light from the window above the doorway blazed straight into my eyeballs, searing them. A stadium full of people were stomping on my brain. A truck-load of ibuprofen might be a good start.

This was what happened when you were a senior year lightweight. Other guys could drink their body weight in booze, but I hadn't been blitzed in a long time. I'd always needed to be ready during the season and off-season practices. Right now, though, I felt more like I'd been scrambled.

Last night had been a shit show of epic proportions. I'd hoped to sleep it off for the next two to three months. No such luck.

Shielding my eyes, I opened the door.

"Quinn, what are you doing here?" My eighteen-year-old sister stood on the porch in a jacket she'd painted by hand that was reminiscent of the pattern I'd splattered all over the toilet last night.

My parents' sedan idled, double parked, outside the house. "Do Mom and Dad know you have the car?" I dropped my head, squeezing my eyes shut.

"They left for Florida yesterday. Do you really want to bother them with a pesky little detail like me borrowing the car?" She held up her thumb and pointer finger less than half an inch apart.

"What have you done?" I squinted, opening one eye.

She rolled her eyes. "Can you drop out of Dad Mode for a whole ten minutes? I'm here to make a delivery." Held in her hand at eye level was a folded piece of lined notebook paper —the same kind Marisa and I used to trade during high school chemistry. My initials were scrawled over the front of the paper.

I hesitated.

"Like you're not going to take it." She shoved it against my chest.

My hands pressed against the smooth paper, heart punching against my ribs. "Why'd she send you?"

"She wanted to make sure you wouldn't back out of what-ever she has planned."

"She didn't tell you?"

I guess things hadn't changed much.

"About you two dating? And boning constantly? And then her screwing things up? Of course she did."

Spit lodged in my throat at Quinn's bubbly reply.

"Kidding. I'm kidding. She didn't mention anything about sex." She shuddered. "But she said you two had been secretly dating and she'd messed up and wanted to talk to you." Rocking back on her heels, she chewed on the inside of her cheek. "And I totally wasn't supposed to say any of that to you. All I was supposed to say was please read the note and come with me if you wanted to talk to her. Don't tell her I threw in the stuff about boning." She cringed, her cheeks flushing. "That was more of a punishment to myself than I anticipated."

I stared down at the paper in my hands.

"You are coming, aren't you?" Quinn's voice wobbled in panic.

The smooth paper glided under my fingertips. I unfolded it and looked up at Quinn trying to read over the top of the paper.

I closed the door in her face and rested my back against it, staring at the ink and lines, focusing enough to read her note.

———

L,

I know I have no right to ask for this after what happened at the museum, but I'd really like to speak with you. I need to talk to you. After that, well, we'll see, but I need to finally tell you everything. You deserve to know everything. Please meet me at the treehouse.

———

MARISA

———

MY FINGERS GRIPPED EITHER SIDE OF THE PAPER, READING AND re-reading it.

Furious pounding rattled the door.

I jerked it open.

Quinn's hands were anchored to her hips. "Serious—"

"I'll be there, but I need to get ready."

"I can wait." She stepped into the doorway.

"No, I'll be there. I just need some time, okay?"

Chewing on her cheek, she stepped back and nodded. "Don't make me drive back over the bridge, or I'm charging you for the toll."

"Bye, Quinn." I closed the door and stared down at the paper, now crumbled in my hand.

The first thing I needed was coffee. I made myself a gallon and went back upstairs.

In my room, I picked up my clothes off the floor and dumped them into the hamper. Sitting on the edge of my bed, I ran my fingers through my hair and downed the coffee as quickly as I could without scalding myself. Black with no sugar—it was punishment for being such a colossal idiot last night.

Going through the motions, I pulled myself together. I took a scouring shower set as hot as it would go, and then shaved properly. I spent way too long finding clothes to wear, finally settling on a t-shirt and jeans after the fifth change.

Long shadows stretched across the street by the time I pulled myself together enough to get into my car. The sun hung low in the horizon when I pulled into my parent's driveway, parking beside their car.

The curtains at the front of the house ruffled.

I walked up the path to the front door, trying to keep my mind blank. There was a hurricane of emotions roiling inside me, and I didn't know which way this was going. I wasn't sure which were safe to even explore until I spoke to her, which made me want to run the other way and head back into the city.

The front door flew open before I could get out my key.

"The backyard." Quinn whisper-shouted. "Go around the side. That way." She pointed to the left of the house. The well-worn path around the back of the house had recovered over the years.

We used to ditch our bikes right beside the fence and take off toward the back of the house without even stopping inside.

Rounding the corner of the house, I spotted us. Our picture was stuck to a stake driven into the grass. String lights twinkled, wrapped around the stakes and guiding my path lined with even more pictures.

Me and Marisa in the third grade, our arms linked around each other's necks as we sported big, gap-toothed smiles. My mom had been the chaperone on our class trip to the Philly Zoo, and I'd told her to make sure Marisa was in our group. She'd shared one of her chocolate iced TastyKakes with me.

That might've been when I'd fallen in love with her.

There were more stakes—one for each year we'd known each other.

There was the summer after sixth grade, when she'd tagged along with my family to the shore while her mom had been out of town. We'd binged on funnel cake and puked under the boardwalk, so my parents didn't find out and ban us from eating any more.

There we were standing on the stairs with our dates for the eighth-grade dance. She'd been beautiful. I'd gotten jealous—the first time I realized what that felt like—when she'd agreed to go to the dance with Sean McCormack. She'd said it was only because he'd asked her and no one else had. But I'd kissed her beside the bleachers in the gym.

More memories appeared with each step, every one banging into my chest. We had so much history between us. So much of our pasts was intertwined and connected.

The whole family playing board games in the hospital room while my dad recovered after a surgery.

Another stake. Us at high school graduation. My mortar board had poked her in the eye after someone called my name when we'd tried to take a selfie. I laughed, the sound catching in my throat.

I made it to the back of the house.

And there she stood in her museum outfit, like she hadn't changed since that day, but so much had changed. It was hard to catch my breath with the whirlwind in my chest stealing away every inhalation.

The overly-long grass covered the sides of her shoes. Flowers my mom would plant when they came back were lined up along the flowerbeds surrounding the ten feet of paved stone patio outside the back door.

"You came." Her voice wavered, and her lips twitched into an almost-smile, but her eyes were watery.

"I told Quinn I would." I shoved my keys into my pocket and crossed the patio to where she stood in the grass. "She gave me your note." Keeping the restraint on, I kept my hands in my pockets. "What did you want to tell me?"

She fidgeted with her hands in front of her. "I was an idiot. An asshole and an idiot. Everything you said in the museum was true. I was scared and ready to run at the slightest hint that you might leave me first." A deep, shuddering breath. "It's one thing that's been inevitable in my life. But that wasn't fair, because you've never been that person." Her voice cracked. "You've been the one person who I've always been able to be myself with, who's always been there for me, and that made it the hardest to think of you leaving me.

"I don't want to lie to you anymore. And no matter what, whether you can forgive me or not, I need you to know the truth about how I feel. The only thing that comes from people not saying their true feelings is hurt and pain, and I don't want that for you. I'd never want that for you. I don't want to hide any part of myself from you anymore. You leaving…it would've broken me, but—shocker of the century—that happened anyway. Only I did it to myself because I was terrified of what would happen when you moved on."

My mouth was cotton ball dry. "How do you feel now?"

"I'm scared shitless. I'm worried about what will happen when you get drafted. What will happen if I go to Italy. What happens when you find out I know nothing about healthy, caring relationships like your parents, and I make mistakes. I worry you'll finally realize that I'm not good enough for you. And that you'll get tired of trying to choke down my food.

"But most of all, I worry I've destroyed the one relationship that means the most to me in the world. More than anything, I want to be with you in whatever form that takes.

"I love you, LJ. With everything I have, I love you, and even though I'm scared out of my mind, I want to be with you."

The rush of emotions bearing down on me locked me in place, like I'd been soldered to the ground. I couldn't move. I could barely breathe. She'd finally said the words—said them so I felt them. They reached into my chest and bear-hugged my heart.

But she wasn't the only one she needed to come clean about a few things. I licked my lips, trying to figure out the best way to say what I needed her to know.

"There's something…." The words turned to pennies in my mouth, vile, metallic, and acidic. Running my fingers through my hair, I blurted it out. "Last night we went out for drinks and there was a woman."

CHAPTER 31
MARISA

swayed, catching myself before I stumbled. "A woman. At the bar."

I wasn't sure how I'd expected this to go, but puking in the backyard hadn't been in my plans.

"I was looking to numb everything. I ordered two shots just for myself, and she started flirting with me. I gave her one of my shots. We toasted them and downed them both."

The blood drained from my face, pooling at my feet. Burning nudged at the back of my nose. The cool April air singed my nostrils.

"I kept thinking how she looked a lot like you."

My brain, of course, flashed to images of LJ and my evil twin making out at the bar, hands all over one another.

"She invited me to join her at the bar. To have a few more drinks." He stepped closer and I wanted to back up, to run away from the thought of LJ with my doppelgänger falling into bed together or tearing each other's clothes off.

"Did you?" The whisper was barely audible even to my own ears.

He took my hands, stopping my fidgeting, and I stared at the center of his chest.

With his finger under my chin, he raised my head to look me in the eye. "No, I didn't. I had a second where I considered having another drink with her, but I couldn't do more than walk away, because I felt absolutely nothing for her. All I could do was find all the ways you were similar, and discounting each one in her as not measuring up. Because she wasn't you."

A relieved and borderline-hysterical laugh escaped my lips. "I thought you were confessing to taking her home."

"No, Risa." His thumb brushed along the side of my cheek. "Even after everything, a drink with another woman was pushing it for me. I couldn't have done anything more. Not when I'm completely, irrevocably in love with you. You can't rewrite fourteen years of history in a couple weeks."

Tears I'd sworn had run out while we'd been apart came bubbling back, only this time they were happy ones. Everything shone so brightly it felt like my chest was filled with a sunrise. This was the dawn of a whole new era of Marisa and LJ.

"You couldn't have led with that part?" I laughed and flung my arms around his neck, holding him close and breathing in the LJ smell I'd missed.

"I felt a mini-heart attack was warranted after what you put me through."

I held his face between my hands and kissed him—a shoulders up, full body press with his arms trapped between our chests.

His lips were even hungrier than mine. He gulped me down and savored every taste with the flick of his tongue.

My knees dipped, but he had me.

His arm wrapped around my back, holding me, keeping me steady like he always did.

"I missed you." I traced my fingers along his jawline.

"Not nearly as much as I missed you." He peppered my face and neck with kisses, tickling me until I yelped and struggled from his grip. He didn't let go, though—he held onto my hand, our fingers intertwined.

"I've loved you from as far back as I can remember."

He huffed. "As long as you can remember?"

"Let me show you." I took his hand and led him to the treehouse we'd hung out in as kids. Back when we were younger it had felt like it was thirty feet in the air. Now, the tops of our heads reached the bottom edge of the house his dad had made a couple summers before we'd met.

The six-runged ladder wasn't the long scramble it had been when we were two feet shorter.

LJ followed me, and we crammed into the space that had once felt like our own house. Now we were folded into it, on our knees with our heads bumping the roof.

"I haven't been up here in forever." He swatted at a spider web.

This place held so many memories. I used to sneak in here sometimes to sleep when my mom didn't come home. Somehow, staying in the dark back yard of the Lewis house was more comforting than being in my own home alone.

"What did you want to show me?"

Using the flashlight on my phone, I shined the light on the underside of the sill of the small window. We'd had a pulley set up outside the window, and would use it for water balloon ammo storage against other kids in the neighborhood. "It's here."

His eyebrows dipped and he rolled over onto his back, staring up at the worn wooden shelf.

I lay down beside him and stared up at the marks above us, joined together over ten years ago.

"When did you do this?" His head whipped to the side and he stared into my eyes.

"The spring of seventh grade. You guys went to Disneyworld and I hung out here for a while."

"By yourself." Present LJ was angry and scared for Past Marisa.

"It was comfy up here. I had blankets and everything."

He ran his fingers over the markings in the wood. *M + LJ with a heart around it.*

With a Swiss army knife Charlie had given me, I lain here with a camping lantern I'd taken from their garage and etched the wood, staking my middle school claim on LJ.

I rested my head on his shoulder and hugged myself to him. "Younger me had her shit together way before I did."

His lips brushed against my temple. "I'm glad both versions of you are in total agreement now."

Lifting my head, I ran my fingers across his chest. "Totally."

———

TUCKED IN ON THE BOTTOM BUNK OF THE DOUBLE-SIZED BUNK bed, we finished the last of the pizza Quinn had piping hot on the dining room table when we'd come in from the treehouse.

"I was willing to cook for you." I picked up LJ's discarded crust.

He shuddered. "How about a condition of us being together is that you never, ever cook for me or anyone else again unless under direct supervision?"

"Does this mean you'll teach me how to cook?"

"I'll try, but no promises. And no surprise meal preparation." He leveled his crust at me.

I took it from him. "Deal."

He handed me my soda and sat back against the wall that was still covered in posters from high school.

The high from all the declarations was wearing off, and we'd sunk into a comfortable silence like we always had.

"We should talk about Italy."

I stopped chewing, choking down the crust half eaten. "I was thinking about that too."

Professor Morgan would be disappointed, but...

"I don't have to go."

"You have to go."

We said at the same time.

"What?" Again in stereo.

"You have to go."

"I don't have to go. Then we can figure things out after the draft. I can stay here, or find a local job wherever you're going to be."

"You worked hard for this. And it's your dream. The season is nineteen weeks long. Twenty-three once you factor in training camp and the pre-season."

"But—"

He pressed his finger against my lips. "Being with me doesn't mean you have to be with me every minute of the day. As much as I've loved living with you for the past year, I'll be on the road. I'll have a workout schedule and all kinds of other things I'll need to do. Knowing you're off working a job you love and sharing that passion with the people around you—it'll keep me from missing you too much. That and some pretty hot and heavy phone and video chat sessions."

I chuckled.

"Don't think for a second that I don't want you there. But you need to tell me if you can honestly say you wouldn't go regardless of what happened in the backyard."

I leaned back, nibbling on my bottom lip. I wanted to be with him through all these big changes. Taking a moment, I thought about where that need came from. It was a place of fear and worry that somehow, being out of sight, I'd slip from his mind. That wasn't possible. It wasn't true. He loved me, and nothing would change that.

"I want to go." It was whisper-quiet. Looking to him, I took his hand. "I want it."

"Then you'll get it. Once we know what kind of money we're talking about, I'll find a place in Venice. It might be a shoebox, but we'll make it work."

"You'd move to Italy for me?"

"For your fellowship? Of course. Between football seasons, traveling leagues back in high school, and training, I've barely been out of the country for more than a few weeks. I'd love to explore Italy with you." He tucked my hair behind my ear and cupped my cheek.

This heart fluttering every time he looked at me would never get old. The idiot of the century award definitely went to me for ever doubting him.

"My parents and Quinn would love to visit too. Once you're finished, we'll figure it out—together." He squeezed my hand, and the warm sureness of his skin pressed against mine filled my chest with a hopeful happiness I hadn't thought possible. "They'd love it there. Quinn will freak."

"I'll freak about what?"

Quinn poked her head in the door.

"Way to eavesdrop. How long have you been out there?"

She rolled her eyes. "No eavesdropping. I wanted to let you know I'm sleeping over at Stacey's." Her backpack strap hung off one shoulder.

LJ sat up straighter. "Do Mom and Dad know?"

"Do Mom and Dad know you're in here making out with Marisa?"

"Quinn…"

I held onto LJ to keep him from going full brother bear.

"That's Stacey, love you both! Bye!" She bolted, thundered down the stairs, and slammed the door behind her.

"She'll be fine."

His lips thinned into an unhappy line.

I brushed my lips against his to break the gridlock. "In a few months, she'll be in college, remember?"

"You're right, but it doesn't mean I have to be happy about it."

"True. Although her leaving does mean we have the whole house to ourselves." I scooted away from the wall, shifting to my knees, and flicked open the top button of my shirt.

His eyes widened and dropped to my chest.

I popped one more open. "I mean, if we're being practical here. You'll probably want to stay here, since no one else is home. And you'll be close by in case Quinn needs anything." The top of my bra peeked out from between the gap in my shirt.

"You make a persuasive argument."

I ran my hands over his chest and pushed him down onto his back. Throwing a leg over his hips, I worked my fingers down over the rest of the buttons on my shirt.

His hands shot out and he stilled mine. "Since we are both in confession mode, there's one other thing I have to tell you."

My hands froze and my muscles locked.

"Since we've promised not to keep secrets anymore, I need to confess I subsidized your rent for The Brothel and took out an extra loan to cover the difference."

I shot up, slamming my head into the bunk above me. "You did what?"

He sat up and rubbed the spot on the top of my head.

Swatting his hands away, I cursed his name. "Are you serious? Why would you do something so stupid? An extra loan? What if you don't get drafted? What if you're walking across the street and a runaway bus runs you over? Of all the stupid—"

He cut off my rant with a kiss.

I melted into it before breaking apart. "No, you're not going to win that easily. Why—"

"Because I love you. And I knew you wouldn't take the help, so I did it for you."

My head dropped back and I stared up at the slats of the bunk with pictures of us slotted in them.

In his own annoyingly perfect way, he'd protected me. Even if I didn't like his methods, I couldn't doubt the outcome. "When you put it like that...I'm paying you back."

"I'm sure we can work out a generous payment schedule." His hands gripped my ass and he pulled me forward until I fell against his chest. Our lips met and we were in a race to see who could get the other undressed first. No matter who was victorious, we were both winners.

EPILOGUE

LJ

I sat in the room buzzing with anticipatory energy I'd never felt before—not before playoffs or a championship, not even before signing the letter to come to Fulton U. Fifty ten-seater tables were crammed into the room with pro banners hanging behind a stage with a podium and a massive LED screen.

Cameras were set up all over the perimeter of the room in the belly of Madison Square Garden. My feet rested on a cable bundle taped down to the concrete floor. I was surrounded by players, agents, and parents decked out and ready for the big moment.

Roving cameras moved throughout the tables, stopping off for interviews with the other draft prospects. An electric energy reverberated in the room. Everyone sized everyone else up, trying to work out when their name would be called. It would be the difference between an eight-figure signing bonus and a five-figure one, and contracts for tens of millions spread out over a few years.

When my agent called, nearly bursting my ear drum to let

me know I'd gotten the invite, so many of my worries had fallen away. I'd be selected tonight, the question now was when and where.

Marisa slid her hand onto my leg and squeezed, tickling me right behind my knee.

I jerked forward, trying to knock her hand loose.

She leaned in and whispered in my ear. "No matter what, we're all here for you and we love you." Her peck on my cheek calmed some of the nerves bouncing off the walls inside my head.

Sucking in a deep breath, I closed my eyes and leaned back in my chair. A contented calm washed over me.

My mom leaned over. "Should we all get a peck on the cheek from Marisa, if it'll calm us down like that?"

Marisa laughed. "Kisses for everyone." She hopped up and pecked Mom and Dad on the cheek before taking her seat.

Her comfort with my parents had always warmed a special place in my heart, but now it meant even more to me. Our lives would be forever entangled, intertwined in an inseparable way, and I wanted her to know they'd always love her as much as I did. Flashes strobed through my head of how I'd loved her all last night and this afternoon before we got dressed up to come down to the draft ceremony.

Okay, maybe not exactly the way I did, but she'd always be a daughter to them.

Finally being able to tell everyone had been a relief. Berk walking in on us making out during our spring break party had certainly sped up our timeline for making things official. But I wouldn't have had it any other way—not that sneaking about wasn't hot as fuck for a while.

The lights strobed and the announcements began. The team with who'd had the worst season had the first draft pick. Utah. Marisa's grip tightened on my hand beside the place settings on the table.

The face of the commissioner of the league loomed over us on the giant screen. He was out on the field packed with fans from the different teams, all cordoned off in sections with faces painted and waving flags.

My lips brushed over the shell of her ear. "They need a QB way more than a linebacker."

The announcement was made and the other side of the room broke out into cheers. Polite applause followed.

Through the heads of a few people, I spotted Berk with his agent still on the phone. Jules waved at us and we waved back.

The newly minted professional quarterback walked toward the doorway leading out to the screaming fans. A clip package played on the screen and he was handed his hat on the walk up to the podium for even more pictures.

Player after player was selected and took their walk out to the stage. Agents, managers, and parents were all on phones fielding calls, screaming and laughing together.

The food and drinks on the table sat untouched. Berk hadn't come back to his table after being the seventeenth draft pick. He'd even shaken hands with the STFU asshole he'd fought on his way out to the podium as the fifteenth draft pick. From a fistfight in the tunnel in the middle of a game to handshakes. I guess the promise of a few million had a way of calming people the hell down.

But not me. At least not yet.

My freshly tailored suit would need dry cleaning with the sweat situation I had going on. From almost anywhere in the Northeast, I'd be a ten-hour flight from Marisa. My parents would be able to come to games, and I could drop by and visit Quinn.

Marisa rubbed her hand on my neck and rested her head on my shoulder.

There were no issues with PDA now. Not that we were making out in front of my parents, but I didn't take the ability to take her hand or kiss her or hug her no matter where we were for granted.

"With the thirty-first pick of the draft, Philadelphia selects."

We all held hands, gripped way too tightly.

"LJ Lewis, defensive lineman from Fulton U."

Our table erupted. Thirty-one. Elation exploded, erupting from every angle. I was tackled. Arms wrapped around me, rocking me back and forth. Their grins were touchdown-pass wide, just like mine.

I straightened my suit and held onto Marisa's hand. I walked toward the doorway, not letting go until the last moment, our fingertips skimming across one another.

Walking out onto the stage, the fans in the Philly section cheered. The video roll played and the commentators spoke over it all. I took the hat from the commissioner and shook his hand, posing for pictures and trying not to grin like an absolute moron. No such luck.

When I left the stage, my agent was already in the walkway before the green room spouting off numbers and names. And the main number. My signing bonus and contract terms.

My hand shot out, bracing myself on the wall. I didn't need a concussion from learning I was one signature on the dotted line from becoming a millionaire.

"Just give me a second, Glenn." I stared at the jerseys lining the wall leading to the green room and imagined having one with my name on it. Everything drowned out and I spotted myself in the reflection of the framed jerseys with my Philly hat. "I did it."

A lightness. A release of tension. A feeling radiating straight through my chest that should've been a beam cast in the sky. I'd done it.

———

THE SUV PULLED AWAY FROM MY PARENTS' HOUSE. I HELD ONTO Marisa's hand, running my fingers over her knuckles. We'd driven down after the draft instead of staying in New York. There would be time for that later, but we only had two weeks left of The Brothel and our time living all together.

"I can't believe we only have two weeks until graduation. This semester feels like it's lasted a year."

She looked at me in the way she never shied from now, the one that never failed to charge straight to my heart like jumper cables attached to a fresh battery.

My phone buzzed in my pocket. Running my thumb along the side of her knee, I pulled it out and checked my message. "Rain check on our private celebration. We've got an important matter to attend to back at the house." I showed her the screen.

Her eyes widened and she grabbed her bag, digging around inside and finding a hair tie. She piled her hair on top of her head in a tactical bun, and her face meant business.

The driver dropped us off in front of the house and we rushed inside. The trace of light from the kitchen didn't make it out to the living room window, but we knew they were there. Extra cars were parked on the street outside the house.

Inside, we were met with our first full house in a long time. There were old and new roommates, along with the ladies who'd won their hearts. Reece and Seph, Nix and Elle, Berk and Jules, and Keyton with flashlights in hand.

Nix cupped his hands around his mouth and shouted at the ceiling. "It seems we have three pro football players in the house."

The room collapsed into a chaotic strobe of flashing lights and cheers, hugs, and laughter. Raised voices went over every detail of the night. Keyton hadn't been invited to Madison Square Garden, but he'd been drafted in the third round, heading out to LA with the Lions. Berk was going to Boston. And I'd be staying here in Philly.

Reece stepped to the center of our circle. "Okay, enough of all this celebrating. You know what we're all here to do."

Looks of determination settled over everyone's face. "We're changing things up tonight. It's going to be men versus women."

All the women shifted to one side with a challenging glint in their eyes.

Keyton stepped forward. "No crossing enemy lines. No making out with the enemy." His shoulders relaxed a little and he softened. "I mean for my sake. Please, no making out. I've been scarred enough already."

Marisa and I were fascinated by the ceiling and windows.

"For the late arrivals, you've got five minutes to change."

Berk and Jules hadn't had the New Jersey detour, and were already in their battle gear.

Marisa and I rushed upstairs, bodying one another the whole way.

She darted into her room and I ducked into mine. My suit jacket, fancy dress shoes and dress pants were gone, and I grabbed a pair of sweats and took off the dress shirt.

"You're going down, LJ!" She called from the other side of the wall.

"You might think that, but you'd be wrong. I'm stealthy and I've taught you everything you know." I threw on some sweatpants and a t-shirt and dumped out my arsenal in the basket in my closet.

"Did you steal my Commander Blaster?"

I picked up the blue and orange plastic gun and tucked it into the waistband at the back of my sweats. "Nope, haven't seen it anywhere." Grabbing an ammo belt of orange-tipped foam, I slung two over my chest.

The racket from Marisa's room died down a bit.

"That's time." Keyton shouted from downstairs.

I bolted back out into the hallway at the same time as Marisa.

She shoved me into the wall and rushed past me down the stairs.

A gentle knock stopped all of us. No one was missing.

The front door opened. "Hey Coach. Wha—what are you doing here?" Uncertainty radiated from Berk's voice. Things hadn't gone so well the last time—scratch that, anytime—Coach had shown up at our front door.

"I wanted congratulate you boys on how well you did today." He held out his hand and shook Berk's.

Keyton walked up next and shook it. "You did a hell of a job for the team this season."

Marisa walked around the open door and I came down behind her.

"You looked beautiful tonight." He hugged her.

Looking over her shoulder, he looked at me. "The city will be lucky to have you playing here. It'll be a hell of a motivator for the next crop of kids showing up here." He pulled off his hat. "And I know you could've gotten a higher—"

"It's okay, Coach. I made it." I wrapped my arm around Marisa, bits of plastic and foam jamming into my chest and looked into her eyes. "And we'll make it."

Marisa had let me read the emails from her dad. As much as I wanted to hate him or be angry with him, every one of them hammered home how much she meant to him. Anyone who cared about her half as much as I did was someone I wanted on my team. The team who'd make it their life's mission to show her how much love there was in the world for her, and that it was never going away.

"I know you will. I can see you're all getting ready to celebrate."

Behind me, the whole gang was locked and loaded with more Nerf gear than a toy warehouse.

"It's a tradition."

"Have fun. I'll see you both later."

Marisa shot forward and hugged him. "See you on Monday, Dad."

He stood there in stunned silence for a moment before wrapping his arms around her, barred against her back. A tremble rocked his body. "See you." He let her go with a sheen to his eyes.

She closed the door and turned, sniffling a little.

"You okay?"

Her arm wrapped around my waist and she held me close. "Yeah, I'm good."

Breathing in, I closed my eyes and kissed the side of her head. There was a fidget of her fingers.

"And even better now." She jerked the blaster out of my waistband and backed away with it trained on me.

"You little sneak."

"Takes one to know one. 'Nope, haven't seen it.'" She deepened her voice to imitate mine and evaded my grasp, jumping behind Seph and Elle.

I lined up beside Berk, Keyton and Reece. The girls faced us.

Keyton stepped forward before the two teams. "We all get five minutes to strategize. No going outside. No making out. Does everyone understand the rules?"

"You're going down, LJ." Marisa glared with a smile tickling her cheeks.

"Not if you go down first."

Keyton cleared his throat.

"I didn't mean…not…"

Everyone burst into laughter, and the guys shoved at my shoulders.

"Okay, back on track. Everyone has five minutes. Go!"

There was a scramble for the best defensive positions. Marisa brushed past me and I couldn't help it. I snagged her around the waist and kissed her. Quick, playful and full of desire. "I love you, Risa."

Her eyes twinkled with mischief. "I love you too, L. And I wasn't joking about you going down tonight. One way or another."

"Sounds like I'm the winner no matter what the game has in store for me." Another quick peck.

Keyton's voice broke us apart. "What did I say? I swear. You can't make it a whole ninety seconds…"

Marisa burst into laughter and charged back up the stairs with the rest of the ladies.

"I know. Something about this woman just drives me crazy."

———

THANK YOU SO MUCH FOR SPENDING SOME TIME WITH THESE TWO best friends! For another day with LJ and Marisa, you can check out their bonus scene. Who says football and a London adventure don't mix!

———

There's another story in the Fulton U Universe. Don't miss The Art of Falling for You!

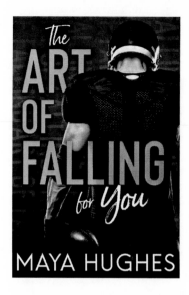

There's no flashing scoreboard.
There's no cheering crowd.
There's only her and me.
The countdown clock is ticking. The only thing scarier about
finding my first love will be losing her.

Your next binge read is here!

Ready for some more college sports action?

Shameless King - Enemies to Lovers

ENEMIES TO LOVERS HAS NEVER FELT SO GOOD!

Declan McAvoy. Voted Biggest Flirt. Highest goal scorer in Kings of Rittenhouse Prep history.

Everyone's impressed, well except one person…

I can't deny it. I want her. More than I ever thought I could want a woman. I've got one semester–only four months–to convince her everything she thought about me was wrong.

Will my queen let me prove to her I'm the King she can't live without?

Only one way to find out…

One-click SHAMELESS KING now!

———

Want to start Fulton U where it all began?

The Perfect First - Reece + Seph

"How long do you last in bed?" Those were her first words to me, swiftly followed up with, "And how big would you say you are?"

Cue the record scratching, what?!

Persephone Alexander. Math genius. Lover of blazers. The only girl I know who can make Heidi braids look sexy as hell. And she's on a mission. Lose her virginity by the end of the semester.

Grab The Perfect First today!

THE END?

I can't believe it's truly the end for Fulton U. Or is it? While the Fulton U series is complete, this doesn't mean other characters won't pop up in the future.

Writing this group of friends has been a wild ride. I'm never quite sure where things will go, but I love the ride no matter how frustrating these characters make me.

A special thank you to my editors, Dawn, Sarah, and Sarah. To my assistant, Karen! Oh man, I couldn't do it without you.

And thank you to you! Time is limited in our crazy world, so thank you for taking the time out of your busy schedule to hang out with this lovable group of people and for loving them as much as I do.

If you were wondering, Keyton will get his own story. I'm working on it now and it's different than anything I've done before.

If you're looking for Liv and Ford's story, you can grab, Fearless King right now and start the whole series for FREE with the novella, Kings of Rittenhouse.

Happy reading!

Maya xx

EXCERPT FROM THE PERFECT FIRST

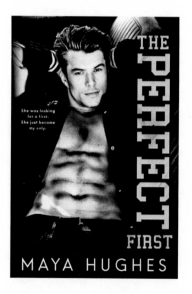

Seph - Project De-virginization

The jingle sounded again as the door to the coffee shop swung open. My head snapped up and my bouncing leg froze. The sun shone through the doorway and a figure stood there. He was tall, taller than anyone who'd come in before. His muscles were obvious even under his coat. He paused at the entrance, his head moving from side to side like he knew people would be looking back, like he was giving everyone a chance to soak in his presence. His jet black hair was tousled just right, like he'd been running his fingers through it on the walk over from wherever he'd come from. The jacket fit him perfectly, like it had been tailored just for his body.

I glanced around; I wasn't the only one who'd noticed him walk in. He seemed familiar, but I couldn't place him. He bent forward, and I thought he was going to tie his shoes, but instead he wiped a wet leaf off his pristine white sneaker. Heads turned as he crossed the floor toward me. Squeezing my fingers tighter around the notecards, I reminded myself to breathe.

He glanced around again and spotted me. The green in his eyes was clear even from across the coffee shop. Dark hair with eyes like that wasn't a usual combo. He froze and his lips squeezed together. With his hands shoved into his pockets, he stalked toward me with a *Let's get this over with* look. That didn't bode well. He stood beside the seat on the other side of the booth, staring at me expectantly.

My gaze ran over his face. Square jaw. Hint of stubble on his cheeks and chin. My skin flushed. He had beautiful lips. What would his feel like on my mouth? I ran my finger over my bottom lip. What would they feel like on other parts of me? My body responded and I thanked God I had on a bra, shirt, and blazer or I'd have been flashing him some serious high beams. This was a good sign.

He cleared his throat.

Jumping, I dropped my hand, and the heat in my cheeks turned into a flamethrower on my neck. "Sorry, have a seat." I half stood from my spot in the booth and extended my hand toward the other side across from me. The table dug into my thighs and I fell back into the soft seat.

Sliding in opposite me, he unzipped his coat and put his arm over the back of the shiny booth.

"Hi, very nice to meet you. I'm Seph." I shot my hand out across the table between us. The cuff of my blazer tightened as it rode up my arm.

His eyebrows scrunched together. "Seth?" He leaned in, his forearms resting on the edge of the table. He was nothing like the guys from the math department. They were quiet, sometimes obnoxious, and none of them made my stomach ricochet around inside me like it was trying to win a gold medal in gymnastics at the Olympics.

I tamped down a giggle. I did *not* giggle. The sound came out like a sharp snort, and I resisted the urge to slam my eyes shut and crawl under the table. *Be cool, Seph. Be cool.* "No— Seph. It's short for Persephone."

He lifted one eyebrow.

"Greek goddess of spring. Daughter of Demeter and Zeus. You know what, never mind. I'm glad you agreed to meet with me today."

"Not like I had much choice." He leaned back and ran his knuckles along the table top, rapping out a haphazard rhythm.

I licked my lips and parted them. Not like he had much choice? Had someone put him up to this? Had something in my post made him feel obligated to come? I hadn't been able to bring myself to go back and look at it after posting it. Shaking my head, I stuck my hand out again. "Nice to meet you…"

He looked down at my hand and back up at me, letting out a bored breath. "Reece. Reece Michaels."

"Very nice to meet you, Reece. I'm Persephone Alexander.

I have a few questions we can get started with, if you don't mind."

"The quicker we get started, the quicker we can finish." He looked around like he would have rather been anywhere but there.

Those giddy bubbles soured in my stomach. A server came by with the bottled waters I'd ordered. I arranged them in a neat pyramid at the end of the table.

"Would you like a water?" I held one out to him.

He eyed me like I was offering him an illicit substance, but then reached out. His fingers brushed against the backs of mine and shooting sparks of excitement rushed through me. Pulling the bottle out of my grasp, he cracked it open and took a gulp.

My cheeks heated and I glanced down at my cards, flipping the ones at the front to the back.

"I have a notecard with some information for you to fill out."

Sliding it across the table, I held out a pen for him. He took it from me, careful that our fingers didn't touch this time. I'd have been lying if I'd said I didn't want another touch, just to test whether or not that first one had been something more than static electricity. He filled out the biographical data on the card and handed it back to me.

I scanned it. He was twenty-one. Had a birthday coming up just after the New Year. Good height-to-weight ratio. Grabbing my pen, I scanned over the questions I'd prepared for my meetings.

"Let's get started." *Just rip the Band-Aid off.* Clearing my throat, I tapped the cards on the table. A few heads turned in our direction at the sharp, rapping sound. "When were you last tested for sexually transmitted diseases?"

Setting the bottle down on the table, he stared at me like I was an equation he was suddenly interested in figuring out. And then it was gone. "At the beginning of the season. Clean bill of health." He looked over his shoulder, the boredom back, leaking from every pore. *Wow.* I'd thought guys were all over this whole sex thing, but he looked like he was sitting in the waiting room of a dentist's office.

"When did you last have sexual intercourse?"

His head snapped back to me, eyes bugged out. "What?" I had his full attention now.

"Sex? When did you last have sex?" I tapped my pen against the notecard.

He sputtered and stared back at me. His eyes narrowed and he rested his elbows on the table.

I scooted my neatly lain out cards back toward me, away from him.

"No comment."

"Given the circumstances, it's an appropriate question."

The muscles in his neck tightened and his lips crumpled together. "Fine, at the beginning of the season."

"What season?" I looked up from my pen. That was an odd way to put it. "Like, the beginning of fall?"

"Like football season."

The pieces fit together—the body, the looks from other people around the coffee house. "You play football." That made sense, and he seemed like the perfect all-American person for the job.

"Yes, I play football."

"When did the season start?"

He shook his head like he was trying to clear away a fog and stared back at me like I'd started speaking a different language. "September."

"And…" I ran my hand along the back of my neck. "How long would you say it lasted?"

His eyebrows dipped. "It didn't last. It was a one-night thing. I don't do relationships."

Of course not. He was playing the field. Sowing his oats.

Banging his way through as many co-eds as possible. Experienced. Excellent.

I cleared my throat. "No, I didn't mean how long did you date the woman. I meant, how long was the sex?"

The steady drumming on the table stopped. "Are you serious?"

I licked my Sahara-dry lips. "It's a reasonable question. How long did it last?"

"I didn't exactly set a timer, but let's just say we both got our reward."

"Interesting." I made another note on the card.

"These are the types of questions I'm going to be asked for the draft?" He took the lid off the bottled water.

The draft? Pushing ahead, I went to the next line one my card and cringed a bit. "Okay, this might seem a little invasive." I cleared my throat again. "But how big is your penis? Length is fine. I don't need to know the circumference, you know—the girth."

A fine spray of water from his mouth washed over me. "What the hell kind of question is that? I know you're trying to throw me off my game, but holy shit, lady."

———

Persephone Alexander. Math genius. Lover of blazers. The only girl I know who can make Heidi braids look sexy as hell. And she's on a mission. Lose her virginity by the end of the semester.

I walked in on her interview session for potential candidates (who even does that?) and saw straight through her brave front. She's got a list of Firsts to accomplish like she's only got months to live. I've decided to be her guide for all her firsts except one. Someone's got to keep her out of trouble. I have one rule, no sex. We even shook on it.

I'll help her find the right guy for the job. Someone like

her doesn't need someone like me and my massive...baggage for her first time.

Drinking at a bar. Check.

Partying all night. Double check.

Skinny dipping. Triple check.

She's unlike anyone I've ever met. The walls I'd put up around my heart are slowly crumbling with each touch that sets fire to my soul.

I'm the first to bend the rules. One electrifying kiss changes everything and suddenly I don't want to be her first, I want to be her only. But her plan was written before I came onto the scene and now I'm determined to get her to re-write her future with me.

Grab your copy of The Perfect First or read it for FREE in Kindle Unlimited at https://amzn.to/2ZqEMzl

ALSO BY MAYA HUGHES

Fulton U

The Perfect First - First Time/Friends to Lovers Romance

The Third Best Thing

The Fourth Time Charm

The Fulton U Trilogy

The Art of Falling for You

The Sin of Kissing You

The Hate of Loving You

Kings of Rittenhouse

Kings of Rittenhouse - FREE

Shameless King - Enemies to Lovers

Reckless King - Off Limits Lover

Ruthless King - Second Chance Romance

Fearless King - Brother's Best Friend Romance

Heartless King - Accidental Pregnancy

CONNECT WITH MAYA

Sign up for my newsletter to get exclusive bonus content, ARC opportunities, sneak peeks, new release alerts and to find out just what I'm books are coming up next.

Join my reader group for teasers, giveaways and more!

Follow my Amazon author page for new release alerts!

Follow me on Instagram, where I try and fail to take pretty pictures!

Follow me on Twitter, just because :)

I'd love to hear from you! Drop me a line anytime :)
https://www.mayahughes.com/
maya@mayahughes.com

Made in United States
North Haven, CT
25 April 2023

35880618R00200